ENDLESS POSSIBILITIES

BOOK 1 IN THE SPIRITUAL GIFTS SERIES

KIMBERLY MCKAY

Endless Possibilities

by

Kimberly McKay

by
Kimberly McKay

FINDING KYLIE

FACING REDEMPTION

COMING HOME

SAVING GRACE

SECOND CHANCES

ENDLESS POSSIBILITIES

DANGEROUS VISIONS

Coming soon:
Blind Instincts
Miss Givings

ENDLESS POSSIBILITIES

Copyright 2017 Kimberly McKay

All rights reserved. No part of this book may be reproduced or transmitted in any means, electronic or mechanical, including photocopying, recording or by information storage and retrieval system without written permission from the publisher or author, except for the inclusion of brief quotation in a review.

This book is a work of fiction. Names, characters, places, and incidents are either the product of the author's imagination or are used fictitiously, and any resemblance to places, events, or persons living or deceased is purely coincidental.

ISBN: 978-1544800851
First Edition

First Printing, September 2017
Printed in the United States of America

❀ Created with Vellum

To my grandparents, who always remind me they still watch over me in the thin place where heaven and earth meet.

1

It was a typical day for Evelyn Bozeman. Even at the seasoned age of ninety-two, she could hoist her small frame onto her trusted tractor to work the thirty acres outside her ranch style home. As she buckled herself into her seat, she took a second to smell the sweet air as the morning breeze danced through her hair.

It is nothing short of a miracle. Evelyn inhaled, knowing how blessed she was to have her life.

"Time to bale the hay, you old goat." She tapped the steering wheel. "Let's get going."

Marshall Bozeman, just within earshot, watched from the barn and stepped out into the morning dusk. He slipped off his work gloves to rest his arms on the steel fence line and chuckled, asking, "Did you check the fuel tank?"

At the sight of her stepson, Evelyn grinned from ear to ear. Marshall was always double-checking her as if she'd forget.

"I'm old, not dumb." She waved him off.

"Aren't we all?" He rubbed his shoulder. "Feels like rain is coming this way."

She looked up at the billowy clouds and sighed. "Maybe? Maybe not."

"My shoulder never lies." He raised an eyebrow in Evelyn's direction. "Sure, I can't do this for you?"

Even though he knew better, he had to ask. His stepmother may have been spry for her age, but accidents happen. He shook his head. She'd never give up working her land.

To her, it was a part of something bigger than herself. God blessed her with the farm, something for which she'd be eternally grateful. It came to her at a time in life when she had nothing and no one to turn to.

Evelyn gave him a look that left no interpretation and pushed in the clutch.

"Why don't you tend to the horses and leave me to my hay? And, tell Amelia I'll be in to help with the chores in a couple of hours."

"Yes, ma'am." At the mention of his stepsister, Amelia, Marshall's lips upturned, bringing a twinkle to his gray eyes. Amelia was sure to give her mother an earful for driving the tractor even a foot, let alone working some of the land.

As he turned toward the stables, he heard the familiar rumble of the tractor as Evelyn started toward the field. Before Marshall could reach for the door, something prompted him to turn and search for her along the horizon.

His chest filled with pride as the morning rays greeted her profile, giving her a golden halo. His heart warmed for the woman who not only raised him but single-handedly saved his father from losing their land. As if she could read his thoughts, she turned to wave her arm in the air. Marshall slipped off his cowboy hat and enthusiastically waved it in return.

He dipped his head to slip his hat back in place when his body was thrown against the barn as a blast encompassed everything around him. A sonic boom echoed through the air, shaking everything in its wake.

Marshal shook his head from the shock of the blast and popped up, hoping to see Evelyn waving from afar. His heart lurched as he searched the empty horizon to find nothing but flames and particles falling from the sky.

A yell tore from his chest as he took off in the direction of the accident. At that same moment, his stepsister screamed from afar.

"Mom!" Amelia cried at the top of her lungs. Amelia stumbled out the front door of their family home and ran as fast as her legs could carry her toward the explosion, only to get pulled back. She struggled to free herself, but it was of no use. All she could do was watch the fire as it told a grim tale.

"I have to save her!" She continued to fight her way from the porch. "I knew I shouldn't have let her on that thing!"

"Let Marshall handle it." Hank reined in his wife, hoping she'd succumb to his grasp as it was evident there was no saving Evelyn from this disaster. There was nothing left except flames and a few pieces of scrap metal that had blown across their property.

As she soaked his shirt with tears, he stroked her hair and whispered, "Let's go inside and call 9-1-1. Then we've got to call Anderson and Alexis."

Amelia's face twisted at the mention of Alexis, who had already lost so much.

"I don't know if I can do this." She glanced once more at the flames that lapped at everything within reach of the accident. "Mom." Her shaky intake of breath led to more tears.

Hank led his wife onto the porch swing and sat her down. He kissed the top of her head and said a silent prayer for strength.

EVELYN WATCHED from above as her family twisted in anguish. In an attempt to grab Marshall's arm as he attacked the scene with a fire extinguisher, her hand passed straight through. Without notice, Evelyn appeared next to her daughter, who was sobbing in Hank's arms.

Wondering what happened and how she could reach her family, her soul ached with remorse. Now that she'd passed, she could feel the outpouring of sorrow that ripped through the air like lightning rippling through a storm.

"I'm sorry," she whispered without much time to lament.

It was then that Evelyn heard her mother's loving voice echo through the wind. She turned to find the billowy clouds she'd previously admired parting. Then, what she saw was nothing short of heavenly.

2

If he closed his eyes and listened, it would have seemed like another ordinary evening on the farm. Hank Evans inhaled the sweet scent of rain and tried to ignore the burned grass that mingled in the air.

Repetitive pounding sounded as his young neighbor swung a hammer nearby. It was another reminder of why they had all gathered. While he wished it was as simple as a social call, it was a community gathering around loved ones during a time of need.

Eyes still closed, he focused on the sounds Tyler made with the hammer, trying to block out the ache in his chest as it synced in cadence with his young friend's swing.

Tyler, who'd grown up on the adjacent land, watched his surrogate family with anguish he never expected to come so soon. As a wild pre-teen, he used to sneak over their property lines to spy on Hank and Amelia's kids, who were about his age, as he yearned for that sort of family closeness. They were what a healthy and loving family should be.

Once Evelyn caught him, she waved him over to her front porch. She gave him an insightful look, making it seem like she could see to the core of his soul and discover every desire he held dear. With a reassuring smile, she invited him to spend time with the whole family any time he was free.

That moment changed his life. It was an offer and a bond he could never repay. Tyler shook his head at the memories that came flooding back.

"That should do it." Tyler set the hammer down. "Thankfully, we got your windows boarded up before the rain made it this far east."

Hank finally opened his eyes, wishing that repairing his family's pain could be as easy as boarding up a few windows. Those planks of wood would seal his home from further damage, but what would protect their hearts from the rolls of agony that would continue to blow through?

He took a sip of coffee and looked out at the charred grass remembering how Marshall and his farmhands fought the flames off with their hoses until the fire department arrived.

If only I had double-checked the fuel line. He grimaced at the memory of the explosion. *Maybe I could have caught the problem before anything dangerous happened.*

Tyler saw the flash of guilt on his face and slapped a hand on the older man's shoulder, saying, "There's nothing you could have done any differently. Anyone that knew Evelyn understood she was determined to work as hard and long as she could."

Just then, Amelia stepped to the front porch with a steaming mug for Tyler. She shook her head at her husband with consternation.

"That's right." She turned the mug handle toward Tyler. "She went out on her terms. There's nowhere else she'd rather be than working her land."

"Thanks for the coffee." Tyler took the mug from her. "Have you talked to them?" He looked Amelia over, referring to her kids with whom he'd grown up until adulthood. The dark circles around her eyes and pained expression spoke volumes. She'd been up all night in tears.

"The kids or the police?" She sat on the porch swing and drew her thick sweater around her tiny frame. She was built just like her mother, who was small but sturdy.

"Anderson and Alexis, but I guess the cops too. Have they been out to investigate?"

"You just missed 'em." She nodded toward the extended drive. "They said nothing seemed out of place - just a routine farming accident."

Marshall slipped off his work gloves and stepped up to the porch to join the group. His gut burned as he overheard his stepsister's words. He turned to Amelia with a determined look in his eyes.

"Except I keep my equipment in tip-top shape. No way that should have happened."

"It's called an accident for a reason, Marshall." Amelia turned back to Tyler and continued, "They still have to finish their official report. The fire department will investigate. I'm sure." She drew in a breath, wondering how much she should or could divulge to Tyler about her kids.

Everything was so taboo when it came to sharing details of their life. Her oldest, Anderson, was only in contact when he was able, which was few and far between. Even when he did reach out, it was usually via cryptic postcards or short phone calls from whatever remote corner of the world he was in at the moment.

And with Alexis ... Amelia sighed. Her daughter had cut her off years ago from sharing anything with Tyler for personal reasons unbeknownst to her.

"I bet it seems like ages since you've seen them. None of you are kids anymore." She pursed her lips and stared out at the field, wishing she could turn back the clock to simpler times when the three of them, Tyler, Alexis, and Anderson, raced across the area on horseback without a care in the world.

"I haven't seen them since college." He sat next to Amelia and put his arm around the woman who was like a second mom to him. "Anderson and I kept in touch for a while. His career kept him so busy, like mine, and we drifted. And Alexis, well, I haven't seen or heard from her since she got married."

"Yup. I never saw that one coming." Amelia's gaze temporarily locked with Hank's. Tyler watched as something unspoken transferred between them before she finally said, "But Clay was good for her in many ways. Even if his job was hard on them both, and in the end..."

"I was sorry to hear about his passing," Tyler took up where she left off. "Although I vaguely knew him, he seemed like a nice guy, who adored Alexis. Then again, who wouldn't?"

His mind wandered to the young girl, whose coy smile could have gotten under his skin if he hadn't kept up his guard. She was Anderson's younger sister, and there was no way he'd allow their flirting to exceed harmless banter until she did the unexpected. He flashed back to the kiss they shared the night before she ran off. Though it should have been water under the bridge, to his dismay, it still left a lasting impression.

"How is she taking it?" he asked, referring to Evelyn's accident. When Amelia shrugged, he could have kicked himself and recovered by saying, "Well, of course, not well. She and Evelyn had an exceptional relationship."

Amelia's thoughts wandered to yesterday's phone conversation. After trying to call her daughter throughout the day, she finally heard back from Alexis after nightfall when she and her young daughter, Lani, settled into a hotel. Alexis, who had already decided to pack everything the two owned and move home, was shocked to hear of her grandmother's passing.

Amelia's heart broke for her daughter, who still had two more days with a young child in tow to pull over state lines and then had another five hours to drive home.

"Yeah. They were close." She sent him a sad smile, wondering how her daughter and granddaughter would handle their newest loss after losing Clay only a few years ago.

"So, when is she? I mean, when are Anderson and Alexis getting here?" He covered his flub. Although things between him and Alexis never were serious, a part of him always wondered what could have happened between them if their circumstances were different.

Marshall raised an eyebrow at his stepsister and pursed his lips. It was no secret to either of them that both Tyler and Alexis had eyes for one another when they were kids, even if Tyler wouldn't admit it.

"Day after tomorrow for Alexis, and we're still waiting to hear back from Anderson. He's a bit hard to reach." Marshall leaned against the banister and drained the last of his coffee. He sent a backward glance to the news truck, in which Tyler had arrived, and said, "Looks like your cameraman is ready."

"Yeah," Tyler sighed. "Thanks for the coffee, Amelia. Hank, Marshall, please call if you need anything."

"Thanks for the help," Amelia stared into his weary eyes. "You didn't have to come out here when the story broke."

"I was out of town yesterday but got back as fast as I could. When my team was slated to come back for more footage, I wanted to be here too. Besides, it's what we do. You guys are like family, even if it's been a while." He rose from the swing and sent her a look. "You know I'd do anything for you."

As Tyler dropped down the steps from the front porch, he surveyed the damage around him. It broke his heart to see how much was lost.

He turned to face the three of them and said, "Have Anderson call me when he gets in when he's ready. I know you'll have a lot on your hands. And tell Alexis I asked about her, okay?"

Amelia nodded with a wave as Tyler jogged to his truck and slipped inside.

"So, this is where the elusive T.J. grew up?" Ryan, his photographer, sent him a look.

"It's Tyler James to them." He grimaced. "And this was a lifetime ago."

"It looks like a world away." Ryan started the engine, and slowly backed away from the property down the long drive. "The only time I get called out this way is for grass fires or ..."

Ryan stopped short of finishing. When covering most stories, he'd learned to grow a thick skin, but in this case, he knew T.J. couldn't be impartial. It hit too close to home.

"Yeah." Tyler stared at the horizon, where his family property lay just over the fence line. "I still come out on weekends, but it's been a while since I've stopped for a visit. Too long."

"Sorry, boss." Ryan's heart went out to him.

As a top-ranked news director, T.J. ran a tight ship. He had a stern reputation in the newsroom yet was also someone you could trust to do the right thing. Everyone who worked for him knew they could approach him with anything, and he'd show compassion.

When T.J. insisted on coming with him to the scene of the explosion, which seemed like an everyday farming accident, it hinted to something that could be out of the ordinary.

Since when does someone in T.J.'s position have time to leave the newsroom, let alone ride along? Especially when it probably wouldn't even make the lead into to the five o'clock news? Ryan had no way of knowing just how important it was.

"Everything upload okay?" Tyler nodded to the equipment in the back of the truck.

"Yes, sir," Ryan answered. "You know. I wondered why you insisted on the mobile unit."

"I wanted to make sure I could stay a bit – to take care of whatever they needed."

Ryan nodded. "I get it. I'm sorry, man."

Tyler nodded. There was a time when he could say this was like a second home. He, Anderson, and Alexis were inseparable as kids, until one day they weren't. Tyler couldn't pinpoint what it was, but after Alexis' high school graduation, everything changed. It was as if overnight, his world slipped away.

After Alexis' graduation party at the Bozeman ranch, Anderson returned to Texas for training, and Alexis, adoring eyes turned to steel. Then, unexpectedly, she ran off to marry someone from her graduating class and followed him three states away.

Tyler sent his photog a steely smile and shook off the waves of emotions that threatened to overtake him.

"It's okay, Ryan. Time to get back. The news never waits for anyone."

As the truck bumped along the gravel road, Tyler let out a ragged breath and wondered if he'd ever be a part of something that was fulfilling again. He used to think climbing the ladder at one of the top-ranked news stations in the market could give him that, but in seeing how much had changed back home, he wasn't sure any longer.

3

When Evelyn passed, it was nothing short of the typical, out-of-body experience that she'd read about from those who'd come back from the dead. She followed the quintessential light toward a place full of bold colors, which were so vibrant that she couldn't even put them on a color scale. As she traveled for what seemed like days, she finally saw a looming, beautiful, and magnificent city on the horizon.

She blinked to find herself standing amid clouds that became infused with a road paved with gold. She walked closer toward an emerging horizon that held a heavenly glow that beckoned.

While on earth, Evelyn had wondered what was beyond death. There were certainly a lot of theories out there. Catholics called it purgatory while Protestants said souls were sleeping until the rapture when Christ would come for those who were in their grave.

Now, seeing first-hand, she could put all theories to rest. Evelyn sensed how real heaven was and what lay behind the gates that looked as though they spanned toward eternity.

As the skyline dazzled from what seemed like a stone's throw - in her heart, she knew it was heaven. The closer she came, the more she yearned to walk through the gates and enter what she'd been taught and believed her whole life.

As she stepped past a beautiful garden, her mother appeared at her side. At the sight of her smiling face, Evelyn's soul filled with love and peace. It was as if her insides took flight and were soaring for all to see.

She looked from her mother to more familiar faces that suddenly appeared around her. Their benevolent eyes gleamed, urging her to run toward them with tender appreciation as to what lay beyond. However, her mother laid a hand on her arm and gave her pause.

It was the first time she experienced her mother's delicate touch since Evelyn left home to marry a man who had less than honorable intentions. Evelyn shook her head free of thoughts of her first husband to focus on the glory of this moment in which she was reunited with her gentle-hearted mother. It was then that she saw the worry in her mother's eyes transform to tender resignation.

Her mother, the strongest prayer warrior of them all, drew her into an overdue embrace only to pull back and say, "It's not time for you yet. You've got some work to do first."

The next thing she knew, she was standing by the oak tree near their family cemetery, staring down at her second husband's headstone, which lay next to her plot.

Usually, when you hear stories of someone returning from the beyond, it's to their earthly life. Yet, here Evelyn stood, still a soul without her body. The cryptic message from her mother replayed over and over, leaving her with a sense of dread and disappointment.

It's not my time? I'd say the fact that I'm not breathing in my earthly body means that I'd truly met my expiration date. Isn't that about as close to my time as it can get?

She was more confused than ever. Evelyn sat near her gravesite for what seemed like years until Alexis and Lani drove by on route to their ranch-style home. When her flesh and blood came within range, Evelyn forgot about her burial plot. She peered inside the truck as Alexis made the turn for the makeshift cemetery near their house.

Before then, Evelyn's confusion had bound her by the family gravesite with no direction; until she saw the clairvoyant look in her great-granddaughter Lani's eyes. It was then that Evelyn knew what her task was and how she prayed Lani played a part in it.

4

As Alexis navigated the road that spanned the perimeter of her family's property, she drew in an anxious breath. Although it had been ages since she'd been home, the thoroughbreds galloped along the fence line and greeted her and Lani as if they'd never left. The usual excitement of seeing their manes toss wildly in the wind was replaced with a profound sense of loss. How would they exist in that home now that her grandmother was gone?

I'm not gone.

Alexis glanced in the rearview mirror, expecting to see a shapely silhouette in her backseat, only to shake her head free from the words she clearly heard as though her daughter had spoken them. Instead, she observed Lani's cherub face as her daughter studied the horses from her booster seat.

At the tender young age of seven, her sweet daughter was more sensitive than most. When Lani was born, she and Clay celebrated their precious gift from God. After a miscarriage early in their relationship, they prayed for a healthy pregnancy. Lani, which meant sky or heaven in Hawaiian, was the answer to their prayers.

From birth, Lani was different than any other child. On the

surface, she was developmentally on target, yet anyone could see the depth of her soul through her eyes. It was as if she was born with the wisdom of a clever old woman who could see through every thought or emotion another had.

The locals on Oahu, where Clay was stationed at the time, said she had the heart of a wise sage that transcended time. Alexis shook her head at some of her neighbor's superstitions but said nothing. Just because their faith was different than hers, didn't make it less relevant to those in their neighborhood. Alexis nodded at their input and thanked them for the sweet words while also giving her two cents. She often responded that God had given her daughter a thoughtful and tender spirit to everything around her, which meant He had big plans for her in the years to come.

Alexis beamed over her shoulder at her daughter, knowing she was blessed with a gift. In moments like these, though, it could be emotionally taxing as her daughter took everything in more deeply than most. Clay and his mother passed within a couple years of one another. Lani was close to both, which was why Alexis made the call to move home, as nothing was keeping her in Michigan any longer.

Never in a million years did she imagine she'd be driving home to face her own grandmother's passing. The losses they'd suffered were too many and too soon.

Alexis patted her swollen eyes and sighed, hoping she could keep a sunny disposition up for Lani. Lord knows she needed it.

"How's my angel?" she asked her daughter, whose sullen eyes were still puffy from the tears she'd shed. The knowledge that they were no longer driving to live with Great Grams had them both distraught.

"I'm okay." Lani's small voice came from the back seat.

Alexis sought out her daughter's luminous eyes, which resembled her father's and blinked back some tears. She offered a reassuring smile, putting on a brave face for Lani.

"As well as I can be, considering." Lani's tiny voice dropped.

"Yeah." Alexis' voice stilled. *She sounds like such a grown-up.* And yet, she was still only seven-years-old with so much to learn.

With her free hand, Alexis stroked her daughter's legs, which were stretched out between the front seats. Her heart warmed as Lani took her hand in her two small ones and leaned forward to give it a soft kiss.

"I love you, sweetheart," Alexis said in a hushed voice. When she heard her daughter respond in kind, a sense of bittersweet peace swept through her. In moments like these, she truly wished Clay could see what an amazing child she was becoming. Lani had just turned five when he died.

Suddenly, the looming gates at the entrance of the Bozeman ranch were upon them. She slowed to a stop and took a deep breath in before twisting to face her daughter.

"You ready to see where your mom grew up?"

As her child's full cheeks displayed dimples from her slow smile, she watched the curls bounce as Lani enthusiastically shook her head.

"I am. She said I'm going to love it here."

"She, who, sweetheart?"

"Great Grams. She told me."

Alexis' wide eyes blinked. "Honey, we've talked about this. My grandmother had an accident."

"I know. She's sorry about that."

Alexis shook her head, knowing how active her daughter's imagination could be. After Clay's and then his parent's passing had taken place, she had imaginary conversations with them too. She shouldn't have been shocked to know that Lani was doing the same with her Grandmother, except they'd only met once.

Alexis would never have expected that her daughter would create stories about someone she'd not formed a bond with, not like she'd had with Clay or his parents.

"Okay." Alexis sighed. "Hold on. It's a bumpy ride from here."

As they pulled down the gravel drive, Evelyn watched her great granddaughter's puffy, but wise eyes fill with wonder as she turned to her with a look of recognition.

"Can you see me?" she whispered to Lani.

Why am I whispering? No one can hear me.

Lani enthusiastically nodded. A sense of hope crept into Evelyn's soul. She squinted, unsure if her great-granddaughter was answering her mom's questions from the front seat or hers.

Evelyn sent Lani a sly grin, thinking she looked so much like she had at that age. Evelyn sat humbled at the legacy that she'd left behind. Slowly, she narrowed her eyes and asked once more, "Can you see me?"

"Yup. I can. And you're pretty. You look much younger than the pictures I saw of you," she whispered across the seat.

"What's that?" Alexis asked from the front seat.

"Nothing, Mommy. I'm just back here talking to Great Grams."

Alexis rolled her eyes and shook her head, saying to herself, "Of course you are."

She sighed a deep breath of resignation and slowly turned the car around to head toward the cemetery, which was only a few yards away.

"Speaking of Grams. I know her funeral isn't for a couple of days, but this is where she'll be laid to rest." Alexis stopped her engine and looked through her windshield at Evelyn's future gravesite. "And, I want to spend some time under her favorite tree before we do anything else."

Lani rolled her eyes. All her mom had to do was open her eyes to see who was right behind her.

5

Alexis wove through a few headstones toward her grandmother's plot, clutching her daughter's small hand with one hand and a wildflower in the other. She came to a stop at her grandmother's favorite bench, which sat by an oak tree near her Grandpa Bozeman's grave. The plot was marked by a double headstone, in which Tennessee Bozeman's name was engraved next to the spot where her grandmother's name had yet to be engraved.

She laid the dandelion on the bench as she sat where her grandmother often would. She slowly squeezed her eyes shut, trying to imagine her grandmother's face.

"Hey, Grams. I know your funeral isn't until next week, especially since Mom and Dad haven't reached Anderson, so...," Her gaze landed above her grandfather's headstone. "I figured here was as good as any place to visit you."

Alexis slid her hands over Lani's ears and added with a shaky voice, "Mom said there's not much of a body to bury." As a warm tear escaped, Alexis dropped her hands from Lani's head and slid off the bench to kneel on the ground. "How could this have happened?"

As tears overflowed, her daughter's strong little arms quickly wrapped around her neck.

"Momma, it's okay."

The sense of Lani's warm breath on her neck brought her back to the present. The soft comfort enveloped her, giving her a sense of peace. Her daughter's hugs always had a way of centering her.

"I know, baby." She leaned back to wipe a few tears away while kissing her daughter's full cheeks. "You make everything alright."

"She wouldn't want you to be sad." She sniffed. Seeing her mother so sad broke her heart. Her mom had already cried too much.

EVELYN SENT her granddaughter a sad smile. When Alexis placed her favorite wildflower on the bench, Evelyn sensed the pain emanating from Alexis' soul. To comfort her, Evelyn reached for her, but her hand slipped right through to the air around them.

Evelyn felt like screaming. Why couldn't she achieve something as simple as a hug? It was then that her frustration mingled through the air, mixing with the sorrow that poured from Alexis. Evelyn blinked. The things she experienced now that she had passed were incredible. She could visualize emotions as they cascaded from her loved one's hearts as well as her soul.

When Alexis drew Lani into her lap, Evelyn blinked, determined to reach them. She pushed every ounce of passion she had through her spirit as she wrapped her arms around them both. When she opened her eyes, Evelyn was ecstatic to find that she was enveloping her family without passing through.

"Oh, my dear child," she whispered.

Alexis' head suddenly popped up, and she searched the air around her. She swore she could hear her grandmother's sweet words of endearment but shook it off like a memory. Her Grandmother used those words often when she'd take her into her arms, especially during times of turbulence.

"Did you hear that?" Lani asked her mom.

She cocked her head, unsure if her daughter heard it too, or if it was a figment of both of their imaginations.

Seeing the look of confusion that crossed her mother's face, Lani added, "She's with us."

She dropped her forehead to Lani's with a sigh, before running her fingers across the stone bench where her grandmother sat almost every afternoon. Her heart ached for the one person who could give her direction; only she wasn't here to give her guidance anymore.

I'm still with you.

Alexis' eyes widened in awe. She searched the sky above and blinked, wondering if she was going crazy.

"Is that you?" She paused, cutting her eyes to the side, wondering if she'd hear a reply. When Alexis neither heard nor felt anything in return, she reluctantly reached for Lani's hand and winked at her dark-headed angel.

As her daughter's dark curls bounced in the breeze, Alexis ran her hand through the soft layers saying, "Time to go, sweetie."

Lani knowingly nodded her head. Her mother couldn't see what she could, and that was okay. She knew the truth.

Both girls stood and dusted off their jeans. Alexis turned her face to the sky with a heavy heart and said, "I'm sorry I got here too late. I wish I had a chance to say goodbye. I know you had a rocky past, Grams. I just wish I could have found out more before you left us. I'd give anything to know what makes us Bozeman girls tick."

"I thought your last name was Evans before you married Daddy." Lani's face scrunched with confusion.

Alexis let out a sound that was almost a laugh, saying, "You're right. My dad, your Papa, is an Evans. He married your grandma, my mother, who was a Bozeman. She was adopted by Great-Grams' second husband, Tennessee. See, that's his name right there." She pointed to the headstone.

"If you say so. That's a lot of names." Her round eyes went wide.

Alexis shook her head at her daughter's face and pulled her inward for a hug.

According to her Uncle Marshall, Evelyn, who was widowed and pregnant, stumbled into the Bozeman's' life under mysterious circumstances. Eventually, she married Marshall's father, Tennessee. She evolved from a shell of a widow to the fulfilled mother and dedicated wife Marshall finally knew her to be. However, neither Tennessee nor Evelyn ever talked about her past or how she came to live on their ranch. All Marshall remembered was the day Evelyn arrived in his father's truck. He was only three when she entered their world, and he'd adored her ever since.

Since Marshall's father honored her need for privacy, he never divulged her secrets. And now, any chance of discovering anything about Evelyn had died along with her.

Alexis knew more than anyone that a girl had a right to her past. Still, more than anything, she wanted the ability to give her daughter a full history of her family tree. With the passing of her Grandmother, their family lineage was locked away forever.

Regret clung to Evelyn's soul. She understood the importance of the answers Alexis was searching for yet was afraid of what could happen if her granddaughter found them. She slowly outstretched her arms, hoping the love embodied for the girls would cascade around them, giving Alexis the peace she needed.

Alexis wrapped her arms around her midsection as a slow warmth spread through her heart. She looked down at her daughter, who gave her a knowing look.

Within seconds, a soft and gentle breeze swept through the leaves above her and wrapped around her grandmother's favorite bench. With a soft gust, it whipped toward her enveloping her in what she would describe as a loving embrace. Alexis couldn't swear to it, but if she believed in ghosts – she'd lay money on the fact that her grandmother was comforting her now.

Evelyn noticed Alexis' face twist beneath her. She wished she could caress the tears away like she'd done throughout her life. As she beamed down at her, she prayed her granddaughter knew how proud she was of her.

"What am I supposed to do now?" Alexis laughed and shook her head. "What am I doing? You can't answer me."

Her daughter giggled and rolled her eyes, saying, "Just open your eyes, Mom."

Alexis took a deep breath, contemplating what was in front of them with this massive void in their life. Now, it was only her mom, herself, and Lani.

"I wasn't ready to lose you, too." A final errant tear slid down her cheek.

After Clay died, you were my rock. You called me every week to check on me. You told me you understood what it was like to lose the man you loved.

Alexis gave a wry laugh before saying, "I bet you can't fathom how much it hurts to lose you."

"You still have me, Mom." Lani's concerned eyes darkened as her lip quivered.

Alexis dropped to her knees once more, saying, "Oh, I know, sweetheart. We'll always have each other."

"But what if we don't?" Her daughter's voice broke.

"I promise. When have I ever broken a promise?"

Lani slowly shook her head. "Never."

"Okay, then. Know I'm never leaving you."

"It's part of the reason we moved back here." She pushed some curls behind her daughter's ear and stroked her face saying, "Grams would have loved getting to know you better."

"Uh huh." Her small hands gripped her mother's face. "I love you, Mommy."

"I love you, baby."

"Let's get home. I can see my mom from here. She's waiting on the porch."

Lani looked across the cemetery to where a grand two-story house sat in an open field.

"Is that where we're going to live?"

"Yes, baby."

"Whoa. That's massive."

"Massive. Your vocabulary kills me, kid." Alexis let out a breath with a shake of her head.

"Bye, Grams!" Lani waved to her departed great grandmother, who was now standing beneath the oak tree.

Alexis studied the spot where her daughter waved at and wondered for the first time if she actually saw something.

A surge of hope pulsed through Alexis' heart as if her grandmother was there, lifting her spirits.

"Honey, do you really see Grams?"

"What do you think?" Lani pursed her lips and gave her mom an incredulous look.

Evelyn smirked. Her great-granddaughter was wise beyond her years.

Alexis inhaled and brought her fingertips to her heart as it tingled from something unknown.

"It's possible that she's here – that's for sure. I don't see her, but I imagine you think you do."

"I don't think I do. I know I do."

Alexis shrugged her shoulders. "Okay, ask her for me then. What do I do next?"

Alexis gazed upon her daughter, who looked once more to the same spot and stood to wait with her ear to the wind.

Evelyn slipped forward to whisper as Lani cocked her head, intently listening.

"She told me you should apply to the news station. She told me you want it - so go for it." Lani grinned.

Stunned, Alexis took a step back as her mind raced. *I never told anyone I was planning that.*

"Oh," Lani blurted out with a giggle. "She also said to help your mom with the chickens."

Alexis dropped her head back and let out a belly laugh before saying, "I hate getting up that early." She looked at her grandmother's headstone and said, "But you lived for it."

Evelyn's eyes danced with joy. "Do something you love. Go ahead, Lani. Tell your mom."

"She said to do something you love." Lani stroked her mother's leg.

Alexis' heart dropped. That was how she and her grandmother ended every phone call. Lani wouldn't have been privy to that. She quickly pulled her daughter in and stared into her soulful eyes.

"You *can* hear her," she whispered.

"I heard Daddy, too, before he finally stepped toward Heaven."

Alexis' jaw dropped as a jolt of pain tore through her chest. *Why didn't he ever come to me?*

Lani patted her shoulder.

"Don't be mad, Mommy. He only wanted to make sure we were going to be okay. And I think Grams does too. You are just too big to see them, I think."

"Oh, honey. I'm not mad. I thought you were having pretend conversations. I never imagined you could see them."

"Well, to be fair. Daddy only came to me in my dreams. I never actually saw him. I would just wake up and remember our conversations. Seeing Grams, well, this is something new."

"Sweetheart." Alexis sat, stunned.

Evelyn dropped to her knees next to her girls and stroked Alexis' hair. Although it was seventy-five degrees with the full sun outside, a small shiver ran down Alexis' spine.

Evelyn whispered into her ear, hoping she'd understand her. "Sweetheart, let the past stay in the past. You have your whole life ahead of you. Take care of yourself and your baby."

Alexis slowly stood. Her voice faltered as she took in her surroundings. "So, she said to do something I love, huh?"

"Yup." Lani grinned a toothless smile as her two front teeth had recently fallen out.

"Okay, kiddo. Go ahead and get in the truck, and I'll be right there."

As Lani skipped toward their beat-up truck, Evelyn's eyes darted to the bench, where the dandelion still lay. Unsure if it would work, she repeated the same steps that allowed her to hug her family only moments before.

She closed her eyes, intent on focusing her movements with her whole heart before pushing every ounce of energy toward the seeds from the dandelion puff toward Alexis' slender frame. When Evelyn opened her eyes, she grinned as wildflower seeds cascaded around her granddaughter's amazed face. It looked as if she were in the middle of a snowstorm, only instead of snowflakes – fuzzy white seeds fell around her.

When a gust of wind swirled, bringing with it a shower of dandelion droppings - Alexis sensed her grandmother's spirit and had hope for the first time in days.

"Is that you?" she whispered. Although the air stilled with no response, there was something that was undeniably Evelyn Bozeman in the air. She let out a satisfied sigh at the tangible emotion that clung to her heart. At that moment, she knew she had her grandmother's blessing.

Evelyn was glowing with the joy that flowed from her soul. Alexis' shining expression lifted her spirits more than she could ever imagine. As her granddaughter made her way toward her truck, Alexis clearly left a different person than when she arrived.

"See you soon, sweet girl," she whispered through the wind.

"I love you, Grandma." Alexis lifted her face to the sky.

While Evelyn knew Alexis couldn't hear her, neither couldn't deny the unspoken bond that still tied them together.

6

It had been two weeks since her grandmother's funeral, and Alexis still couldn't fathom the idea of being without her presence on the ranch. However, if she were to listen to Lani – her spirit was always around them.

There were some moments, like at the oak tree when they first arrived, that she thought her daughter had a gift. And then there were days like today, where she was convinced her intuition ran deep, yet her imagination was still that of a seven-year-old.

Alexis let out a deep sigh, thinking about how many people came to support them at their humble family cemetery to lay her grandmother to rest. She had impacted the whole community in one way or another.

"Deep thoughts, Sis?" Anderson stood in the narrow doorway of their family kitchen, leaning into it with his arms crossed.

"Yeah." She nodded. "While you get to return to God knows where I live in this empty tomb. At least it seems that way without Grams."

"It was your choice to move back." He shrugged. "And, who says I'm going back?"

Alexis turned and slowly contemplated his statement while

taking him in. Although two years apart, they looked like they could be twins. The strong family resemblance gave her pause. She wished she knew to whom they resembled other than their grandmother. Although she and Anderson counted themselves of Bozeman decent, their biological grandfather was someone utterly unknown to them.

As she stared into her older brother's eyes, a look of worry crossed her face. He had always been the taller of the two with a stocky build, but today as she surveyed him – he looked a bit gaunt. And, his eyes held shadows that she knew ran deeper than his grief from their grandmother's passing.

"You doing okay?" She blinked and waved him over. "I mean other than the obvious."

Anderson nodded and gave her a look that she couldn't quite interpret. It was guarded and a bit unsure, but he said, "Of course. I'm a tough guy, remember?"

She raised an eyebrow at him, saying she thought differently. He had always had a tender heart, and part of her wondered when his career in the CIA might get the best of him.

Anderson cleared his throat. "If the funeral was any indication of how tough one of us was, I'd say you won the jackpot on that one, Sis."

He snatched a carrot from the table and poked her in the arm before sitting at the table.

"What? I cried. Just like you did." She frowned, unsure of where this was going, and turned back to peeling potatoes in the sink.

"That's not what I'm talking about. I saw the way you brushed off Tyler." She glared from across the kitchen, but he continued, "When he approached us, you gave him a look that would stop most men in their tracks. Then, you turned on your heel and hightailed it out like he was a leper."

Alexis' stomach dropped at the memory of how good Tyler looked in his designer suit, which was a far cry from the jeans and t-shirt kid she used to know. She sent her brother a sideways glance with an innocent look.

"I don't know what you're talking about."

Anderson bit his cheek and smiled. "Admit it. You have a thing for him. You always did."

"I do not have a thing for Tyler James." She brought a hand up to her hip in protest and turned to lean on the counter. "He's the most irritating and egotistical man I've ever known."

"No, actually, he's not." Anderson shook his head. "He's one of the nice guys. You used to think so too. So, what happened?"

"Drop it, okay?" Alexis spun back to the counter and turned on the faucet to rinse more vegetables. "It's nothing."

Anderson was about to push the subject when Lani rushed in from the living room to ambush him at the table.

"Unc!" She yelled and scrambled up in his lap, taking his face in her hands. She searched his eyes, thinking they were the most beautiful shade of turquoise she'd ever seen.

"I thought I heard you in here." She squeezed his cheeks and stared a little too long into his eyes before taking note of her mother's irritation. Her face broke into a wide grin as she continued, "Mom's giving you the look that she gives me when I've had one too many sour patch candies. Did you spoil your dinner too?"

Anderson held up his carrot and shook his head. "I'm only questioning her on her manners, Lani. She was rude to a close friend of ours recently."

Lani dropped her eyes and then whispered, "That's because she's lonely, but don't tell her I said that."

Alexis released the potato she was peeling in the sink and spun to face them. "I am not lonely."

Anderson smirked in her direction.

"And even if I was – the last man on earth I'd go for is Tyler James. To him, I'll always be..." Alexis stopped short and dragged in a calming breath. "Never mind. I've got to finish peeling these. And if you both want to get in my business, then you may as well be helpful."

She dropped a peeler to the kitchen table and nodded toward her daughter before handing some potatoes to her brother.

"Be careful with that," she said, before giving Anderson a look. "And the subject of my life is off-limits."

Lani giggled. "You're in trouble."

"Since when am I not, kid? Trouble is the business I'm in."

Alexis gave them both a look and turned to fill a pan with water and set it on the stovetop to boil. Although fuming at the thought of spending one second in Tyler's presence, there was a time when it was all she dreamed of.

Her mind settled on the last time she was within close quarters of Tyler when he shut her advances down and mortified her by taking up with the next girl who came his way.

No, getting cozy with the likes of Tyler James was not on her list. To be honest, she wished everyone would stop making her out to be a heathen by not giving him the red-carpet treatment. She couldn't have cared less if she ever saw him again.

"Mom?" Lani asked for the third time.

Alexis swung to face her family, who looked at her as if she'd committed a mortal sin.

"What?" She frowned in response.

Her mother, who snuck in without her knowledge, raised her eyebrow and said, "I've only asked you something twice without any response. Where were you in that mind of yours?"

Anderson grinned. "I bet I know where she was."

Alexis sent her brother an evil eye before turning her back on him.

"Sorry, Ma." She shrugged. "I've got a lot on my mind. What did you need?"

Amelia looked from Anderson's smug smile to Alexis' tight face and wondered what she'd interrupted but ignored it for the moment.

"Just wondered if either of you would be here tomorrow. I just got a call from an inspector from the fire department who said he wanted to swing by and talk about the accident."

Anderson straightened in his chair. "That doesn't sound good."

"I can't let myself go there yet, Anderson." Amelia blinked back the concern that filled her large almond eyes. "What else could it be but an accident?"

Alexis threw an arm over her mother's shoulders. "Let's cross that bridge when we come to it, Mom. You don't know that it's anything more than a final report telling us what we already know. The tractor malfunctioned."

Amelia nodded as she pulled back, hoping her daughter was right.

"What time is he coming by?" Anderson set Lani on the ground and rounded the kitchen island to join his mom on the other side.

Before she could answer, it dawned on her that Alexis may not be available. Her eyes went wide with recognition, and she said, "You have your interview tomorrow."

"Yeah. Will that be okay?" Alexis blinked. "I can push it back."

"No, you need this." Amelia stroked her daughter's arm with a reassuring smile.

"What interview?" Anderson interjected.

"At the news station – in downtown Dallas," Amelia answered for her daughter.

"Hey, isn't that where-"

Before Anderson could blurt out Tyler's name, his mother cut him off. "Yeah, she applied last week. Now, it's just a matter of acing the interview." She gave Anderson a look as she turned from Alexis' view.

"Oh - okay, then." He responded to his mom before nodding at Alexis. "Well, break a leg, Sis."

"Mom, I can reschedule," Alexis replied, clueless to the silent conversation that had taken place between her mother and brother.

Amelia shook her head. "No, I'll ask him to come out after you get back. It can wait until you're done."

"Okay, if you're sure." She wobbled her head from side to side. "After all – I gave up my career once. I'd like to think I still have a shot."

"You'll do just fine. It's like riding a bike." Anderson's searched her eyes with a smirk and added, "And something tells me you've got this one in the bag."

Amelia stepped on her son's foot with a look before she batted her eyes at her daughter. To keep the pain from registering on his face, Anderson spun, lips clamped. The last thing they needed was to raise her suspicions.

Alexis watched the exchange between them and was about to comment until her daughter tugged on her hand.

"Mom, you've got to see the face I made on this potato."

Alexis let out a belly laugh as Lani plopped a sopping wet spud that resembled something from her cartoon books in the palm of her hand.

"I took the peeler and gave it googly eyes and a mouth." Lani shot her a toothless grin. "Come look at the family I made for him."

A row of potato faces was lined up on their kitchen table. Alexis leaned over to inspect them and sent her daughter a smile of approval.

Anderson leaned in and whispered in his mom's ear. "Tell me why I'm not allowed to mention that Tyler works at the station."

"Because after all this time, she still has a bug stuck up her butt about something he may or may not have done in I don't know how many years. She won't interview if she knows she'd have to work with him," Amelia whispered in return. Her eyes lit up with mischief, before adding, "I wonder how much trouble I'm going to be in after tomorrow?"

"Why?"

"Because the person she's interviewing with is the News Director."

"So?"

"You've not stayed in touch with Tyler very much, have you?"

"I've not been in a position to pick up the phone and reach out to anyone."

His mother gave him a look that said, 'Don't I know it?'

"Well, he got a promotion last year. Tyler is the News Director."

Anderson stifled a laugh.

"Oh, that's rich." He glanced at his sister, who was still eyeing them with suspicion.

"What's up with you two today?" Alexis frowned.

"Us?" Anderson shrugged and looked at his mom with a blank stare.

Amelia raised her eyebrows in return as Anderson said, "I could tell you, but..."

Alexis rolled her eyes, knowing her brother's favorite cliché. "I know. I know. But you'd have to kill me."

"Something like that." He shot her a smug look before grabbing another carrot and sailing out of the door.

"Mom?" Alexis raised an eyebrow in her direction.

"Oh, don't mind us. I'm just trying to get him to loosen up." Her mother waved her off.

"You noticed it, too, huh?" She looked to the door where her brother disappeared. "There's something he's not telling us."

Amelia nodded with worry. "It's been two weeks, and he's still here. Typically, when he takes leave, which is next to never, he only drops in before practically disappearing in the middle of the night for his next assignment."

Alexis twisted her lips and gave her mother a look. "And he looks like he's lost at least twenty pounds."

"I know." Amelia drew in a worried breath before shaking her head. "Look, first, focus on your interview, and then we'll meet with the inspector. Afterward, we'll corner your brother - together."

Alexis walked toward the window that faced the front lawn, where Anderson stood staring off into the horizon. She clicked her tongue and shook her head.

Alexis hoped whatever was behind her brother's aloof behavior wasn't more tragedy, because she wasn't sure her family or her heart could handle it.

7

    Alexis navigated Dallas traffic, thankful she had her GPS to give her step-by-step instructions. The oversized, stacked overpasses seemed to stretch for miles, looping in all directions. If she wasn't careful, she could get lost in a heartbeat with one missed turn.

As Natasha Bedingfield's distinctive voice blared through the stereo system with her favorite song, Alexis narrowed her eyes and imagined herself on a racetrack, zipping in and out of cars. In a few short seconds, she slowed and shook her head.

Her dearly departed Clay would be making fun of her if he could see her now. Clay was a fan of anything with a motor. He was the one who taught her how to hug the turns and when her lead foot could take it all the way.

She peeked in her rearview mirror before pulling across a lane of traffic. She was almost to her exit when she recalled the image of Clay leaning over the side of one of his last projects in his garage. Clay would inspect every curve, his hand running along each edge on any number of cars he'd work on. He was a classic car lover all the way. She winced, trying to free herself of the memory.

It's been almost three years. Come on, Alexis.

She banged her hand on the steering wheel and turned up the volume on the radio. Recently, Alexis considered the option of dating again, but a memory like this sabotaged any desire for companionship.

"I don't have time for this right now," she growled to no one.

Evelyn, who seemed tied to Alexis, appeared at her side as if she sensed her unease.

"Time for what?" Evelyn asked.

Even though Alexis was utterly unaware of Evelyn's presence on a conscious level, a part of her must have discerned her spirit. Because she sighed and sent a sad smile in her direction.

"Focus, Alexis," she told herself. "There's too much to lose if you can't nail this interview." *And if I get this job, I could use my newfound contacts to dig a little.*

During her short time back home, Alexis had made up her mind to research her grandmother's background. Come hell or high water, she wanted to add more branches to her family tree. Her first step in investigating was to go through Grandmother Evelyn's personal items in the next couple of days. She thought she'd go to her interview first before uncovering anything too dramatic. She just hoped there was something of value in her grandmother's room.

As if Evelyn could read her mind, she laid her hand on Alexis' shoulder as she changed lanes. A small shiver shot through Alexis. She immediately drew back as her granddaughter brought shoulders in with an abrupt shrug.

At that moment, Alexis smiled at the thought of her grandmother, hoping she'd be proud of her as she went for her dream job.

"I gave up my job for Lani years ago, Grams," Alexis said aloud. "Now, I hope I still have a chance to take it back. Now that we're here with Mom, I don't have to worry that Lani will be alone."

After Clay had died, she gave up most everything, including her dream of becoming a journalist, to help her in-laws who also babysat Lani when needed. However, in two short years, both Clay's parents passed, leaving her at a loss for what should happen next.

It was then that she sold her in-law's property and decided to move home. The intention was to raise Lani with a bit of normalcy, and the ranch could provide that.

If she were to be one-hundred percent honest, another reason for moving back to Purity was to rediscover parts of herself that she lost with Clay's death. The pain that traveled from Alexis' heart was like a dense fog that she had to fight her way from.

Evelyn was surprised how acutely aware she was of her granddaughter's emotions. Alexis' heartache wrapped around Evelyn's spirit like a wet shower curtain, making it seem like she was drowning in sorrow.

To break the somber tone, she ran her hand along Alexis' thick blond curls and whispered in her ear, hoping it resounded somewhere inside.

"You have a bright future in store for you, my dear."

As if her spirit understood, a peaceful wave washed over Alexis. With a lighter heart, she accelerated down the off-ramp.

Once she exited the freeway, the congested traffic from the highway looked like an open road compared to the gridlock that she approached. Alexis scrunched her nose in thought. She had seconds before she missed her turn.

For Evelyn, the next few seconds seemed to slow as if time were diminishing. She watched the emotions that made their way across Alexis' face before catching a glimpse of what was to come if she didn't insert her newfound abilities.

In a split-second decision, Alexis made a judgment call and gunned her engine across two lanes of traffic, hoping she could make a spot where there was none.

Evelyn's eyes went wide as the image of a future collision flashed before her. Without much thought, she aligned her spirit above Alexis's vehicle, giving it a gentle nudge and easing it through traffic. Evelyn let out a sigh of relief once her granddaughter was safely out of harm's way. Without her intervention, Alexis would have been sandwiched in-between a large truck and a speeding Jaguar coupe.

Alexis flinched, unsure how she missed a massive fender bender by a narrow margin but didn't have time to reflect as her destination was around the next corner. She steered onto the next main thoroughfare toward the television station when a deafening horn blast blared from behind.

She looked over her shoulder as the Jaguar vigorously swerved past her. Although she couldn't see the driver, his hand gestures through the window were plain as day. She shrugged and waved out her window with regret before focusing forward. An almost accident wasn't enough to slow her down, and if she didn't hurry, she'd be late.

As she sailed above the pickup, Evelyn grinned down on her granddaughter. Alexis may not have seen who the other driver was, but Evelyn did. Things were about to get interesting.

8

Tyler stormed toward his office, wiping his shirt with one hand and shaking coffee from his cell with the other.

"Of all the Mondays," he grumbled, passing his assistant who was tidying up her desk.

"Good morning, TJ." She flashed her pearly whites without hesitation. "Isn't it a beautiful day outside?"

Tyler took a deep breath, thankful for her genuine smile. Fran always brightened everyone's day. He quickly forgave the idiot driver who ruined his morning and decided to leave his anger outside.

"Good morning." He returned her smile with genuine effort. "I bought us some bagels, but right now, they're drenched in coffee in my passenger seat."

Fran's eyes gleamed in anticipation of whatever story had TJ in disarray. Instead of clarifying what transpired, he asked, "How were things while I was gone?"

"Busy as always. I'd say welcome back, but I know you took a vacation for some reprieve. I'm sorry for your loss."

"Thank you." His pained face strained as the memory of Evelyn's face flashed before him. He shook off the memory of her boisterous laugh with a resigned sigh. He could have sworn he could still hear it when he was home alone but shook off the notion.

With a gleam in her eye, she wagged a finger at his shirt. "Well, if that stain has anything to say about the start to your week..." She tried to stifle a giggle but failed miserably. Her boss may have been in a bad mood, but he wasn't without humor.

Tyler let out a chuckle and nodded in agreement. "I know, right? I've got a lot to catch up on. Is the staff meeting still set for later this morning?"

"Yes," Fran paused before adding, "but there's one thing added to your schedule today."

As she started for his office door, he hesitated, asking, "And what would that be?"

Fran grimaced. "Dan put an interview on your calendar."

"Why didn't you tell me?"

Her eyes widened at his tone. "I only found out seconds before you came in. He said the applicant reached out to him last week, and he was impressed with her gumption. He told me to schedule her with you for an interview. I thought you knew. Besides, he's the boss." She tilted her chin. "If he says, 'Get her ready' - I jump to it."

When Tyler playfully narrowed his eyes in her direction, she added, "I mean – you're my boss, but he's bigger than you."

Tyler chuckled. Fran had been with the station for a long time and understood more than anyone how intimidating their general manager could be.

Fran's shoulders sagged with relief. "Dan's in his office waiting for you. He asked that you stop in before seeing her."

"You mean she's here now? Why didn't you tell me?" He grabbed his notebook and stuck his phone in his pocket.

"I just did." She grinned.

"Will you let the team know where I am and that I won't be long? Text me with anything breaking," he said referring to the news. "Please retrieve whoever it is I'm interviewing. I'll be with her shortly."

She clucked her tongue at Tyler's back as he exited the office.

∽

ALEXIS SURVEYED THE LOBBY, her gaze landing on the young woman behind the oversized front desk, who nodded in return. The area was much like the station where she'd worked in her earlier years, but she was sure the technology had changed some. Sitting out here as an outsider was foreign, but the comfort of knowing what was behind those doors soothed her frazzled spirit.

"You can do this," she murmured.

"Ms. Mathers?"

She looked up as a perky blonde strode across the lobby with a hand outstretched.

"I'm Fran. You're meeting with TJ, our news director today. He'll be with you in just a few minutes."

Alexis stood to shake her slender hand. "Nice to meet you."

"Would you like something to drink?"

"No, thank you."

"Okay, then." Fran drew in a breath with a genuine smile. "Why don't you follow me, and I'll give you a short tour of the newsroom while we're waiting? He shouldn't be too long."

Alexis glanced at her watch, noticing that it was already fifteen minutes past the time for her interview.

Fran pretended not to notice and pursed her lips. She appreciated punctuality as well, but today wasn't a typical scenario.

"Right this way, please. She held the door open before nodding to the receptionists in dismissal.

∽

TYLER'S CLIPPED stride could be heard down the hall. As he poked his head in the doorway, Dan waved him in.

"Hurry up. I want you to see this before talking with Ms. Mathers."

Tyler's eyebrows shot up. *It couldn't be.* "Ms. Mathers?" He grinned.

"Has a nice ring to it, doesn't it?" Dan turned his computer to give Tyler a clear view of his laptop.

As Alexis' soft eyes peered at him from the monitor, Tyler almost forgot to breathe.

Dan anticipated his reaction and knowingly grinned. He tapped a pen on his desk and searched his new director's eyes for any sign of interest.

"Quite a looker, huh? And she has a brain to go with it."

"Well, that's a deadly combination," Tyler murmured, already too familiar with how dangerous her attributes were.

As he sat down with a thud, his stomach clenched, giving him pause. It was clear that his world was about to turn upside down. Alexis was a reminder of his past, from which he worked hard to overcome, but she had been his saving grace day after day when he'd come to her home seeking refuge.

After college, Tyler quickly built a life for himself as TJ – a man unaffected by any issues from his younger years. Yet now, as her image flashed on his boss' monitor, he glanced over the desk, hoping to discover a roll of antacids. She could be even more dangerous to him now than she was to him then.

Get a handle on yourself. Tyler turned his attention back to the story she was covering.

While the footage was a bit dated, what still shined through was how composed and controlled Alexis was in the middle of a chaotic outburst. As dozens of looters ran behind her in the streets of Washington, DC, she was clear, concise, and conscious of how to deliver a stellar broadcast. Even if the story had Emmy written all over it, what mattered was how her velvety voice disrupted his thoughts.

"She has a face that begs to be watched." Dan's serious tone brought him back to the matter at hand. "You think you can find room for her on your team?"

Tyler dragged his eyes away from the screen and blinked. "After your last budget meeting, you're asking me that?"

"Okay, well, it's not like she has to break a contract to move to this market. What do you have open?" He leaned back in his overstuffed chair.

"You know what we need as much as I do that I could use someone to take the incoming calls to the news desk, and I can always use a good photographer."

"A college intern could do that." Dan frowned and leaned back in his chair. "You could make room on your team if you need to. If she's any good, you'll know what to do."

"I'll figure something out." Tyler dropped his eyes back to the image on his boss' screen.

After all the times Alexis had shunned him, he wasn't sure mixing her into his work life was the smartest decision, especially considering how confused it left him. For the life of him, he couldn't figure out her shift in nature toward him, and even more - why it bothered him so much.

"You do that." Dan gave a look that left nothing to interpretation. "Contract negotiations are coming up. We could cut some of the dead weight around here and bring in some new life." He tapped his finger on the desk before pointing at Tyler. "I have a feeling about her."

Tyler nodded, saying nothing. What could he say? His boss had a nose for these things. Usually, he did too when he could make fair or logical decisions, but when it came to Alexis, being impartial would be like fighting the tides of a tsunami. If he wasn't careful, he could be swept away.

～

As fifteen minutes late turned into half an hour, Alexis impatiently tapped her foot on the tile floor. Although she appreciated the tour from Fran, she now waited, minutes dragging by in a vacant room with a clock that was ticking each second away to oblivion. Her calm façade was beginning to crumble when she noticed the interview wasn't as much of a priority to them as it was to her.

Not to mention the upcoming meeting her mom had about

Grandmother Evelyn's accident. Alexis glanced at her watch, thinking she'd miss that too if the elusive TJ didn't hurry.

"This is ridiculous," she said just as someone entered behind her.

When Tyler pushed the door open, the first thing he saw was a set of long, shapely legs that led to a red pair of stilettos. If he didn't know who they belonged to, he might have been tempted to let his mind wander, but this was his childhood friend. Even if the sight of her made his heart race, Tyler would dismiss any thoughts that he had no right to.

He quickly shifted gears as he stepped inside and asked, "What's ridiculous?"

As he slipped into the seat across from her, shock registered on her face. His gut twisted with the desire to know what he'd ever done to change her attitude toward him. Especially since she used to send him adoring glances as a teen. They had even shared a kiss after her high school graduation. Yet, since then, she disappeared from his life without explanation.

Through his previous family drama, Alexis' presence in his life had been a treasure. Their inside jokes, summer expeditions across their adjoined their property, and quiet moments in her treehouse was paramount to who he became despite his drunkard mom and a non-existent father. After everything he and the Bozeman kids shared, her overnight transformation from friend to foe was baffling.

He swallowed and moved forward. After all, Alexis was here for an interview. That meant he had the control, but something about her look had him glaring right back whether he liked it or not.

He stuffed down the resentment threatening his calm demeanor and sent her a steely smile. If she wanted to pretend that he was someone foreign to her, then two could play at that game.

He extended his hand for a formal handshake as if meeting for the first time.

"Hi, Tyler James, well they call me TJ. I'm the news director of KTXT."

As Alexis' cheeks burned from embarrassment, she slowly

slipped her hand in his, ignoring the warmth that traveled up her arm and swirled down to the depths of her toes.

"Cut it out, Tyler. I know who you are."

"You do?" He leaned back, slowly accessing her collected and controlled appearance. "Could have fooled me."

Her mouth went dry as he gave her the once over. The wild boy who ran around their property with dark circles under his eyes was no longer. His boyish charm and unruly hair were now refined with a stylish cut, a designer suit, and a chilled attitude to match.

"I have had a lot on my plate if you haven't noticed." She side-stepped the truth and glanced down to her hands as she fiddled with the hem of her jacket.

Get a hold of yourself.

She glanced back up to find his dark piercing eyes were not only alluring but seemingly wise beyond his years.

"I know you have. I'm sorry for your loss. Well, your losses. Your mom kept me up to date."

"She did. Did she?" Her eyes narrowed.

Tyler bit his lip and glanced at his watch, unwilling to go *there* just yet. "Well, I'd love to catch up further, but we are here for an interview."

"Maybe this was a mistake." She leaned down for her briefcase.

Tyler continued and motioned for her to stay, which she surprised herself by doing.

"From the footage I just saw of one of your news stories, I'd say you have a lot to be proud of," he said.

"That was a long time ago," she blurted before thinking. "But I've by no means lost my edge. I just don't know if this is the right station for me now that..."

Tyler raised an eyebrow. "Now that you know you'd be working for me?"

"That's not what I meant."

"Look, do you want the job or not?"

"I do, but I don't know if I could work for..." She finally added, "you."

Tyler sat, stupefied for a brief second, unsure of how to respond. Just what was it that he had done that was so offensive? He was tempted to dismiss her from the interview until the image of Dan's face flashed before him. His boss' not-so-gentle advice to find her a spot rang through his ears.

He drew in a frustrated breath. "Well, if the footage I watched is any indication of the professional that I know you are, then I think you can handle it. Around here, I'm not Tyler James. I'm TJ, and I'd be your boss."

Alexis had never been more tongue-tied in her life. As she looked at Tyler, she thought he seemed comfortable in his designer suit. Still, his masculinity beckoned as if he could strip down to a rugged pair of jeans and go riding at a moment's notice. He may have had the rest of the station fooled into thinking he fit the corporate mold, but to her, he'd always be the boy next door - the one whose dimples used to make her daydream until the day they didn't.

Tyler cleared his throat at the slight frown that crossed her beautiful face. It was clear Alexis' mind was spinning in all sorts of directions. For the life of him, he wished he could read what was going on behind her sparkling eyes. He stared down into the almost turquoise pools beneath her thick lashes and blinked.

"Let's get down to business, shall we?" He leaned forward and tapped a pen on the notepad in front of him. "To be honest, I didn't expect to be interviewing anyone today, especially you."

"That makes two of us," she said under her breath.

"But." He paused. "I like what I saw on my monitor. And the camera loves you."

When Alexis' pouty lips parted in a smile, it was as though the room lit up. For a minute, his mind went blank.

"Thank you." She uncrossed her legs and sat straighter in her chair with anticipation.

"First things, first." He dragged his eyes away from her long legs and focused on his words, hoping he could form a sentence. "Dan says you're not under contract with another affiliate?" He flipped through the papers in front of him to find her resume.

"I quit my job a few years back when Clay passed. Lani and I moved in with his parents to help them run their bed and breakfast. Clay's dad was already sick before Clay died. His parents couldn't run it by themselves any longer. So, no, I'm not under contract."

Alexis wanted to kick herself for divulging so much, but Tyler had always been her confidante. It was a hard habit to break, whether she liked it or not.

"I'm sorry." He dropped his eyes to her resume. "And what about now? Will your schedule be free of any family obligations?"

Alexis knew he meant family other than Lani, but his abruptness was more than she was willing to overlook. Their past only covered so much ground before the gloves came off. She pursed her lips. "Family always comes first."

"So do my ratings." His eyes narrowed.

Tyler knew he was pushing a bit too hard, but maybe it would change her indifference to him. While he'd give anything to have an honest conversation with her, now was not the time. Just when he was about to apologize, she spoke.

"Yeah, well, my mom is on standby at any given notice to watch my daughter, so I could boost your ratings, which I hear need a little bit of help." She lifted her chin in defiance.

Tyler watched her eyes blaze with a burning desire to tell him off and waited. After an awkward pause, he clamped his lips to form a straight line. He knew she'd be rating heaven but wondered just how much she wanted to be on his team.

Let's test her ambition, he thought and sent her a crude smile.

"As of now, I don't have an open spot on my desk or my news team," he said, referring to an anchor or field reporter positions.

Alexis nodded. "Well, thank you for your time."

As she gathered her purse to leave, he drummed his fingers on the table. "But if you're interested in working here."

She stopped short of standing and stared at him, wondering what his endgame was.

"For now, I have a position at the news desk, taking inbound calls to feed to the team. Or, if you have any experience behind the camera, I have a photographer position open. We could start you on the floor during a newscast or two and then move you into the field to film breaking news."

Tyler's eyes shone with satisfaction. If he remembered her fiery spirit, she'd probably want to tell him what he could do with his offer – but if she wanted to be a part of this news team, it might be something she'd bend to accept. Contract negotiations were in one short month, and she'd have a spot if she could prove to him that she deserved it.

"And," he continued, "when a reporter position opens, you'll be a shoo-in." He shrugged, sending her a mischievous grin.

What's he up to? She narrowed her eyes. She knew all about budgets and staffing a newsroom. If they wanted her, they could make room. What kind of game was he playing?

She bit her lip, wondering how she could graciously exit without telling him exactly what she thought of his offer without burning a bridge. After all, someone straight out of school could do what he was suggesting.

"While I appreciate that," she paused and put a sarcastic spin on what came next, "very generous offer. I think I am going to..."

"Take the week to think about it." He cut her off. "We're ranked number one in our market."

"Three." She corrected him.

"What?" He stifled a grin. She'd done her homework.

"Three. KTXT is ranked third."

"Well, we won't get to first without believing we can. And part of that is pulling together a winning team." Tyler ran a hand through his thick, dark hair and shot her the boyish grin she remembered. "I'll admit - I wasn't expecting this."

Tell me about it, Alexis thought.

"But, Lexi, I'm inclined to believe that you would be a great addition – when we have the room."

Alexis' stomach took flight when he used her childhood nickname. She glanced at her shoes and wondered when the last time she'd heard anyone call her that.

Tyler saw the disappointment flash across her face and was obligated to give her something.

"I wasn't going to tell you this, but contract negotiations are in a month. So, this trial period wouldn't last long. If you can tough it out, it would be worth your while."

Alexis inhaled through her nose and nodded. "Thank you. I'll think about it and get back with you." She broke eye contact and glanced to the side, wondering what might have progressed between them if only he'd let it happen all those years ago. When she made eye contact once more, she cocked her head and stood.

"Thanks for your time." She offered her hand for a quick handshake only to find that he held it longer than she'd have liked.

The sparks she'd experienced years ago were still there whether she liked it or not. She pulled away, eyes wide, and stared at her shoes, unable to make eye contact. She thought she'd left these nerves behind and wondered if working in the newsroom with him was going to be a detrimental disaster.

Unsure if he'd ever have the chance to dig deeper into what led her to distance herself from their friendship, he quietly said, "It was good to see you again."

Alexis swallowed, saying nothing, and tried to clamp down on anything other than professional courtesy. In what seemed like an eternity, which was in reality only seconds, she nodded and lifted a hand for a parting wave before leaving him behind in the conference room.

∼

As Tyler stared out his office window from the second floor, he all but laughed when he noticed her approach the same little red pickup that cut him off in traffic.

"That was her?" He rubbed a hand over his jaw.

When his assistant heard his laughter booming from outside his office door, she poked her head inside. "Who?"

"Her." He waved her over to the window and pointed at Alexis as she unlocked her door. He emphatically motioned to the stain on his shirt before pointing to the window once more.

Fran watched her boss' face light up and grinned. He couldn't take his eyes from what was transpiring below them.

She glanced down as the striking blonde in high heels exited the cab of her truck to pop her hood like a pro. Although she looked like she could stride down the runway, there was a tomboyish quality about her that had Fran nodding with instant appreciation. Alexis was more than she appeared.

"Looks like she's got car trouble." Fran cut her eyes toward the scene that was unfolding below and then back to her boss.

∼

As Alexis turned her key for the third time, Evelyn clamped her hand over her granddaughter's engine, keeping it from sputtering to life.

"You're going to thank me for this," she whispered. She'd seen the sparks between Tyler and Alexis as they sat across from one another in the conference room.

"Come on!" Alexis urged her engine before finally dropping her hands from the ignition. She glanced at her floorboard, wishing she had a few tools with her. She spotted one of Clay's old rags and reached for it before getting out to pop the hood.

She carefully lifted the hood with the cloth and leaned in to investigate. As old as her truck was and after driving halfway across the country, she was surprised it still ran.

"Everything okay out here?" She turned to see a very smug Tyler, who had slipped off his jacket to reveal a coffee stain across his midsection.

Her mind wandered to what was beneath his shirt before she mentally kicked herself. She sent him a slight frown.

"I think so," she said, turning her attention back to her truck.

Tyler's chest filled with awe as she bent over her engine with ease as if she knew what she was looking for. As if reading his mind, she slowly straightened to slip off her suit jacket and roll up her sleeves before reaching back under the hood, giving Tyler pause. Her backside, now promptly displayed as her short skirt slipped up about an inch, was on display. Out of courtesy, he dropped his eyes.

Emotions he didn't even know he had surfaced. Tyler turned, knowing if she took one glance at him, she'd be able to see everything that lay behind his eyes, which were known to give away his every thought.

Alexis was an enigma, unlike anything he'd ever remembered. Anderson's kid sister was no longer a beautiful yet off-limits distraction. She was a stunning woman who no longer needed anything from anyone.

Does she even know the power she possesses? He loosened his tie.

"Maybe I can help?" He leaned against the side of her truck, admiring her nimble fingers as she checked her engine with a rag to keep from singing her skin.

"No," she frowned. "I need a new starter. I'm almost sure of it." She groaned and reached for the rod clip in dismay. "Watch your fingers." She indicated for him to move back before she eased the hood back into place.

When Tyler noticed the perspiration gleaming across her forehead and down her cheek, he retrieved a handkerchief from his pants pocket.

"Here – let me get this." He wiped her brow with one hand while cupping her face with the other. For what seemed like an eternity, they stood there, transfixed.

Startled by the tender moment, Alexis' breath hitched. As he guided the soft rag across her forehead, a tingling sensation made its way from the base of her neck down to her toes.

This can't be good. She took a step back.

Tyler knowingly smirked. Whatever this was, he knew she felt it too. The desire that flashed in her eyes quickly dampened as she stepped away from his touch.

Since she hadn't answered his question, he pulled his cell out to send a quick text and asked once more.

"Now, how about a ride? I know where you live, you know." He shot her a sly grin that sent her reeling.

"Oh, no. I couldn't impose." Her throat went dry at the thought of sitting in a confined space with him for the drive to Purity.

"It's okay. I just sent my assistant a text. My schedule is now clear for the morning. Come on. My ride is just inside that secured area. It's that little green number in the second row."

Alexis glanced toward the fenced-off parking lot where an expensive sports car sat a few rows over. She swallowed at the sight of the Jaguar and met his knowing eyes.

"That's yours?" She barely got out a whisper. He beamed from ear to ear.

"Come on. I'll be doing the public a favor by getting you off the roads."

Alexis couldn't help it. She let out a nervous laugh wanting nothing more than to crawl into a hole and hide.

"It'll give us time to catch up." He ushered her through the gate and toward the passenger door before opening it.

Evelyn watched the scene unfold with heartfelt awe. To see how much passion pulled at Alexis' heartstrings made Evelyn light up with joy. She spirited forward to lay her hand on Tyler's shoulder out of gratitude.

Unknowingly, he paused before sliding into the driver's seat and wondered when his heart held such a sense of peace.

9

A gentle breeze streamed in as Alexis cracked her window. She watched Tyler from the corner of her eye and grimaced. It was nothing short of excruciating as they rode in silence. The fact that his strong jawline and full lips beckoned to her after all these years infuriated her. It was an insult to Clay's memory, and she silently berated herself.

As Tyler left the city traffic behind and started for the smaller country road that led toward their hometown, he cleared his throat almost desperate to end the awkward silence. It was as if she were a stranger, which couldn't be farther from the truth. And yet, here they were, acting like they had no common ground – or at least she was.

"I tried to approach you after the funeral. I don't think you saw me." He stared her down, daring her to come clean.

Alexis squinted and inwardly bit her lips. She didn't want to go down this road just yet. The last thing she wanted was to rehash old history.

"Yeah." She kept quiet. The path of least resistance was the smartest option.

"Or at least that's what I thought."

Tyler scanned her pensive yet beautiful face, searching for the truth before she turned to look out at the countryside and sighed.

"I've missed this view," she said.

He raised his eyebrow and gave her a pass but wasn't done just yet.

Why was she so dismissive, and what had he done to deserve it? The young girl he knew would never shy away from anything. After everything they'd shared growing up, he wondered how she could push that part of herself away so easily.

"Yeah, I know what you mean." He watched a few stallions tussle on the horizon. There were a few ranches along this stretch of the road that put his and the Bozeman's land to shame. "This area has really changed since school."

Suddenly, Alexis turned in her seat and stared at him with interest. "So, Dad said you didn't sell your property after your mom died."

"I couldn't let go of it." He shrugged. "Even if there were too many ghosts."

Her heart went out to him. Without thinking, she touched his arm but immediately pulled away. Her instincts for comfort took effect before her hardened heart could advise against it.

As she folded her hands in her lap, she shook her head. "I'm sorry, Tyler. I really am."

"To live there would mean seeing her around every corner with a bottle of whiskey." He sent her a soulful stare. "But I couldn't sell it either. In some twisted way – it's still home."

Alexis bit her lip, unsure of what to say. As if he could sense her unease, he quickly added, "It's okay. Now, I rent it out to a family, the Kahle's. They board horses – hence those two running down my fence line." He gestured toward a pair of Mustangs that were racing in the wind. "They take care of it for me."

"They have a daughter about Lani's age who has some challenges. And, riding seems to do wonders for her. So, I built a small house on my land and commute to work. My place sits around the bend from the old house. Sometimes, I still come out to ride."

As their gaze connected, memories of the two of them came

flooding back. Alexis recalled the two of them racing horseback almost every week. Overwhelming images of Tyler's untamed hair and dark eyes flashed before her as they laughed in the summer sun. His transparent charm used to beckon to her even when they were kids, and if the last ten-minute conversation proved anything, it still did.

Although the three of them, Anderson, Alexis, and Tyler, had once been practically inseparable, there had always been an unspoken bond between Tyler and Alexis. All Tyler had to do was show up, and Alexis not only intrinsically knew the depths of his spirit but was able to pull him out of the doldrums if it was a bad day. Her quick wit and heartfelt eyes always calmed him no matter what he'd experienced at home. Alexis had been his lifeline. She'd saved him from allowing his mind to recount the images of his mother, who would lay on the couch without noticing if he came or went.

For the last few minutes of the drive to Alexis's property, it was as quiet as the eye of a storm. The unspoken emotions swirled around them as if ready to choke the life from Tyler. He clenched his teeth to keep from saying something he'd regret.

Instead of steering to the front of her home, he turned and parked behind the barn.

"Um?" She blinked in his direction. "My house is that way."

Tyler turned off his engine and faced her, compelled to discover what had changed between them that had caused her to cut him from her life.

"What happened?" he asked.

When her body tensed, he knew the answers he was searching for wouldn't come easy.

"Well, you made a wrong turn for starters." She pointed toward her house.

"No, I mean after your graduation."

Suddenly, it was as if the summer air swelled by ten degrees. She began fanning herself. "I'm not sure what you mean." She pointed to his ignition. "But, can you please start that thing and crank on the AC?"

Tyler took a slow breath. The car's interior was still chilled from the drive over. Instead of obliging, he ignored her request and continued, "We've been best friends practically our whole lives. On the night of graduation, Clay was following you around like a puppy. You weren't serious about him. Heck, you even kissed me! And then the next thing I know, you run off and get married without saying goodbye - without saying anything to anyone!"

Images of that night infiltrated her thoughts. Tyler's warm lips were a welcome change from Clay's sloppy kisses. She shook her head as the guilt sank into the depths of her spirit. How dare she compare the two? It was like speaking ill of the dead.

She closed her eyes and dropped her head. "Tyler, we were kids. Who knows why we did anything?"

"We were, but we were close too."

"Maybe a little too close." She snapped her head up to meet his earnest eyes, which were filled with confusion.

"What does that mean?" A pained look crossed his face.

She closed her eyes and lowered her voice. "I'm sorry. Maybe this was a bad idea. I can't take a job working for you. I-It wouldn't be good."

"Why not?" He reached for her hand, but she withdrew it to grab her purse. "Why did you cut me out of your life?"

Alexis opened the car door and stepped out. Before she shut it, she leaned down and asked, "You honestly have no idea?"

"No!" He quickly exited from his side and rounded the front to face her head-on. "You were a lifeline for me growing up. I wouldn't have made it without you or your family. And then, one day, you're gone, and you treat me like I'm an ax murderer or something."

Alexis's eyes started to water, but she turned her head before he could tell. Once she was sure her tears were at bay, she hoisted her bag on her shoulder and spun back. "Well, maybe I wasn't the nice kid you thought I was."

"I guess not." His voice was as hard as steel. Tyler shot her a sizzling glare before sinking into the driver's seat and pulling away from the barn, leaving her to walk the distance to her home alone.

Unsettled as he was, he knew there was more to her story. Out of respect for the friendship they used to have, he was determined to figure it out.

"This isn't over," he whispered to himself as she started for the porch.

Alexis was proud of herself. She didn't once look over her shoulder as he drove away – not even once. Her pride crumbled, though, as soon the first of many tears rolled down her face. She angrily wiped them away and stormed up the steps. She'd spent enough time lamenting over Tyler James, and it cost her more than she'd like to admit.

Alexis was proud of herself. She didn't once look over her shoulder as he drove away. Her pride soon crumbled, though, as the first of many tears streaked down her cheeks. She wiped them away and stormed up the porch. She'd spent enough time lamenting over Tyler James, and it cost her more than she'd like to admit.

10

She got up at the crack of dawn to help her father and Uncle Marshall work the ranch. Although the skies were clear now, the storm that was brewing out west would hit home by sunset. It would take all of them to stay ahead of the weather. Now that they were a family member short, the whole Bozeman clan and their crew needed to pitch in.

Well, everyone except Lani. She was still too young to do anything more than gather eggs. Instead of waking her, she peeked her head through the door of her room to blow her a kiss. She paused in the doorway, watching Lani's chest rise and fall with each breath.

If someone had told her before she became a mother how something as simple as a child's breathing in the early morning light could melt your heart, she would have thought them crazy. Now that she had experienced how fragile and fleeting life was, she appreciated every moment she had with her daughter. Especially quiet ones like these.

She pursed her lips and brought her hand to her chest. After the last few days, Lani could sleep in as long as she wanted. Besides, she'd learn a few things around the ranch soon enough. She pulled her daughter's door shut and retreated into the hall.

Boots in hand, Alexis tiptoed down the hallway and grabbed the railing to swing around the corner for the first step before skipping downward for the landing below. It had been ages since she worked her family land. Even though she wasn't conditioned for a full day, like most of their ranch hands, she was looking forward to some of the more menial tasks.

Comfort settled within her chest as she passed a sign at the bottom of their stairwell that read:

Twelve hours a day of being a cowboy is better than an hour of anything else.

There was a time in life when she resented that notion more than anything in the world. Growing up, she was obligated to work the land but didn't dream of living that life. If she stayed here, that's precisely how she'd end up - as a rancher or married to one.

That was why running away with Clay was so enticing. He promised her adventure. The other part was who she tried to forget for the next decade, but Tyler didn't make that easy. His grin and easy nature swept through her dreams over the years, but never more than last night.

Alexis almost tripped over the wool throw rug on the main floor and grumbled.

"Well, good morning to you too." Her mother's face beamed from across the kitchen.

She grunted in return and gave her mother a nod as she stepped out to the porch.

Amelia followed her out and pulled her into a soft embrace.

"It's good to have you home," she sighed. "I couldn't do this without you."

Alexis searched her mother's dark brown eyes and smiled with gratitude. She was never more thankful her mother gave her the option to live her life the way she pleased – even if that didn't include farm life.

"Thanks." She slowly blinked and rubbed her eyes. "I haven't been up this early in a while."

"Better get used to it." Amelia put her hand on the screen door to let her daughter outside. As they walked out to the porch, she added, "I'll start breakfast and get Lani up to help me in a little bit."

Before Amelia could spin for the door, a soft tug pulled at her arm. She immediately turned back to find Alexis' questioning eyes.

"How are you doing, Mom? Can we talk about yesterday?" Alexis tiptoed around the subject they'd all been avoiding last night.

It only took one look at her mother's forlorn expression to understand the burden they all carried. As if Tyler's tongue-lashing wasn't enough to put her in a foul mood, the tail end of the conversation between her mother and the fire inspector would be.

It would be an understatement to say that this morning brought a whole new level of pain to the Bozeman clan, as they emotionally and mentally sorted through yesterday's visit. The fact that an officer from the Purity Police Department was present should have been their first clue that it wasn't your average follow-up appointment.

I'm sorry to tell you folks – that Evelyn's death wasn't an accident. It was sabotage.

As the words echoed in both their minds, they stood in silence until Amelia sucked in a deep breath and stared at the grooved pine ceiling and blinked back tears.

"Are we going to talk about it?" Alexis gently pushed.

Amelia closed her eyes, not ready to open it up for discussion.

"I don't know, to be honest, Sis." Amelia lovingly patted her daughter's arms. "But now is not the time and like Grams always said, 'Each day is a gift from above, so we better use it wisely.'"

After her mom disappeared inside, Alexis took a deep breath of morning air. As she faced the land, she sighed at the memory of her grandmother's catchphrase before grief encompassed her heart. Her grandmother was well known for her compassion. When someone was struggling, somehow Evelyn always knew and would show up with comfort food and a shoulder or a helping hand.

Because of her selfless spirit, many families benefited from her generosity. Most everyone she knew had a soft spot for Evelyn. Her mind instantly flew to Tyler, who, at the age of six, showed up on their doorstep, malnourished and matted. Still, she saw through his angry disposition and nurtured the joy back into his spirit through warm food, love, and friendship.

Evelyn approached everything in life with fierce passion, but she was more than a humble servant. She had a sharp mind for business.

Throughout Purity and the surrounding areas, the Bozeman ranch was known for having the finest timothy grass in the Midwest. When tough times hit, Evelyn didn't buckle. Instead, she thought of ways to diversify and talked her stepson, Marshall, and her family into having a weekly farmer's market. It expanded the business with a broader reach than any of them expected.

Alexis' expression turned tender as she thought of how Evelyn had always been ahead of her time. She ran her hand down the fencing as thoughts of her grandmother pummeled her spirit.

"You were a pioneer, Grams," she whispered to the breeze that picked up. Her grandmother had so many ingenious ideas to increase their revenue. Some of them included hay festivals and mazes in which family or church groups would happily pay every fall to experience.

But the farmer's market was her grandmother's true passion as it offered a way to help their family as well as many other households in the area. Evelyn was insistent that they open the market up to other farmers, so that they, too, would be able to make a profit. It was her way to bolster the whole community, even though the Bozeman's had enough produce to support most of the offerings.

Alexis slowly pushed open the barn doors to reveal what seemed to be a vast cavern inside. To one side lay a row of office doors, where her mother, father, and uncle ran the family business, while the other side housed the stables and supplies. The smell of fresh droppings and hay accosted her senses as the doors creaked open, letting the early morning rays filter in from behind her.

In a heartbeat, she was taken back to when she was a young girl. Saddled with morning chores before school, she often found herself alone working at the crack of dawn until it was time for the bus.

The mundane tasks required became a source of contention, but after all these years, there was comfort in her simple past. After everything she had been through, she welcomed the quiet calm of spreading feed for the chickens and gathering eggs at the break of dawn. She imagined her family felt the same way – especially this morning.

The fire inspector's words replayed within like someone shouting from the depths of a canyon. As she shoved her work gloves in her jeans pocket, she reached for a bucket and filled it with scratch feed.

"What are you doing up so early?" Her brother's voice sounded from the loft above.

Alexis squinted through the dark to see her brother's long legs hanging from a rafter just above some hay bales that had been stacked against the wall.

"What are you doing up there? I thought you'd be out with Uncle Marshall fixing the fence."

"I couldn't sleep."

"When did you get up?"

"I didn't."

Alexis frowned. "What?"

"I haven't gone to bed yet," he mumbled.

"Anderson." She sighed with emotion.

"Don't start in on me," he growled, making his way from the rafters to drop down on the hay. After descending a few bales like stair steps, he plopped down on the one closest to his sister. "How can you expect me to sleep after hearing what happened to Gram's tractor?"

"Look. I didn't get much sleep either, but I went to bed like a sane person. I wasn't climbing the rafters."

"How could you not?" He ran a hand through the blond waves that swept over his temples. Since he'd been home, his uniform cut had grown out just enough to drape over his sea-green eyes.

"I don't know. Yesterday was a roller coaster. First, the job interview from hell, and then my truck broke down. Ugh!" She rolled her eyes in disgust.

"I noticed who brought you home."

Alexis sent him an evil eye. "Then, after narrowly escaping his congenial presence," she added with a sarcastic smirk. "I took the walkway from the barn to see a police cruiser in front of the house." She dropped the bucket and pushed her small frame up on the bale of hay next to Anderson. "I thought I was going to have a heart attack. I didn't have any idea the police would be there too."

"We didn't expect it either. I don't know how Mom is making it." He dropped his gaze to the bucket beneath their feet. "She's a rock."

"She has Dad and us," Alexis added. "But, she's avoiding the subject."

Anderson squeezed his eyes shut, unable to think of who would want to hurt anyone in his family. With his background, he'd seen a lot of darkness in the world. He knew no one was above reproach, but a part of him had been naïve to think his family was safe from the unpleasantries of the world.

To prevent the waves of anxiety that threatened to claim him, he changed the subject.

"So, why didn't Tyler come in?" He sent a sly look to his sister, who shot him another smirk in return.

"Whatever." She hopped down to retrieve the bucket.

"No, seriously. He's family. He'd be welcome."

"He left in a fit, okay? And while we're on the subject, why didn't you guys tell me I'd be interviewing with him?" She spun around to face him with a hand on her hip.

"What?" His lips curled up, almost feigning a smile before shrugging. "I had no idea."

"Yes, you did. Now it makes sense with the way you and Mom were going on in the kitchen yesterday. You both knew!"

"Honest. I didn't!" He put his hands up before sliding off the hay.

Alexis let out a grunt. "It doesn't matter. He's not the guy we grew up with anyway. I could work for him and be fine, but I'm not sure if I'd want to at this point."

"Don't let that stop you from your dream, Sis." Anderson raised an eyebrow. "Just what happened between you guys, anyway?"

"He kept asking me stupid questions, and I sent him on his way."

"I'm not asking what happened yesterday." He stared her down.

She spun on her heel. "Why does everyone think something happened, okay? Nothing happened." *And maybe it's best it didn't.*

"Okay, okay." He followed her outside to the chicken coop just as the sun's rays filled the yard. He stretched and reached inside the bucket. "Here, I'll take some. I thought Lani was going to learn how to do this." He sprayed the yard with feed as she began shaking the bucket, alerting the chickens to their presence.

"She will soon. She needed her sleep today. So, what do we do now?" She looked over the fence to the spot that still showed signs of burns from the explosion.

"Well, now we find out who would want to hurt Grams."

"Who would want to do that?" Her eyes misted. "She helped anyone who needed it. Everyone loved her."

"Well, in my experience – everyone has a past. And we don't know much about hers."

"How do we find out anything? She was a mystery – even to Mom. Even Uncle Marshall was unaware of how she came to be a part of his family."

"Well, then – I suggest we start digging. And I'd start in her room." Anderson nodded toward the family home.

"Mom's not ready yet. Gram's door has been shut since the accident."

Anderson cocked his head and drew in a breath. "It's been almost two weeks since the funeral. She'll be okay. It's time to open it and dig deep."

"Think you could use some of your contacts?" Her question hung in the air between them like a spider clinging to its web. At any moment, it could drop, or it could scurry away.

Her intent with this question was two-fold. Anderson had been elusive about why he was still home, as his typical MO would only give him a small window home before returning to work. Maybe his answer would allow her the ability to delve into why he was still here.

Not that she was complaining. She missed her older brother, but the distant look in his eyes did nothing to ease their mother's nerves.

Amelia had too much on her mind with her mother's passing to have to worry about her eldest child.

Anderson finally broke eye contact. "If we don't find anything in her room, I'll think about it." He threw another handful of feed. "If it comes to that."

When her brother started for the gate, Alexis hollered after him. "Where are you going? I could use your help shoveling out the barn."

"Marshall may need me out in the fields. I told him last night I'd help harvest."

"Anderson, are we going to talk about it?" She took off after him.

"There's nothing to talk about." He shot a look at her over his shoulder. "Let it go, Sis. I've got men's work to do."

Anderson's sly grin did nothing to ease the rock that sat in the pit of her stomach. What was he hiding?

"It's your life." She sighed. "I'll start in Gram's room tonight."

Just then, they heard the rumble of Marshall's truck as he pulled up in the field behind him.

"I've been looking for you. We're short a few men and need you. We've got to get this grass up while it's still dry – before the rain hits." He frowned out the driver's side at his nephew. "You know this job is five to nine – not a nine to five."

"I was just on my way to find you," Anderson said unapologetically and waved back to his sister before hopping inside the passenger side.

Alexis shook her head and headed for the barn to muck the stalls.

"Great," she mumbled. "Just what I had in mind when I moved back home."

11

It seemed fitting that storm clouds pressed toward the ranch as if enveloping it. Alexis' heart swirled with uncertainty, much like the skies. As hard rains pelted the ground, Alexis dropped to her knees in front of Evelyn's grave. Freezing cold water penetrated her jeans, chilling her skin. It was then she realized the dirt around her was quickly turning to mud.

Alexis pushed her wet, matted hair away from her eyes, and stared at Evelyn's headstone. "What happened, Gram? Who are you, really?"

Evelyn wished with all her might she could take the confusion and pain from her granddaughter's soul. She wanted to infuse comfort within as she wrapped her arms around her granddaughter's slender frame.

"I'm still the same woman you always knew," she whispered to Alexis over the thunder.

Living, if that is what you would call it, somewhere in this thin place where heaven and earth met was a confusing task. Evelyn was privy to some of what transpired as she faded in and out of her family's everyday activity, but she wasn't there all of the time. When she was absent, it was as though she was asleep.

"I wish I had the answers." Evelyn sighed, knowing Alexis couldn't hear her. She hadn't seen what brought her flesh and blood to her grave in this state. She could only guess Alexis had gone through her room and found a clue that could lead her to the truth. Yet, it was just a breadcrumb, and it would likely confuse her more than educate her.

"Why would you hide it, Grams?" Alexis frowned.

"Because it wasn't something that anyone needed to know," Evelyn answered, hoping the truth would somehow settle into her granddaughter's heart.

Evelyn watched Alexis' full pouty lips tremble and felt like screaming.

Why am I still here? What is the point of watching my family suffer like this?

Alexis dropped her head into her hands and cried as a strong set of arms lifted her from behind.

"Are you crazy?" Tyler spun her to face him as lighting cracked loudly above them. They both jumped as the sky lit like it were on fire. "Come on!" He grabbed her hand and practically dragged her to the barn for shelter.

"What are you doing here?" Her teeth chattered.

Instead of answering, he reached for a couple of horse blankets and gathered the material around her shoulders to keep her warm.

"The question is – what are you doing here? You're soaking wet." He frowned. "Does your family know you're missing and in a storm no less?"

She shook her head. "I put Lani down for a nap. She sleeps hard, especially through storms, and then." She paused to draw the blankets closer as Tyler wrapped his arms around her. She shivered in response, unsure if it was the cold rain or his embrace that had her body responding.

"And then?" he prodded.

"Then I went through some of Grandmother's things. We got some disturbing news yesterday after you... left."

"Yeah, that's why I swung by – to apologize. I was harsh."

When she made eye contact, she noticed a few rain droplets clinging to his thick, black hair. She fought the urge to brush them away, keeping her hands tightly wrapped inside the blanket. Inwardly grimacing, she turned to stare at the rain that pelted the side of the barn.

"It's really coming down," she whispered as a few horses neighed in the background. "I'm glad they're all tucked in safely."

Tyler looked toward the stalls and nodded. "That they are. And what about you? What on earth would make you run out in this storm? You know how dangerous flash floods are."

"That's the pot calling the kettle black!" Her eyes flashed.

"You're avoiding the subject. Since when did you get so persnickety?"

"Persnickety?" She laughed. "Is that even a word?"

"Yes, and you are. Every time I've seen you." He faltered. "Well, you're not you."

"Life has a way of changing someone." She dropped her gaze.

"Don't I know it?" His eyes blazed as he stared through the storm toward his property that sat a mile away.

Alexis could have kicked herself. She knew he had survived so much more than she had, and he didn't sit around wallowing in it. So, why was she?

"I found a letter." She dropped the blanket from her shoulders to pull a damp piece of paper from within her windbreaker.

As she pushed it into his hands, he sent her a questioning look.

"Go ahead. Read it." Her eyes urged him to proceed.

He peeled the tri-folded paper apart. It was just damp enough that it stuck, but the writing was still intact. He took a step back and motioned for Alexis to sit with him on a bale of hay. When she declined, he took a seat but couldn't quite read yet since Alexis began to ramble.

"I was going through her clothing to donate to the church like she'd want." Alexis paced the floor. "Since Mom wasn't ready, I did it myself. After Anderson took the boxes of donations to the garage, I started sifting through her roll-top desk and found this." She finally stopped in front of him and reached for the letter to lovingly stroke the letters that spelled Evelyn's name.

This time, before she could put distance between them, Tyler gently took her hand and guided her to sit next to him on the hay bale near one of the stalls.

As her thigh brushed up next to his, she nervously continued, "She had so many papers, which I almost dismissed until this one caught my eye. It was in a manila envelope that I left in her desk after pulling the letter out. There was a large logo on the outside of the envelope. It stood out so much from the rest that I was compelled to read what was inside."

As the couple sat on the hay safe from the storm, shock rocked Evelyn's spirit. As Alexis continued, she found it hard to focus on the sound of her granddaughter's voice. All she could think of was how long that secret had been buried and what it might do to her family to finally know.

Evelyn whispered to herself, *why did I keep it?*

"Why did she keep it?" Alexis asked in unison, staring at the letter. "What does it mean?" She wiped her nose with her sleeve as Tyler sent her an adorable grin.

"I haven't even read it. How would I know?" His heart lifted as he watched her face, seemingly transform back to the vulnerable young girl he used to know.

Alexis brought her knees in and tucked them in the blanket. "Read it. Tell me what to do."

Evelyn sighed as the sorrow pouring from her heart mingled with the confusion that seeped from Alexis's.

It doesn't matter, Alexis.

Evelyn settled next to her and laid a hand on her shoulder and said, "I'm okay. You don't need to do this."

Evelyn's heart tore in two at how her past still dredged up turmoil for her family.

"Why the urge to uncover this now?" She searched her granddaughter's determined face.

Compelled to answer the unspoken question, Alexis explained aloud what her spirit desired to confess.

"I need to find out what happened to her." She dropped her head, realizing he didn't yet know about the investigator's visit. "After you left, we got some bad news. Her tractor had some sort of timing device on it. Her accident was..."

Tyler's mouth parted in shock. "It wasn't an accident?"

"If someone meant to harm her, does that mean the rest of my family is at risk?" Alexis swallowed, unsure if she wanted to go there.

As the answer hung between them, he dropped his eyes to read the letter in question.

My Dearest Evelyn,

After much thought, I've decided that it is best for us to part. I never thought my family would have suffered from my decisions and can't put any scandal on them right now. Know that I've loved you the best I could, but it just wasn't good enough.

However, I am a man of my word, and I promised to take care of you and your unborn child. My father still thinks it's mine, so find solace that my financial support will last through the years for as long as we're both alive.

Take this check as a promise of what is to come. After all, a promise is a promise.

Take care,

William

Tyler's head snapped up to meet Alexis' unwavering gaze.

"Now, I can see why you're so upset." His eyes widened. "Who is William?"

"My grandmother never spoke of anyone from her past, except her parents and her sister. I have no idea who he is." She shook her head. "And what about his promise? As long as they're both alive?"

She left the unspoken question to settle in the back of her mind. *What if her death was only the beginning?*

Tyler laid the letter on the hay next to them and drew her back against him. His gesture was meant to be one of loyal support, but having her pressed against his chest set off warning bells. Ignoring them, he held her close. She needed a friend right now. And no matter what had caused her to run out of his life all those years ago, he was still her friend.

"We'll figure this out. I promise," he whispered into her hair.

"Should I tell Mom?"

As she sat within his embrace, the scent of fresh soap transported her to a place of comfort while at the same time making her stomach spin as if she were inside a washing machine. Although it was what she needed, she begrudgingly pulled away. She had to keep her wits about her, and whether she liked it or not, Tyler was quickly becoming a distraction.

"I don't know if Mom can handle this letter. She's already reeling from Gram's death."

Tyler nodded. "Yeah, but this is pretty big news. It's not the kind of thing you keep from your mom, especially since it's about her mother."

He gazed at her, wondering when she'd grown into such a beautiful woman. He couldn't equate her as a childhood friend any longer. As they stared into one another's eyes, the urge to kiss her almost drove him over the edge.

Alexis blinked as his chocolate eyes softened. The intimacy that silently transpired clung to them like the droplets from the storm, and it was a shock to them both.

"There you are!" Hank stomped in out of the rain.

Whatever moment they had shared shattered the second Alexis' father stepped in, causing both Alexis and Tyler to scoot uncomfortably in opposite directions.

"We were worried, sick!" Hank yanked a drenched ball cap from his head and smacked it against his jeans for good measure before slipping it back on.

"Why?" Alexis slid from her place and stepped forward. "Is Lani okay?"

"She's fine, but she woke up and came downstairs looking for you. And you weren't anywhere inside. After the news about Evelyn," his voice dropped, "Your momma kinda panicked, although she'd never admit it."

"I'm sorry, Dad. I didn't think." She reached for the letter next to Tyler and slipped it inside her jacket. "Of course, you guys would worry. That was irresponsible of me to run out into the rain."

Tyler watched as her nerves took a dive and slid off the hay to join her. His touch was firm but gentle as he turned her to face him. Without breaking eye contact with Alexis, he asked, "Hank, can you give us a few minutes?"

Hank looked between the two and stood for a few seconds. "Well, I, uh, yeah. As long as you're alright."

She nodded, afraid of what might tumble out if she opened her mouth.

After Hank left, Tyler lifted her chin with his finger and said, "I'm glad to see you again."

She squinted and shook her head. "What?"

"Although I would do anything to take this pain from you, at least I got to be your confidante again. I've missed this." He waved his hand between them. "Us."

Alexis straightened her back as her expression changed from confusion to a steely stare. "There has never been an us."

He shook his head. "There go your walls. Did you know you're the spitting image of your grandmother when you smile? Then, you tense up, and everything changes, even your eye color. It turns from deep turquoise to almost a greenish-gray. It's like nothing I've ever seen except when the sky changes during a storm."

Alexis ignored the fact he was paying too much attention and got back to the subject at hand.

She tapped her jacket. "So, what do I do?"

"Come on. I'll go with you. We'll tell your family together, and then you'll need to call the police."

Tyler stepped forward and reached back for her hand, which she begrudgingly obliged.

Evelyn watched as they walked hand-in-hand toward the main house. Although a bit of bright blue shone through the dissipating storm clouds, she knew the storm was far from over.

12

It had been three weeks since Alexis discovered the letter and come to the realization she had just as many emotions for Tyler as all those years ago. Since she was no closer to finding clues about the mysterious *William* and how he fit into her grandmother's life, she finally accepted Tyler's job offer, thinking it would give her access to more records.

Running a camera wasn't what she wanted but knew it could provide her access to doing more research while she waited for an opening on his news team. Alexis, however, took one look at her monitor at the over-polished news anchor onset and pursed her lips. She gave a look that, thankfully, no one could see in the dark interior of the studio. All the studio lighting was angled toward the anchor's perfect hair and expertly applied makeup.

"How'd I let him talk me into this?" Alexis grumbled to no one, as she listened to the producer's instruction through her earpiece.

"Okay, camera two. Zoom in to give me a tight headshot."

After making the smooth transition to the next segment, she nodded into her monitor. At least she still had skills from her first job in television. After she and Clay married and moved to Virginia, she answered an ad in the newspaper for a camera operator for the local news. She thought it would be something fun to do while Clay was in training, and it turned out she was good at it.

It only took about six months before the news director decided he'd like to see her in front of the camera instead of behind it.

After a few small news stories, she gained her composure and realized she had a knack for it. Although no formal training, her career took off. The audience responded to her genuine likeability and ease.

It got to the point that no matter where Clay's duty stations took them, she knew she could get a job at almost any network due to her hard work and excellent references. Wherever she went, ratings followed.

"And in five, four, three, two, one. And we're out."

Alexis nodded toward her crew after the final instructions bled through her earpiece. She unhooked her cable from the camera and grinned, thinking it was like riding a bike. Although the cameras had come a long way with technology, they still had the same controls.

"Not bad, rookie." Grant winked in her direction as they walked out of the studio. "You look pretty comfortable behind that thing."

"Thanks. It's not my first time, but it's been a while."

"I'd have never known you weren't a pro. You did great." Grant studied his new co-worker out of the corner of his eye and wondered if she would be working the noon news every day or if the boss had her working a few swing shifts first.

He hesitated slightly before saying, "Hey, if you're interested, a few of us may head over to this bar down the street for a few drinks after work."

Before she could reply, Tyler appeared at her side as if on cue and answered for her.

"Alexis already has plans. We have to go over that paperwork, remember?" He squared off with Grant before raising an eyebrow in his direction.

"Um, yeah. I guess." She gave him a blank look.

"Okay, boss. Well, maybe another time." Grant sent her a wink. "I'll take that as a yes."

"Maybe." Alexis nodded before turning to Tyler with a hiss. "What was that about?"

"Trust me. He only has one thing in mind."

"Ugh. Please! What man doesn't? Besides, he was being friendly, and I can handle myself." She huffed and made her way past him, only to pause as he lightly touched her arm. Her stomach immediately flipped. "Now what?"

She feigned frustration to cover the excitement that soared through her veins at his touch.

"Look. I'm sorry." Tyler's voice almost dropped to a whisper when he saw the attention they were garnering. "Come to my office for a second."

When Alexis followed him from the studio, she noticed the curious eyes of everyone in the newsroom.

"Are you trying to ruin my first week here? Everyone is staring. Do you generally act this territorial with all your employees?"

"No, but maybe they're staring because no one else speaks to me the way you have been. I shouldn't have to remind you that I'm the boss here."

He quietly closed his door, although he wanted to slam it. When he spun, he found himself practically face to face with Alexis. At that moment, he didn't know if he wanted to shake some sense into her or kiss her. He took a step back and calmly sat on the corner of his desk. "You may not like me telling you who you can and cannot hang out with, but you won't speak back to me here? Got it?"

As his piercing eyes clouded, she couldn't tell if he was angry or confused. She bit her lip and narrowed her eyes.

She used to be able to read him like a book, but it was obvious things had changed. This Tyler - the one who ran the office – was a stranger to her. Alexis chewed her lip, thinking she liked him better when he was sitting in her barn, giving her comfort.

"Do you tell everyone else who they can and can't hang out with?" She frowned.

"No."

"If you did, they'd tell you off too." She crossed her arms.

"You're not everyone. You're Lexi."

"No, it's Alexis. Just like they call you TJ here." She shook her head. "We're not kids anymore, TJ."

As the sound of his new nickname rolled off her tongue, he winced. It sounded so foreign. It was as if she'd erased any history they'd shared by stepping into the station.

"Oh, I know. You keep reminding me." He ran his hand through his hair. She had to be the most infuriating woman he'd ever known. There was a part him that wanted to throttle her, but the majority of him wanted to pull her in to taste what lay beneath that smart mouth.

"Just let me do my job." She backed away to open his office door when she heard a hard tapping on the other side.

"Come in," he said half-heartedly. The last thing he wanted right now was an interruption.

Before Alexis could move out of the way, a striking, exotic woman barged in, wearing a tight red dress. She brushed past Alexis without giving her a glance. Although her back was to her, Alexis could clearly see this woman's curves were enough to put Alexis' small frame to shame.

"TJ," the woman almost purred. "When are you going to put me in the five o'clock spot? You know I'm better that than ditzy blonde out there."

"Sharena, we've gone over this. Elly has proven herself and has seniority. Keep working hard, and you may get a shot."

"Ugh." Sharena tossed her thick black hair over her shoulder, hitting Alexis in the face.

Alexis turned her head, coughed, and gave Tyler a grimace that left nothing to be interpreted.

Sharena slowly turned and said, "Oh, I didn't see you there." After giving Alexis a once over, she added, "Nice jeans."

Alexis blinked in return and said nothing, knowing it would get her nowhere, except into the center of this woman's drama.

As Sharena sashayed from Tyler's office, Alexis blinked in awe.

"Wow. And you'd rather have her than me out in the field?"

"I told you contract negotiations are soon. Just sit tight."

Alexis blinked and let out a breath. "Okay, whatever."

"Please stay clear of Grant. Trust me. Okay?" Tyler lifted from the corner of his desk. "He's not the only one who thinks you look great in those jeans."

Alexis raised an eyebrow and ignored his backhanded compliment. "Apparently, your diva out there didn't think too much of them."

Tyler wished he could express how the sight of her backside had his pulse racing. He blinked and let out a slow breath.

"And Grant?" he pushed.

"I'll be good. I won't let him near me unless we're in the office and its work."

"I'm just looking out for you."

"I understand, but could you keep it on the down-low? I have to make my way here. I don't need a target on my back because you act like my older brother. I want to earn my way here. The last thing I need is to earn a reporter spot and for people thinking you gave it to me because you like me."

Tyler shook his head. "Not gonna happen again." He crossed his heart and gave her his most charming smile.

"Okay. See you around, boss."

As she left his office, he kept his focus on the floor instead of continuing to appreciate how well she filled out her jeans. It became quite clear that whatever reasons he had for keeping the male office staff away from her wasn't for brotherly reasons.

13

"I'm home!" Alexis dropped her keys into the dish on the entry table. When she heard nothing but silence in return, she cocked her head and yelled, "Hello? Anyone?"

She groaned and stepped out of her tennis shoes, thankful for the one luxury her new position at the station afforded her – comfortable shoes. As for lugging around a heavy camera on-site at today's wildfires, well, that part she wasn't a fan of. She lifted the front of her shirt and sniffed.

"Ew," she said as the scent of burnt embers brought tears to her eyes. She blinked a few times, trying to get them to come back in focus, thankful to be home.

Although she was only on-site for a few hours, it seemed like days, especially since she and her crew got a little too close to the smoke. As a result, the heat irritated her eyes, and now, her throat was rough like sandpaper.

"Mom!" Lani yelled as she tumbled in from the back yard. "I saw the fires on the news." Her daughter almost bowled her over as she wrapped her tiny, yet powerful arms around Alexis' waist.

Alexis caught her daughter to keep them both from falling as the rest of her family came in from the back yard.

"You're a sight for sore eyes." Anderson raised an eyebrow in her direction.

She nodded in return as Lani buried her nose in her blouse.

"Mom, you stink." Her little nose wrinkled up.

"I know, Sweetheart. I'm going to get a shower in just a bit, but right now, I'm starving." She guided her daughter to the kitchen, where her mom and dad were putting away the leftovers.

"I made you a plate." Amelia's face softened. "We grilled dinner in the back yard."

"Grama Amelia says we can have s'mores! Want to join us?" Lani's eyes glowed with excitement.

Alexis hated to disappoint her daughter, but she'd seen enough fires to last a lifetime. As she grabbed a hot dog from the plate, she shook her head down at her daughter with a full mouth and mumbled through her food, "I'm afraid Momma needs a shower more."

"Okay. Come on, Unc!" Lani grabbed Anderson's hand and beamed up at him with an angelic face.

"Now, how could anyone say no to that?" Anderson smirked at Alexis. "Apparently, Mommy can."

Hank nudged his son in the arm and gave him a warning glare.

"She knows I'm kidding," he responded before addressing Lani. "You know I'm joking, right?"

Amelia leaned down to kiss Lani's cheek. "Don't let Uncle Anderson give your mom a hard time. She's had a long day and deserves a long hot shower. If she has the time, I'm sure she'll find her way outside."

Alexis sighed. "Come here, baby."

Alexis opened her arms and sat down, waiting for Lani to curl up in her lap. "Tell me about your day before you go back outside."

"Uh, not much to tell. Great Grams told me you were safe when I saw the fires on the TV. I was really worried."

At the mention of Evelyn, a pained look flashed through her mother's eyes. Alexis sent her mother a tender expression before stroking Lani's face. "I told you that I'd never leave you. You're stuck with me, kid." Then, she tapped her daughter on the nose.

"I love you, Momma." Lani slid to the ground and reached for Anderson's hand once more. "Now, where were we?"

Anderson scooped her up in his arms and kissed her cheek. "Okay, kiddo. Let's go."

"I'm right behind you guys," Hank hollered as the screen door slammed shut. "But not before I do this."

He slipped an arm around Amelia's waist and kissed her on the lips while grabbing the matches from the counter.

"Grandpa!" They all heard from outside. "Don't forget the chocolate!"

Hank winked at his wife. "You heard our little princess. Can't disappoint."

Amelia watched her husband snatch up a package of Hershey bars and said, "No, we can't. See you in a bit, Alexis?"

She gave her daughter a hopeful look to which Alexis shrugged. "Maybe. Hey, Ma?"

Amelia cracked the screen door to step out toward the night air, but stopped and turned toward Alexis, who pulled her in for a hug.

"What was that for?" She chuckled.

"For earlier. I'm sorry about what Lani said." Alexis' eyes filled with remorse.

"What did she say?"

"Her comment about Grams? She swears that Grams is talking to her."

"Well, who is to say she's not?" She took a step back inside the kitchen.

Alexis shook her head and stared up at the ceiling. "I don't know. I don't see how. Grams was a strong Christian, so how could Lani be seeing or speaking with her when she's supposed to be in heaven?"

Amelia chuckled. "Honey, God works in mysterious ways, and you know His timing is not ours."

Alexis sent her a look of confusion. "Isn't that the truth? He also has a strange sense of humor."

"How so?" Amelia's voice went up a notch.

"Oh, come on, Mom. Don't get all preachy on my now."

"Far be it for me to tell you what to think." Her lips flattened. "You're the one who brought this up. If I were going to get preachy on you, I'd drag your butt out of bed on Sundays and force you to attend a service with the rest of the family instead of taking Lani with us and not saying a word to you."

"Mom." Alexis slumped. This was the perfect ending to the perfect day. *Great. Now I've upset her.*

"Don't 'Mom' – me. We're all suffering in our own way. You get solace by going inside your head, where hardly anyone can pull you out. And I receive comfort and strength by leaning on something bigger. If Lani is getting some peace through either making these stories up in her head or actually having communication with my mom, then far be it for me to judge."

Alexis dropped the fork to her plate and stared her mother down. "Okay, then. Tell me what you really think! And don't hold back." Her eyes watered.

Amelia instantly regretted losing her temper but didn't regret telling the truth even if she could have reigned it in a bit.

"I'm sorry. You've had a rough day – a rough year or two for that matter." She dropped to the stool next to her daughter and reached for her hand.

Alexis tensed as her mother covered her hand. She didn't want to forgive and forget. Alexis wanted the anger and hurt to surge through her veins. In fact, she wanted nothing more than to yell - but didn't.

"You're right. I have." She sniffed, as the emotions that swirled through her heart took their physical toll. "But, so have you, Mom." She finally relented and gave in.

"Honey, death is part of living. And our family is suffering a huge loss, but it seems to be par-for-the-course for you lately. You've dealt with so much more. And I know living with Clay's parents wasn't an easy task."

Alexis groaned and rolled her telling eyes. "You have no idea.

Everything I did was wrong. Every move I made was watched. My motives were never good enough."

"Oh, Sweetheart. Why didn't you just come home after he passed?"

"I wanted to." Her voice quivered.

When Amelia pulled her close, she saw the pain that tore through her daughter's eyes. She kissed her cheek and pulled Alexis into a mother's embrace, which could only be described as home. There, she allowed her daughter to sob for as long as she needed.

Once Alexis's tears subsided, she stayed there within her mother's arms and allowed herself to be loved, which was something she hadn't done in a very long time.

"Thank you," she said, before pulling away.

"I wish I could have talked you into moving back." Amelia pushed a few loose strands of hair away from her daughter's wet face.

"It wouldn't have done any good. I promised Clay I'd watch out for his parents. His dad was so sick, and his mom couldn't run the bed and breakfast without us. Toward the end, before his accident, we took shifts around Clay's job to help out." Alexis sighed. "And Lani was the only thing that made them happy. Besides, his mom helped with Lani in so many ways. It would have been horrible to leave them high and dry even if they always thought they knew better."

"You're an angel. I remember how bitter that woman was. God rest her soul and forgive me for speaking ill of the dead." Amelia winced.

"No, I owed it to Clay. It was the least I could do. You know Lani says he visited her after he passed – in her dreams." Alexis choked up again. "At first, I wondered why he chose her and why he wouldn't visit me, but deep down, I know."

"He loved you."

"He did." She nodded through a few more tears, before adding, "But I think he always thought that he wasn't good enough."

"Honey, why would he think that? You had a good marriage."

Alexis shook her head. "Yes, yet there was always a sense of doubt with him. He thought something was missing from our relationship and questioned if I truly loved him. I hated that he felt that way because he was always enough," she sniffed, and continued, "I'm sorry. I'm overly emotional right now. The third anniversary of his death is coming up. And it's just hard. Ya know?"

"I know, baby." Amelia sniffed. As more tears freely streamed down her daughter's face, Amelia grabbed a soft kitchen towel to dab them dry. Before she could, Alexis blocked her hand with a curious look.

"What?" Amelia asked, holding back a laugh as she watched her daughter's face.

"You're not going to lick that thing and try to wipe my face clean, are you?"

"Of course not, Alexis Olivia!" Amelia laughed. "Come here, you rascal."

Alexis giggled as her mother wiped her face dry, remembering all the times she'd chased her down with a rag to wipe her clean.

"At least this time, I'm not covered in mud." She sent her mother a weak smile as she wiped away the last streak that had tumbled from her eyes.

"No, but I'd trade your pain for mud any day. I hate seeing how much you've suffered. No mother wants to see her child hurt."

Alexis nodded in understanding. Anytime Lani scraped a knee or took a tumble, it broke her heart. She could only imagine what her daughter's first heartbreak would do. She held a whole new appreciation for her mother and how deeply she loved her.

"How about - you explain how Grams could still be here? I'll shut up and listen. Okay?" Alexis gently pulled her mother's hands into hers.

"You asked if I thought it was possible that Mom and Lani could talk?"

Alexis nodded.

"Well, what if it is?"

"For how long?"

Amelia threw her hands up. "How the heck do I know? I don't even have proof that she's here. I can only say that God's ways and timing are mysterious. And there are endless possibilities when it comes to what his plans are between heaven and earth."

"So, you think she's somewhere in between?"

"Now, don't get me wrong. Your grandmother made her path known while on earth, and what she lived is how she will be judged when she gets to see the Almighty. There's no praying her into heaven, but, yes, I believe she's still on her way."

Alexis raised an eyebrow. "I guess anything is possible."

"Grama!" Lani attacked the porch steps and yell through the screen door, "It's time for s'mores. You're missing it."

Amelia's grin was contagious. "Life with her here is…"

"I know." Alexis' face softened. She took one last bite of her hot dog and started for the sink. "Thanks for saving dinner for me, Ma."

"I know it wasn't our normal family dinner, but your daughter begged me for hot dogs and s'mores." She lifted an eyebrow and shot her daughter a look of pure joy. "There's not much I can deny her."

"You're going to spoil her."

"That's my job."

"Then, I guess you're doing it well." She chuckled. "Hot dogs are her favorite. I'm surprised she didn't talk you into tapioca pudding too."

"She tried, but I didn't have any." Amelia stopped short of the porch. "Remember, I have a doctor's appointment tomorrow. I may not be able to watch her for a few hours."

"It's okay. If Anderson can't help, I can take her to work with me. Don't worry. Is everything okay with you?"

"Just a check-up. Your dad likes to drive me, and I let him." Amelia grinned like a schoolgirl. "He thinks it's his job to cart me everywhere."

"Not much has changed there." She laughed. "I'm off to get cleaned up. Tell Lani I'll see her in a bit."

Amelia nodded before stepping outside. She stood in the shadows of her porch to watch her family as they bonded over chocolate and graham crackers. As the soft glow from the fire pit illuminated their faces, her heart took flight. It was evident how much joy

Lani created wherever she went, and her boys were suckers for her charm.

She stepped from her porch steps just as Alexis's bedroom light popped on upstairs. She could barely make out her daughter's profile as she grabbed a few clean things from her closet before turning off the light.

When will she find true happiness?

She lifted her hand to her neck. "God, if Mom's still around, could you use her? My family, especially my kids, could use a guardian angel."

"Who are you talking to, Grama?" Lani quietly snuck up behind her to offer a gooey marshmallow treat.

Amelia shook her head. "I was just saying a prayer, Kiddo."

"That's always nice. Did you say hi to Grams, too?"

"No." Amelia leaned down and looked deep into her slate eyes. "Why? Is she here?"

When Lani nodded, her grin exposed the gap where her front two teeth used to be. She pointed toward the tree over the porch.

"She likes sitting up there so she can keep an eye on all of us."

Amelia glanced over her shoulder to the branch where her mother supposedly sat and watched the leaves shimmer under the moonlit sky. She hoped that if she stared long enough, she'd see a silhouette or something that could be a telling sign that her mother's presence was upon them.

"I don't see anything," she whispered to Lani.

"That's okay. You don't have to see to believe." Lani took her by the hand. "Come on. Let's make more of these."

Amelia popped the warm chocolate in her mouth and happily followed her granddaughter toward the fire, but not before turning once more to study the tree. For a split second, she thought she saw a hint of something, but once she blinked, it was gone.

Evelyn grinned from the branch as Amelia struggled to see her. She didn't understand why some could see her while others who clearly wanted to couldn't. All she knew was that while she was stuck here, she was going to make sure her family would be alright. It made her heart light up to see them creating memories by doing something as simple as roasting marshmallows by the fire.

"I'm here, Amelia," she whispered.

Amelia glanced up once more and took in the night sky with awe. She couldn't see a hint of her mother, but her presence was as thick as the summer heat that lingered around them.

14

In the short time she was home, Alexis discovered a handful of things, like the soft sounds of crickets under the veil of the night's sky, that she had unknowingly missed. Simple things, like the way the fresh breeze skimmed her skin as fan blades sliced through the summer air, made her sigh with ease she'd not experienced in a long time. Other than spending time with her family, these were quickly becoming some of her favorite things about being back in Purity.

As Alexis strolled down the hall, she dragged her fingers along the textured and tattered wallpaper in the hallway outside her bedroom.

If these walls could talk. The thought prompted some favorite memories from childhood, and her heart filled with peace.

Slowly, she peeked into her daughter's room in time to see Lani on her knees with head bowed. Alexis' heart swelled at the sight.

"Were you going to wait for me?" she whispered and leaned over to lovingly stroke her daughter's chubby cheeks.

Lani's eyes lit up as she sent her mother a look of adoration. She gently pulled Alexis next to her.

As Alexis bowed her head, she heard her daughter's soft voice say, "You got here just in time, Mom."

"Well, don't let me stop you," she whispered in return.

Lani closed her eyes and grasped her mother's hands and continued her prayer.

"As I was saying – thank you for bringing Mommy home safe. Thank you that we have a nice place to live and food on our table."

Alexis nodded in agreement. Her daughter's prayers were the highlight of her night. Although she couldn't remember the last time she had prayed, she knew her daughter's prayers were enough for them both. Or, she hoped so.

"And God," Lani paused and drew in a deep breath. "Please tell Daddy we miss him. It's been too long, and I wish he were here. And, please help us sleep through the night."

Alexis' throat constricted. She fought back the tears that threatened, and breathed deep before saying, "Amen."

As her daughter buried herself under her covers, Alexis tucked them around Lani's shoulders before leaning in and kissing her goodnight.

Lani's hands quickly shot out from underneath the covers despite her mother's efforts to tuck her in. Lani cupped her mother's face next to hers for a tight embrace.

When Lani's arms encircled her neck, she took in the scent of honeysuckle. She peppered her daughter's face with kisses and drew back with a grin. "You used Grama's night cream, didn't you?"

"Uh huh." Her little head bobbed. "It makes me smell good, and it reminds me of home."

Alexis' heart melted at the thought. "This is home already, huh?"

"Yeah," she sighed. "The only thing missing is-" She stopped short of saying it.

"Daddy?" Alexis traced a finger along Lani's face and brushed back a few locks from her eyes.

"Do you miss him?" Her little voice sounded so vulnerable.

"Of course, I do, Sweetheart. And I know you do too." Alexis' heart broke a bit more for the vast hole in her daughter's life.

Although no one could replace her dad, she wondered if Lani needed a father figure.

"I do." Lani pouted. "Every day. And it's coming up on three years very soon."

Next week, Alexis mentally added and bit her lip.

"You know you will always carry him right here." She lightly tapped Lani's chest. "In the pocket of your heart."

What a cop-out. There was nothing Alexis could say to soothe the pain her daughter carried.

"Sometimes that's just not enough." Lani's eyes watered.

"I know. "Alexis lowered herself next to her daughter's tiny frame and pulled her into her side.

As they cuddled, Alexis stroked her daughter's hair until her soft sobs turned into soft, even breathing. When she was sure she could rise without waking her, she slowly slipped her arm out from underneath Lani and rolled off the bed. Gently, she leaned over to kiss Lani's forehead before exiting and closing the door behind her.

∽

ANDERSON WATCHED Alexis tip-toe from Lani's room and quietly close her door before leaning against the wall with a deep sigh. As he took the last step up the stairwell, he rested at the top and cleared his throat.

Her eyes flew open to meet his concerned gaze only to narrow before she said, "What?"

"Long day?" His boots thudded against the hardwood floors as he approached.

"Shhh. You're louder than a bull in a china closet. You'll wake her up."

"That kid sleeps like the dead. What's got you all riled up?"

"Nothing." The thought of Lani's tearful voice tore at her heart. "She's just having a hard time. That's all."

"Clay?"

"Yeah." Alexis sent him a blank stare. "Between that and Grandma's mystery letter, I need some air. Will you be here to watch her if she wakes?"

Anderson nodded as his sister took the short flight down the stairs. He quickly pursued. "Mom's here. You need company?"

"That depends. Have you made a phone call to your contacts to help me uncover anything on Gram's mystery man?"

Anderson dropped his eyes. The police had no leads, and although he promised to help if there weren't any options, he'd yet to make any calls.

"I thought you were going to use your contacts first. You work with investigative reporters, right?"

Alexis clamped her mouth and said nothing as she gathered her purse. Shaking her head, she frantically searched the entryway table. "Where are my keys? Darn it. Where are they?"

"Here." Anderson lifted her keys from the hook next to the door but held them at an arm's distance. "You're not going to do something stupid, are you?"

Alexis snatched them from his hand before briefly giving him eye contact and kissing his cheek. "I never do. I'll be back."

"Alexis, wait for me to get my wallet. I'm coming with you."

She sighed and stopped in her tracks. She turned to give him a look of reassurance. "I promise I'll take care of myself. I need to get out. Right now, the walls are closing in on me."

Anderson snorted. "The last time you said something like that, you ran off and got married. You're not making things any better here, Sis. I don't like it when you get that look."

"What look?" She frowned. "The look of someone who can't seem to do anything right? The look of someone who needs some closure? The look of someone who just needs to breathe?" Her voice raised an octave with every question.

"No, the look of someone who thinks there aren't any other options." He raised an eyebrow. "What kind of big brother would I be if I let you go like this?"

"One that trusts his sister. I'm a big girl now."

"I know, but Lani doesn't need for you to go off the rails right now."

"Trust me. Lani needs for me to take a breather tonight so I can be my normal self tomorrow. Besides, that look in her eyes when she talks about him." Her voice broke. "I can't. I can't talk about this."

"Alexis!" he hollered as she escaped to the porch.

"I'm all right, Anderson. Give me some credit." She gave him a look over her shoulder. "I'll be back later. Watch her for me." She nodded to the window above them before unlocking her truck.

Anderson watched his sister back out into the night and said a prayer of protection. He waited for her to turn from their property to the main road toward the highway, knowing that if she chose that route, it would provide mindless driving.

When her taillights swung in the opposite direction toward the main strip of Purity, he shook his head with dismay. That meant she only had one destination in mind – Shelty's Bar and Billiard room.

"You going after her?" His Uncle Marshall's voice sounded through the dark.

Anderson turned the porch light on as his uncle raised a hand to shield his eyes.

"Watch it," Marshall grumbled from his rocking chair.

"Why didn't you stop her?" Anderson flicked the light back off before joining him on the porch.

"She's an adult. Not like she'd listen to me."

"You're her uncle."

"You're her brother. Go after her. You know she's heading into dangerous territory. Darn headstrong woman," Marshall grumbled.

Anderson bit his lip and dug for his phone. "When she gets like this – there's only one person she listens to."

15

After Anderson's call, Tyler threw on a pair of faded jeans, donned a plain, white t-shirt, and darted for his pickup. On the drive over, he was never more grateful he opted out of staying at his apartment in the city and drove to his ranch, which was close to the main strip of Purity.

As his tires crunched along the gravel of Shelty's parking lot, his eyes narrowed in search of Alexis' red truck. When he saw it next to a handful of motorcycles, he quickly parked and stormed the entrance like a soldier on a mission. This was the last place she needed to be to blow off some steam.

Why was the urge to come here winning out over mounting one of the many horses she had access to in her barn? When they were young, she often would ride as a release. Yet, now, as the music blared, Tyler realized that Alexis had a life outside his experience. He wondered how much he knew her anymore.

Once inside, it took a few minutes for his eyes to adjust. The stench of cigarettes and Lysol accosted him as he scanned the room. There were a handful of people on the dance floor and a few scattered at tables, but none of them resembled Alexis. Without a clear view of her, he gave the bartender, a former acquaintance from school, an expectant look.

Before Tyler could ask if he'd seen her, Jack, who was cleaning off the bar top, gave him a nod, and said, "Hey, old friend. You looking for Alexis?"

Although lack of privacy was a downside to a small town, in this case, it gave Tyler comfort as he reached over the bar to shake Jake's hand.

"Yeah. Where is she?" He frowned.

"I was about to call her folks. She's around the corner by the jukebox. She looks like she could use a friend, and Lenny made his way over there a few minutes ago."

"Lenny Franks?" Tyler's stomach turned. While in school, Lenny always had a thing for Alexis, even though she never thought twice about him.

"The one and only, and he's only gotten more obnoxious with age."

"Great," Tyler groaned. He hoped to get out of here without a conflict with Alexis. Now he had to worry about an oversized egomaniac, who didn't take no for an answer.

Alexis swayed to the sounds of *The Pretenders* as the tequila dulled the anxiety that drove her to drink. She dipped her head back and closed her eyes, allowing the warmth of the liquor to spread through her limbs. In no time, a numbness settled her nerves also put distance between her and the guilt over her failed marriage.

She slowly opened her eyes and made a noise that was a mixture of surprise and disbelief. Scattered above her were the same rhinestones that had been adhered across the ceiling since the dawn of the '70s. She giggled, wondering if the owner of Shelty's thought it was retro enough that it was still cool.

"Some things never change," she whispered in awe.

Something about the way the light bounced off the tiny stones had her mesmerized. As she drained the last of her drink, she turned to the bar only to lurch forward as a bulky set of arms from behind wound around her. It reminded her of a python as it slowly squeezed the life from its prey.

Alexis spun, trying to get some distance and came nose-to-nose with Lenny. She groaned in distaste.

Lenny was never what she would call unattractive as he had his fair share of admirers, but his eyes were a little too big for his face for Alexis' liking. And right now, those large brown eyes were filled with hunger.

"What are you doing?" She pushed at his arms to no avail. "Lenny, let go!"

"Sexi-Lexi," he slurred. "You're still looking good. Want to dance?"

"No!" She shoved against his chest. "And don't call me that."

Alexis' head swam from the tequila. It seemed that it not only zapped her focus, but her muscle strength too. No matter how hard she tried to free herself, his grip was just too firm. When he called her by her pet name once more, she pummeled his arm with a fist. "Let go! I said - don't call me that!"

"But you are." His eyes danced with dangerous desire. "Your hips are swaying, and they're saying, 'Come here, Lenny.' Come on, Lexi. Let's dance."

"I don't want to." She struggled to get free.

As Lenny aimed for her lips, Alexis dodged his clumsy attempt and dumped the rest of her drink on his head. As it spilled over both of their shirts, including his jeans, he jumped back, putting distance between them.

"Great! You made me look like I peed myself. You bit-"

Before he could finish, Tyler rushed him from the side and slammed him against the wall. Lenny attempted to push back only to find Tyler's forearm securely angled against his neck.

"Take one more step. Please," Tyler said with a growl.

When Tyler rounded the corner toward the back of the bar and saw Alexis struggling against the bulk of Lenny's massive frame, a fury he'd never known coursed through him. Any misgivings he had about taking on someone Lenny's size was thrown out the window when he saw she was in danger.

Just as he was about to pull Lenny away, Alexis dumped her drink on him, giving Tyler the advantage. He rushed Lenny from behind and spun him into the wall next to the jukebox.

With Tyler's arm pressed against his airway, Lenny choked, "Dude. I give."

Distrust flashed across Tyler's face, and he nudged upwards into Lenny's neck a bit further. Lenny's eyes bulged as if he were about to take his last breath. Although he had a good four inches on Tyler, all he wanted was to get to the bathroom.

"Really?" Tyler eased his arm away. "That's all you got?" Relief should have been his first reaction, but disbelief was the only thing that registered.

"Really." He stumbled. "She trashed me with that stuff." Lenny looked down at his zipper with disgust. "Let me get cleaned up, man. She's all yours."

As Lenny left for the men's room, Tyler turned to find Alexis sitting at a table by the jukebox, chewing on a straw with a confused look on her face. She reminded him of a lost little girl.

He approached with caution and slowly spun an empty chair backward before straddling it to sit next to her. He glanced at the table and sighed, pushing a partially empty glass from her reach. "How many have you had?"

"What's it to you?" She grumbled and pushed her bangs from her eyes.

"Well, considering I almost got my butt kicked for you – I'd say you owe me an answer."

"I was doing just fine on my own."

"Right." He lifted his chin and sent her a look. "You look like you're doing just fine."

"Shut up, Tyler." She tossed the straw to the floor only to seize a shot glass from the table next to them and quickly downed whatever liquid was inside.

"Easy, Lexi. You don't even know what's in there." He frowned and placed a gentle hand on hers to remove the now empty shot glass.

He shot an apologetic look toward the stranger, whom Alexis had taken the drink from, and handed him a twenty-dollar bill. "Sorry. Next one's on me."

When the man nodded with acceptance and happily took the cash, Tyler sighed with relief, thankful that he wouldn't need to get into another physical altercation on Alexis' behalf.

Tyler turned his attention back to Alexis and asked, "Want to tell me about it?"

He reached over and pushed a lock of hair from her eyes only to notice the streaks down her face. "You've been crying."

"Yeah, well, I just fought off a mammoth, so," her voice dropped.

Tyler watched her eyes fill up once more before pulling her chair toward him. He ran a hand along her back and leaned his head in, letting his forehead come to rest against hers.

"Alexis," he whispered.

Alexis closed her eyes, wanting nothing more than to kiss him, but that wasn't what he was offering. He was offering an ear, a shoulder, and comfort. If only he were coming on to her, it would make it easier for her to shut him out. This magnanimous gesture was pure Tyler, and that was why it about killed her.

"Don't," she groaned. "Not now of all times."

Tyler pulled back and withdrew his arm. "I don't follow."

She sighed. "Next week will be three years."

Recognition shown in his eyes. "Clay?"

"Yeah." She closed her eyes. "Can you get me another drink?"

"I think you've had enough."

"I'm fine. Get me one more, and that'll be it. And if you do, I'll tell you everything."

Tyler sat, contemplating his options. Without breaking eye contact with her, he finally lifted his hand.

"Hey, Jack!" His voice carried across the bar. The bartender looked up as Tyler continued, "Two lemon drops, please."

"Coming right up." They heard from behind them.

Once the waitress set two shot glasses in front of them, Alexis quickly grabbed both and downed them.

"One of those was for me, you know." He raised an eyebrow but knew neither glass had much alcohol in them. It was more lemon juice and sugar than vodka.

Mischief darted through her eyes. "I know. You can order another."

"No way." He shook his head and crossed his arms.

The two were locked in a challenging stare, both unwilling to be the first to drop their gaze. Without breaking their gaze, Alexis reached for a cocktail napkin and wiped her mouth. Tyler swallowed, fighting the temptation to sample her heart-shaped lips.

"You want anything?" Her lips twitched as if she knew what he was thinking.

Although she was playing with words, he ignored her double entendre and gave a simple answer. "You'd drink anything else Jack would make for me."

"You're probably right." Her mischievous eyes sparkled.

When she giggled, it was evident that what little alcohol she had was taking effect. Tyler signaled once more for the waitress.

"Bring us two coffees and a large glass of water, please." He pulled out a couple of twenties and folded them into the young woman's palm.

"Sure thing." She pushed the money into her pocket and left.

Tyler watched Alexis sit back in her chair and fold her arms comfortably under her breasts. As she raked him over with her eyes, he was befuddled much like a schoolboy with his first crush. His blood pressure spiked as she leaned forward and wiggled her finger at him to come closer.

"You want to know a secret?" she asked with an unsuccessful whisper.

He smirked in return and shrugged. "Sure, Alexis. What's the big secret?"

She nodded and put her fingers to his lips to shush him. "I'll tell you, but you can't tell anyone."

He crossed his heart with his right hand and lifted the other to swear a silent oath.

It was enough to satisfy Alexis because she blurted out, "Clay was always jealous of you."

Tyler choked on the small sip of coffee, unsure if he heard her correctly. Once he regained his composure, he replied, "Of me? Why would he be jealous of me?" He pushed a cup of coffee in her direction. "Here."

Alexis took a sip and sent him a nod. "Because he knew."

Tyler frowned and leaned forward. "Knew what, Lexi?"

"I can't tell." She sat back and crossed her arms once more.

"But you promised you'd tell me everything. And you got two drinks instead of one." He bit his lips from inside his mouth and raised a knowing eyebrow.

Alexis sighed. If she were smart, she'd do the honorable thing and keep her mouth shut. If she told him, it would give life to everything Clay thought about Tyler.

"Alexis, you can tell me anything." His warm eyes beckoned.

"Who needs smart anyway? How far did smart get me all these years?" She voiced her thoughts aloud.

"Huh?" He shook his head, unsure of what she meant.

"Okay, here goes." She sighed as if about to take a nosedive off a cliff without a safety net. "Why do you think I ran off with Clay?"

"I – have – no – idea." He gave her a blank stare. "I've been trying to figure that one out for years, Lex."

"The night of my graduation party?" She paused.

"Yeah," he said in haste.

"I kissed you."

He raised an eyebrow in memory. "I remember." He cocked his head and tried reading her without much success. "Then, you fled from the room."

"You put the brakes on."

"Because I cared for you, and then you ran."

Alexis shook her head. "I ran because of how much I felt when I kissed you. I'd always dreamed of what it would be like. To be honest, it was like rockets and fireworks compared to the kisses I shared with Clay. When he kissed me – it was like puppies or ..."

Tyler stared at her forlorn face. "So, then, why did you leave?"

"Why did you stop?"

"I wanted to make sure you knew what you were getting into. Answer my question, Alexis. I need to know."

She breathed in and paused, searching his eyes, and what she saw in them should have sent her running in the other direction, but the alcohol had her too relaxed to do anything except spill the truth.

"Clay had asked me to marry him that night. I told him I'd think about it, and to think about it, meant kissing you. I had to know..." Her eyes watered.

"You didn't answer my question. Why did you take off after our kiss?" He took her hand in his and made lazy circles in her palm.

As he stroked her skin, sparks raced down Alexis' arm, sending goosebumps over her body. Although she wanted to blame it on the alcohol, she knew that wasn't what flushed her with the desire. She closed her eyes, willing her heart to slow down.

"I ran out after our kiss to find Clay. I needed to tell him that I couldn't marry him. When I found him, I turned him down and left him heartbroken to return to you."

Tyler's soulful eyes filled with regret. "And did you find me?"

As she nodded her head and sighed, a complete understanding set in. After all these years, he knew what happened to make her hate him. He shook his head, which filled with self-loathing thoughts. If only he'd waited.

He'd never forget that night. The second Alexis ran from their kiss, an emptiness overtook him. When their lips met, everything changed for him in an instant. He went from loving and counting on her as his best friend to being unable to live without her.

When she tore away from his embrace, the sting of her rejection was more painful than the hollows of his empty home. At least Tyler expected his parents' betrayal, but with Alexis, well, she was his constant. And to think that she couldn't stand to be in the same room with him after sharing the most intimate and mind-blowing kiss he'd ever imagined was more than he could bear.

Alexis watched his wheels spin and wondered if he'd put two and two together yet. She dropped her eyes and said, "When I came back to find you. You weren't anywhere. I searched high and low until I found you in the barn."

Tyler let out a frustrated breath. "With someone else?"

"Yeah, with one of my so-called friends."

He bit his lips and took a calculated breath, unsure of what to say next. After a few minutes, he said in a raspy voice, "Alexis, I am so sorry. It wasn't what you thought."

She shook her head. "It's okay. It was a long time ago." She paused. "Needless to say, I turned around and backtracked my way to Clay. I finally said yes. And…"

He licked his lips. "And you left the next morning without saying a word to anyone."

Her voice was a raw whisper. "Yeah."

"You have to know something." He dropped his head into his hands.

Alexis waited for what seemed like an eternity for him to speak.

He lifted his head and ran a hand through his hair. "I only turned to her because I thought you didn't want me. And," he paused. "That hurt more than I was prepared to admit."

Alexis' eyes filled with tenderness. "I didn't know."

Tyler searched her face before gently stroking her cheek with the back of his knuckles. Her skin was as smooth as the satin sheets that lined his bed. He closed his eyes at the thought when her full lips gently pressed against his. The sensation sent shock waves through him.

As they kissed, it was as if the missing piece of his puzzle fell into place. Every emotion he'd ever experienced since their first kiss – the confusion – the heartbreak – the desire – came rushing forth as he claimed her mouth. Through it all, he was overcome with a sense of peace.

For Alexis, it was as if she was drowning in a hunger she'd denied herself all these years. The untapped emotions she'd stuffed resurfaced with a vengeance as their passionate kiss took a turn toward fast and furious.

"Dude, get a room." Tyler heard someone say from behind them.

Tyler quickly pulled back and dragged in a breath. He was sure everyone in the room could hear his heart as it beat within his chest. He considered her bright yet confused blue eyes and shook his head. He knew better than this.

"Alexis, you've been drinking. This isn't right." He was trying to do the honorable thing, but it quickly became apparent when her flushed face turned to stone that his moral high ground dumped him into some scorching water.

"What was this? Huh, Tyler? Kiss Alexis back and see if she'll fall for it again?"

"No," he quickly interrupted. "No, Lex. I want this."

"Well, you have a funny way of showing it." Her chair scraped across the concrete floor as she stood in anger.

"Clay was right about you." The second the words escaped, she cringed. While it wasn't fair to blame him, a small part of her didn't care.

Tyler stood to place his hands on her hips to bring her in, but her eyes filled with fury. She side-stepped him and reached for her purse.

"Alexis, wait!" he said to her backside as she ran from the bar.

He attempted to follow her, but a couple from the dance floor blocked his path. By the time he made it to the parking lot, all he could see were her taillights as her truck disappeared around the corner.

16

"Really?" Tyler blinked through his windshield as large drops fell from above.

Great. He grimaced. A steady rain was the exact opposite of what he needed when following Alexis on the soon-to-be-slick roads in the dead of night.

What is she thinking?

He watched her red truck swerve around the next curve in the road. There wasn't much threat of anyone being out this late at night on the back roads, but he was concerned she'd do harm to herself.

He envisioned her truck falling off Old Man's Bridge into the creek that hugged the back of their property lines. A sense of dread filled his heart as the narrow bridge came into sight. When it was time, he punched the gas to cut her off, hoping to slow her down some. If he timed it right, he might even be able to get her to stop altogether.

For the last couple of miles, Alexis had slowed some - partly because she shouldn't be driving, and in part, because she caught herself shifting along the desolated back road. As her wipers thumped back and forth against her windshield, the sounds of rain pelting her truck reminded her of a high-powered car wash. The faster they beat along against it, the more anxiety washed within.

Although the long road didn't provide too many hazards, the narrow bridge, with an old railing and a long drop, gave her pause.

As the rain continued to pelt her roof from above, she struggled to set the right speed for windshield wipers. No matter how fast or slow, it wasn't enough to see clearly. Was it the rain that had her blinking, like Morse Code, or her blurry vision that kept her from seeing ten feet in front of her face?

Alexis shook her head, temporarily taking one hand off the steering wheel to rub her eyes as her tires started a slow drift. She yanked her truck center and let off the gas. If she wasn't careful, she could end up in the ditch, and then how would she explain that to her daughter with a clear conscience?

She leaned forward and squinted into the night, trying to navigate the dark roads, but her headlights only illuminated so much.

Evelyn, who sat in the passenger seat, sadly shook her head. This self-destructive side of her granddaughter was, unfortunately, one that she fully understood, although she wished she could change.

However, Evelyn, even in her most tumultuous years, never took things quite as far as Alexis had tonight. Worried for her errant granddaughter, she urged her with a full heart, hoping she would be able to hear her.

"Alexis, pull over before you hurt yourself."

In her altered state, Alexis stiffened at the sound of her grandmother's voice. She blinked and slowed a bit but refrained from pulling over.

Surely, that wasn't real. Was it? She cut her eyes to the darkness that enveloped the cab around her.

Unbeknownst to Alexis, Tyler's truck flew by in the next lane and pulled in front to slow her down. The bright red lights from his brakes cast a red glow upon Alexis' face sending panic through Evelyn's spirit.

Unaware if her granddaughter was cognizant enough to keep from slamming into his truck bed, she laid a hand on her leg.

"Put the brakes on now!" Evelyn demanded in an authoritative voice.

Alexis, in shock, that she apparently heard Evelyn's words clear as day, saw Tyler swerve in front of her truck just in time to slam on her brakes. As he tapped his lights, she came to a stop and sat in the cab, glaring as he opened his door.

When Tyler stepped onto the wet asphalt, Alexis' heart constricted. Even in her anger, she couldn't deny how much she already missed the warmth of his lips. She shook her head at the confusion that filled her only to hold her breath at the sight of him. Her headlights illuminated a frustrated but breathtaking Tyler as he approached her door.

In the exact moment that Alexis threw her door open, the sky opened with a torrential downpour. Even though she was completely soaked, it wasn't enough to deter her from giving him a piece of her mind.

"What on earth do you think you're doing?" She slammed her door shut and marched toward him.

Tyler's breath hitched. Even through the drenching rain, her eyes breathed fire. She glowed from the moonlight glistening on her wet skin. Her long golden locks flattened around her face and shoulders, and her loose shirt clung to every curve. It took every ounce of restraint to keep from running his hands up her arms and draw her in. Even wet, she was a vision.

"Me?!" He threw his hands in the air before pointing at her. "You're the one who shouldn't be driving. Are you trying to get yourself killed?"

Both stood, waiting for the other to respond. When it was evident Alexis wasn't going to budge, Tyler drew in a short breath and stepped forward to bridge the gap between them. As flashes of anger and confusion flooded her eyes, he rushed to take her face into his hands before claiming her mouth once more.

As the rain poured around them, Alexis' heart soared from her chest. It was as if the Texas winds swept them up and whisked them to another place, where the reality of who they were beyond this kiss would never touch them.

Alexis tried to pull back. If she didn't come up for air, Alexis might never regain the distance she'd fought so hard to keep. Yet, as his tongue danced with hers, she leaned into him as his arms strengthened around her.

Something inside Tyler clicked. Every fiber of his being told him that this was where they belonged, entangled in one another's arms. But the small voice in the back of his head warned him that as soon as this kiss was over, she'd fight it. If it took him every day for the rest of his life, he'd do his best to convince her otherwise.

Alexis had always been his best friend, yet only now had he understood their friendship could blossom into such a beautiful, peaceful place. With one kiss, everything was the way it should be. With her, he was finally home.

As she pulled away, Tyler blinked at the distrust that shone across her face. His heart ached for the young girl he knew was inside who could trust his intentions, but that girl was long gone. Alexis, the woman, was clearly someone who wouldn't easily let him in. At least not yet.

"What was that for?" Her chest heaved as she tried to catch her breath.

"Because you ran out before I could explain."

"What was there to explain?" Her mouth flattened.

Tyler slowly shook his head and took her hand in his as a flash of lightning illuminated the sky.

"Come on." He tugged her toward his truck, grumbling, "It seems I'm constantly saving you from the rain."

Or myself. She pulled her hand free, standing firm in place.

He tossed an angry look over his shoulder to find her with arms crossed, unsure if she wanted his help.

Alexis lifted her eyebrow as if challenging him before taking a deep breath. Although putting on a brave front, she knew if she stepped inside his truck, it could be the point of no return. She wasn't sure if her heart could take another loss.

Tyler shook his head. He was doing everything he could to hold his temper in check, but she had a way of pushing all his buttons. He raised his eyebrows in return, before uncrossing her arms and sliding his hands down them. Treading lightly, he gently held her hands in his and sent her a look that spoke volumes.

As his soft touch sent shivers throughout her, she tried to shut off her emotions. Yet, hard as she tried, Tyler's soulful eyes still beckoned to a place within her that couldn't be denied. No matter what she was going through, she knew he had her back.

But what about your heart?

"Alexis." His voice raised an octave through the rain as it whipped around them. "You can trust me. Now get in the truck." He took a step back and waited.

Alexis wavered. She looked back to her pickup.

"I'll get it. Don't worry about it," Tyler yelled through the wind. "Get in!"

With a quick jerk of her chin, she stepped toward his truck. Once she was safely inside, he ran around the front, slamming his door shut to escape the downpour. They both sat in silence as what sounded like the whole sky fell around them. He glanced at her shivering frame and pulled his jacket from the back of his cab to expertly tuck it around her shoulders.

"Thank you," she whispered through chattering teeth.

"Hand me your keys." His voice was soft but stern.

Alexis did as she was told. She was too tired to fight.

"I'll be right back." He peered in her direction with a slight frown. "Don't do anything stupid while I'm gone."

"Where are you going?" she asked eyes wide.

He gave her a look of assurance. "I'm taking your truck across the bridge. I'll be right back."

"I can get it tomorrow." She frowned.

He lifted an eyebrow and sent her a smirk. "If this rain keeps up, you won't. The bridge could go, and it would be days until you get your truck."

She nodded in understanding, but as she watched him dodge out into the night once more, she worried that it could do just that while he was on the other side.

"Hurry," she whispered to herself.

In the five minutes it took to drive her pickup across the bridge and jog back to his, Tyler wasn't surprised when he opened his door to find Alexis out cold as she lay across the front seat. The jacket he gave her was rolled under her head.

He lifted her head to slide inside and quickly shut the door behind him. With care, he slipped the jacket out from underneath her neck and used it to blot the excess rain from her face. Alexis, already soaked to the bone, was now drenched even further after his re-entry into his truck. With a quick glance in the rearview mirror, he noted that he looked like he'd just come from a swim in the lake.

As thunder shook the cab, he unlocked his phone to check the radar. There was a line of storms that affected everything from the Dallas metro all the way to Purity and the surrounding areas. Instead of pushing through, it settled in place, which meant flash floods were in their immediate future.

When Alexis mumbled something in her sleep, he looked down at her innocent face and stroked another damp lock of hair away from her eyes. She frowned in her sleep and batted his hand away, causing him to suppress a chuckle. Even in her sleep, she was a fighter.

After starting the engine, he reached for his phone once more to call Anderson and noticed he'd already missed a text from him.

Do I need to come out there – or do you have everything under control? Mom is worried.

Tyler quickly responded.

ALEXIS IS WITH ME. *She's okay but probably shouldn't come home tonight. I'm taking her to my place to sleep it off.*

. . .

When Anderson texted back, giving him the green light, Tyler responded once more.

I left her truck on the north side of the bridge. The keys are in the glove box. Pls pick it up, and I'll bring her home in the morning.

Tyler gunned his engine just as Alexis sighed in her sleep. He silently chuckled and stroked her back. "Sleep well, sweet, Lexi."

In a matter of minutes, he navigated to the entrance of his property. His truck slowed to an almost crawl as it bounced over the gravel road. He looked down at his lap, hoping it wouldn't jar Alexis awake.

When he finally arrived, he pulled as close as possible to his porch for cover. He propped Alexis against the passenger door before rounding the front of his truck and sliding her from the seat.

As he lifted Alexis up the front steps, she moaned and nuzzled his neck as she wrapped her arms around it. Tyler closed his eyes and released a breath, knowing that she might not remember their shared kiss or the effects it had on them. How he wished she was sober and fully aware of their last hour together so that tomorrow might have a different tone.

Once inside, he slid her to her feet.

"Where are we?" she mumbled, half asleep.

"I'm putting you to bed. You need rest."

Alexis struggled to peel open her eyes and survey her surroundings.

"This isn't my room." She let out a soft groan.

"You can't go home like this, Lexi." He stroked her hair as he laid her head on his pillow.

"Okay." Her childlike voice softened.

Tyler marveled at the way her mouth turned up. Within seconds, her even breathing turned into a light snore.

He chuckled at the sound and kicked off his boots before he pulled the duvet to tuck around her shoulders.

"Looks like I won't get much sleep tonight." He pulled a lounge chair up to the edge of the bed. Then, he dropped into it and propped his feet on the side opposite of Alexis. He then whispered in her direction, "But I'm glad you will."

17

Soft light slowly illuminated through the shades that cloaked the tall windows in the room. Alexis held her head and struggled to sit as she tried to recognize her surroundings. Although the bold blue walls and white cotton canvas curtains were welcoming, she squinted, trying to shut off the warning bells that rang in her head.

What happened last night? She cradled her head, trying to recall last night. Glimpses of her and Tyler arguing flashed before her eyes before she remembered two glorious kisses they shared. Her stomach dropped. She looked around once more. Was this his room?

She peeked under the sheets and panicked when she noticed she was wearing only her underwear. She searched the room, relieved to discover her jeans and shirt hanging by the fireplace a few feet away. She let out a deep breath, touched by Tyler's thoughtfulness. Of course, he'd have taken care of such details. From what little she remembered, they'd been drenched.

This is why you're not supposed to drink. Alexis shook her head and pushed back the duvet.

Although she enjoyed the taste of liquor in her early years, she quickly learned to limit herself. One to two drinks were usually her cut off. If she stepped over her self-imposed boundaries, she'd end up asleep in the most comfortable spot she could find. In their early married years, Clay made sure to keep her supplied with water, but as they aged, parties and a few drinks became less of a focus.

Becoming a mother, paralleled behaving like a responsible adult. Her daughter became her everything, which meant all else paled in comparison – even Clay.

Alexis shook her head at the memory and groaned. So, if she was such a responsible adult, why did she go to Shelty's last night? She'd not pulled this kind of a stunt since before Lani's birth.

"Alexis," she sighed as an internal lecture was coming on and brought her hands to her temples to rub the ache that beat between them. "What were you thinking?"

Alexis raised an eyebrow in response and slowly propped herself up to see Tyler's boots on the floor next to his oversized bed. Taken aback, she wondered where he slept when she noticed a wingback chair that was sitting at the end of the bed. There was a quilt haphazardly flung along the arm of it. Did Tyler sleep in the chair?

She gave the room a once over. It wasn't what she would call expertly decorated, but the décor was pleasing. The blue paint was accompanied by dark furniture and accented with pops of gray.

"I've got to get home," she whispered while slipping out from under the covers to reach for her shirt.

If it weren't for the fact that her head was pounding and her teeth seemed to have little sweaters on them, she'd bolt from the bed to make her escape. The rushing between her ears made it almost impossible to move any faster than at a snail's pace.

Once her feet were planted on the warm wooden floors, she steadied herself with the intent of slipping on her jeans. It was then that Tyler walked in with a glass of thick green liquid, sending Alexis scurrying for the covers. When she pulled them up, she was never more thankful she was at least wearing a shirt.

She eyed the glass he was carrying and covered her mouth. "Tell me that isn't for me."

His mouth twitched as he sat beside her and set the glass on the nightstand. If he'd learned anything from his childhood, it was how to help someone in Alexis' condition recover. Sadly, this time, it was for his friend, whom he'd never seen hungover. His heart tinged with regret, knowing how much she had to have been hurting to go down that path.

"Morning," he whispered. "This will help." He nodded to the thick green goo that mocked her from the nightstand.

She dropped back to the pillows behind her and rolled away from him with a look of disdain.

"Trust me. I know a thing or two about this." He pulled her wrists toward him and slipped an arm beneath her back.

Alexis' gaze bounced from the glass to his concerned look. She was instantly plagued with guilt, knowing what kind of position she'd put him in. Her eyes dropped, and she mumbled, "I'm sorry."

"What for?" His eyes crinkled at the edges, but his smile didn't truly meet them.

"You didn't have to do this." Her voice fell. She glanced down at the jeans in her hands and back to his soulful eyes. "Did you?"

"Look. You had a rough night. I was a gentleman. I didn't even peek."

Her face burned as she flushed at the thought.

"I'm sure you were." She blinked. "I'm sorry you had to..." Her voice trailed.

"It's not like you make a habit of this sort of thing, right?" His question hung in the air.

She shook her head as he lifted the glass to her. She took a small sniff and wrinkled her nose.

"Are you trying to make me throw up? That smells horrible." She lifted a palm and turned her head.

"It's a guaranteed fix, Alexis."

"No. I need coffee - not that stuff." She nudged his hand away.

He shrugged his shoulders. "Suit yourself. I'll give you a few moments of privacy." His eyes landed on the jeans she had clutched to her chest. "Then, I can come back and help you to the kitchen?"

"I'm hungover, not an invalid," she grumbled.

Tyler snickered. "I know, Evelyn."

Alexis shot him a curious look.

"You remind me of her more and more each day," he said and started for his bedroom door.

Alexis rolled her eyes. "I do too. I'll think something or say something and instantly think that it would be something she would have said." She let out a soft noise that almost resembled a laugh then immediately sobered when she had a flash from last night. Her grandmother's voice rang through her mind, warning her to put on the brakes.

A look crossed her face that had him stopping in his tracks. Before he backed from the room, he asked, "Are you okay?"

She shook off the memory. "Yeah. I dreamed about her last night. I thought I heard her voice, but it must have been a dream."

"I understand." He nodded. "Sometimes, I dream about my mom. And sometimes, when it's quiet, I swear I can hear Evelyn's laughter, but they're just memories, Alexis. It's all part of the process – of grieving or letting go."

"Yeah, that must be it." She agreed as he pulled the door behind him so she could finish getting dressed. Once she was alone, she whispered, "But it seemed so real."

ALEXIS SHUFFLED into the kitchen as the image of her grandmother's smile flooded her memory. Her face softened as she recalled how much her grandmother loved to laugh.

"I miss her." Her voice wavered as she sat on a stool across from Tyler.

"I know," he whispered. "I do too."

She looked up at him from under her eyelids, thankful that she didn't have to explain herself to him. Of course, he'd know who she was talking about. This was Tyler. He knew what her thoughts were before she could conjure them for herself.

Alexis sent him a look before saying, "I keep going back to that letter, which is bold proof I didn't know her at all."

Tyler poured her a steaming mug of black coffee and pushed it toward her. "Alexis, you knew her. She loved you, but everyone has a past."

She nodded and took a sip.

Tyler cleared his throat. "Have you made any progress with regard to her mystery man?"

"William?" She blinked.

He nodded.

"No." She frowned and pinched her fingers on the bridge of her nose. "I've googled her name in a million different ways hoping the name, William, would be associated with hers, and nothing pulls up. No records – no newspaper articles."

"Have you tried ancestry? For marriage records?"

She shook her head. "I plan on it. I have her maiden name and city of birth. I guess I could start from scratch and work my way up?"

"For starters," Tyler said.

Tyler sipped his coffee and stared at her lips over the rim of his mug. All he could think of was how their kiss ignited the long-lost spark between them. He wondered just how much of last night she remembered.

When his warm stare grazed her from top to bottom, Alexis ran a hand along the top of her hair, hoping she wasn't worse for the wear. Although she didn't remember much, the heat she experienced from his kiss was still at the forefront of her mind.

"I must look a wreck." She tucked a few wild curls behind her ears.

His lips turned up at the corners, and this time, his eyes filled with warmth.

"You look beautiful." He set his cup down and leaned toward her.

Panicked, she put her cup down and awkwardly stood.

"Um, thanks for the coffee and the ride." She licked her lips. Alexis needed to brush her teeth and didn't want him coming anywhere near her until she was confident she didn't have dry mouth. The truth was, she didn't even know if she wanted him coming anywhere near her. Period.

Who was she kidding? Of course, she did, but she had Lani to think of. And since her daughter had cried herself to sleep last night - the last thing she needed to do was complicate Lani's life by acting like a lovesick school-girl.

He stopped and gave her a look as if assessing her situation.

"What's on your mind?" He stood to lean a hip on the counter op and face her, his arms crossed.

"I need to get home. I bet my family is worried sick."

He shook his head. "Not particularly."

She gave him a look of disbelief.

"Anderson told them that I picked you up early this morning to spend the day with me." He grinned at her expression. "It's not a lie. I did just that last night – it was just at the bar."

"You didn't pick me up at the bar! You make it sound so..." She sent him an evil eye. "We didn't." She struggled to remember all the details.

"No." He quickly reassured her. "Nothing went on between us other than a kiss or two." He took another step toward her, placed his hands on her hips, and continued, "A really nice kiss that has kept me up all night."

As he closed the gap between them, she put her hand up between their lips, blocking what could have been a replay of the best kiss she could imagine.

"I'm not sure that's such a good idea," she whispered with a heavy heart.

He pulled back and read the confusion in her eyes, intuitively knowing that her endgame was slow and steady. He cocked his head and sent her a sexy grin that said they had time.

"Okay." He dropped his arm and reached for her hand. "Follow me."

"But," she started but never finished. How could he accept her rebuff so easily?

He looked over his shoulder and sent her a wink. "You're okay, Lexi. Relax and enjoy the moment. God knows we haven't had too much of that in our lives."

Unless you count every moment we've spent together. It was why Alexis wasn't sure she could encourage anything between them in case the reality didn't live up to the dream. What if she lost him too?

Tyler led her outside just as the clouds made way for the mid-morning sun. They walked to the fence line outside his home and stood in silence.

"Where are we?" She spun and stared at the house. "Where is this in relation to your mom's place? I don't recognize it."

"Remember the stream that ran just east of my old house?"

Alexis closed her eyes and gave him a half nod.

"My house." He nodded his chin back toward the small home they had walked from. "Is just around the bend from there. It's south of it and closer to the cove. If we were to walk down that path behind my house, it would lead straight to the lake."

Alexis cocked her head and paused. "I like it here."

"Sometimes, when I stand out here long enough, it seems like another world – far away from where I was raised. Once my father died and left this land to me, I figured I could build something good here. I just didn't know what yet."

"What about your place in the city?"

"I stay there during the week for a faster commute. And on the weekends, I come home and ride. Bonnie, the manager of the stables, stays at mom's old house with her daughter and parents." He motioned toward the horizon. "And I'm far enough away that I'm not in their way, and they're not in mine."

Alexis stared at his grave face and wondered how he hadn't been snatched up by now. He was firm, yet tender. He was smart but kept his ego in check. Well, most of the time. And his dark, brooding looks could sweep any girl off her feet. She drew in a slow breath.

He watched her wheels spinning and sent her a dazzling smile.

"You're thinking about me. Aren't you?" He wiggled his eyebrows.

Her belly laugh was all he needed to know. He hit the mark.

"You are." He grabbed her and began tickling her ribs.

Alexis doubled over in a fit of laughter and pushed his hands away. "Stop it! You're such a dork."

When she laughed, it was like a lifetime lifted from her shoulders, and her heart was set free from any burdens. Before Tyler knew it, his face was only a few inches from hers.

Tyler's laughter stilled, and his breathing slowed. As his eyes connected with hers, he noticed desire flickering from beneath the turquoise pools that threatened to drown him, and instinct kicked in. Not wanting to waste another second, he decided that slow and steady never got him anywhere.

"You should do that more often," he said without moving an inch.

Her eyes dilated. "What?"

"Laugh. And this." He tightened his arms around her and placed his full lips on hers, sending her mind spinning.

18

Evelyn's heart soared higher than the heavens when she saw her granddaughter in the arms of the man she loved. With peace, she lifted her head to the sky and transported her spirit among the clouds and patiently waited.

After a few moments, which were immeasurable by human standards, she looked below and waited. Evelyn pursed her lips, wondering how long she sat when it dawned on her that maybe this was her version of eternity. She dropped her head, distraught.

"What are you doing?" She heard from behind.

Evelyn spun around to face a young child that looked so much like Clay that he could have been his twin.

"I'm waiting for. For what, I don't know," she stammered. "I have no idea what I'm doing. Who are you?"

The child's wise eyes filled with mischief. "I think you recognize me."

"Clay?"

"No, but you're close."

It was then that Evelyn remembered the miscarriage that Alexis suffered before she and Clay had Lani.

"Clay is your dad?"

The child nodded with glee. "He told me to tell you 'Hello,' by the way."

"Where is he?"

"He's resting until the final day comes."

"The final day?"

"Yes."

As Evelyn recalled the Bible verses that she'd poured over for many hours on earth, her spirit resounded with the truth about the final day.

"Are you talking about Thessalonians 4:14?"

The child sent her a look to let her know he was pleased.

Evelyn's eyes narrowed, needing more. "I've lived a good life, so why am I unable to sleep awhile until he returns? Why can't I rest?"

"Because you have more to do."

She shook her head with confusion. "But Alexis. I - I thought I was here to help her, and now she seems to be on the right track." She watched the child shrug.

"Then why can't you rest in peace, Grams?"

As Evelyn's heart burst with joy, the emotions wound around the pair drawing them closer. She placed her hand on the head of the child she never knew but intimately mourned.

"You called me Grams." Her lips twitched.

"Well, you are; are you not?"

Evelyn nodded and leaned forward to stare into the child's dark eyes. As she noticed the gold flecks within, she took note of the wise soul that lived behind them.

"You seem to know a lot about what goes on around here." She watched him nod with satisfaction. "So, what is it I'm supposed to do?"

He pointed below them to where Evelyn had once been.

"You're supposed to save her."

"From what?"

"From your secrets and the harm that comes with them."

Evelyn closed her eyes with regret and was about to ask him what to do next, but when she opened them to address him once more, she was alone.

"Hello?" She looked toward where her great-grandson had disappeared only to be whisked away with the wind.

The next thing she knew, she was back on Tyler's land - only Alexis wasn't wrapped in Tyler's arms. Instead, Alexis walked away as Tyler followed, looking as if he'd lost a battle but was gearing up for war.

19

Alexis' emotions bounced back and forth, much like a tennis ball. On the one hand, she basked in the sublime moment. Tyler's tender kiss sent waves of delight through her body. Yet, on the other, she couldn't afford to lose her head or her heart. Within seconds, she pulled back, thoroughly confused.

"I - I can't do this right now," she stammered.

"Why not?" He dropped his hands to her hips.

"Lani needs me."

"You're right; she does. Kissing me won't take anything away from her." Tyler took a step back as his eyes clouded with frustration.

"I can't get distracted by some summer fling." She pulled her hair back and turned with her hands on her head to stare out to the fields past his home toward her family's property.

"Is that all you think I'm offering?" His face flushed with anger.

She spun to face him with her hands on her hips. "I don't know what you're offering. I haven't seen you in however many years it's been."

"Well, whose fault is that?!"

She sent him an evil eye and continued. "And I come home, and suddenly I'm working for you. And, you're at every turn. And, now, it seems that I can't stop you from doing that." She pointed at his mouth.

"Was it that bad?" His sparkling eyes shone as a grin broke across his smug face.

"Ugh." When he looked at her like that, she wanted nothing more than to knock that cocky look from his devilishly handsome face. "You know it wasn't."

"So, you felt it too?" He looked at her from under his eyelids.

"I never said I didn't, Tyler." She jogged in the opposite direction.

"Wait a minute!" He took off after her. "I was just teasing. We have the whole day to ourselves. Let's talk this over."

Alexis spun around, eyes glaring. "We just did. I don't have time for something like this. I have a daughter to think of."

"I know. And she needs a…"

"Don't you say it!" She pointed at him. "Because she has a father."

He put his hands up and gently responded. "I was just going to say she needs another male figure around who can help out. I would never dream of stepping into Clay's shoes, but I'd like to show her what I know – like how to ride a horse for starters." He took a step toward her. "I've not seen either of you roaming the property except on foot. Does she even know how?"

Alexis stared at the ground and kicked a patch of dirt with her boot. She dragged her eyes back up to connect with his and shook her head.

"She was raised in the city. She likes to look at them but hasn't expressed interest in riding."

He took her hands in his. "What's the harm in allowing me to spend some time with both of you? I missed you, Alexis. I'd like to get to know Lani. I knew you like the back of my hand when we were kids." When her eyes softened, he added, "In fact, I'd like to think that our history binds us. Yet, as much as we shared then - I don't know much about you now. If you'd let me, I'd like to try."

She clamped her mouth together and took a deep breath in through her nose. Tyler's eyes twinkled as she shrugged noncommittally.

"That's a start," he said.

"But as friends only." She lifted her eyebrow.

Tyler raised his hand with a silent oath and crossed his heart while crossing his fingers behind his back with the other.

Unsure, she searched the unreadable expression in his eyes but took him at his word. "You said something about spending the day together?"

He nodded.

"What does a person have to do to get something to eat other than that green goo you tried to force-feed me this morning? I'm starving!"

His laughter made her stomach flip as if it were on a trampoline, but she quickly blamed it on the fact that she was famished or still slightly hungover. He grabbed her by the hand and led her to his porch.

"Come on. I'll make you some bacon and eggs. Sound good?"

She licked her lips in anticipation and happily followed.

"As long as they're not green eggs. And, only if you don't try kissing me again." She wasn't sure she could hold her ground again if he did.

He chuckled and led her into his home. "No green eggs. I promise."

Tyler purposely left any mention of kissing out of his promise. He couldn't promise that he wouldn't try again. In fact, when she was ready, that was the first thing he planned to do.

"And, no kissing," she reiterated.

"You're the boss." He sidestepped the subject.

Alexis watched him whisk the eggs as mischief played across his face. Although she knew she should stay clear of him and his intentions, she hated to admit that she might enjoy the chase.

20

The next few weeks at work flew by. Alexis acclimated to her new schedule and even enjoyed working with Tyler. So far, he'd stuck to his word and settled for friendship. It allowed her the comfort she needed to take Lani for riding lessons at his ranch.

As she chewed on the cap of her pen, she tried to focus on the search for Grandmother's mystery man, but all she could think about was how Tyler's soft lips warmed her to the core. As hard as she tried, she couldn't shake the excitement that spiraled through her whenever his eyes trailed her through the newsroom.

"Earth to Alexis." Janelle waved a hand in front of her face, trying to snap her into the present.

"Huh?" Alexis mumbled and came to as one of her co-workers grinned from ear to ear.

"Where did you go off to in that pretty head of yours?" Janelle smirked.

"Oh, sorry." The corners of her mouth indented, showcasing her dimples. "I was doing some research."

She looked to Janelle, whose warm eyes pulled her in. The newsroom was full of divas except for Janelle, who was a producer on staff.

Janelle had always been kind to her, and Alexis appreciated the growing friendship between them.

Just then, Sharena, one of the field reporters, walked by and sneered in Alexis' direction. Alexis rolled her eyes at Janelle.

"Hi, Sharena," Janelle sang. "Have you met Alexis yet?"

"I've seen her around." Sharena talked over her as if she weren't even there.

"Um, hi. Nice to meet you." Alexis stuck her hand out to shake, but Sharena looked at it as if it were covered with mud.

"Yeah. I'm sure." She turned back to Janelle and sent her a grimace before leaving to touch up her make-up.

"Ugh. She's, um, interesting." Alexis made a face.

"Don't worry about her. She has a thing for Tyler." Janelle waved a hand in dismissal. "We all know it, and any new single female is competition in her book."

Alexis spun toward the dressing room where Sharena had disappeared, wondering if they had a shared interest. As if Janelle could read her mind, she said, "Tyler would never date one of his staff. He's too professional, and if he did, it wouldn't be her."

At that moment, Alexis decided that Janelle had become a fast friend. She gave her the reassurance she needed without even knowing it. Not that it mattered, because she and Tyler were friends.

Yeah, right. Alexis' conscience plagued her.

Janelle rolled her chair closer to Alexis to peer over her shoulder toward the monitor.

"So, what are you researching?"

"Nothing work-related. I just shoot the news. I don't work it like you do."

"Anything I can help with?" She cocked her head to peer over the desk toward Alexis' screen.

"I'm not sure." Alexis glanced at the stack of papers and notebooks on Janelle's desk. "I don't want to keep you from anything."

Janelle shrugged. "You're not. I was just going to lunch. Want to join me?"

Alexis' face lit up. "I'd like that. Let me grab my things."

From behind, Grant slid up to her desk to sit on the corner. The amused look on his face was one that both girls had learned by now. It was no wonder Tyler warned her about him when she first started. Grant was good at his job, but he was also an incorrigible flirt.

"You two need company?" He lifted a brow and sent them a cheesy grin.

Janelle rolled her eyes and pulled Alexis by the arm in another direction., "In your dreams, Grant. Besides, we're both taken."

His mouth gaped as an innocent look displayed across his face.

"What? Girls have to eat, right? I was just being friendly."

Alexis giggled as he threw his arms up in retreat, mumbling something about women.

"Nice try, but no dice." Janelle laughed.

As they started for the nearest exit, Alexis stole a glance toward Tyler's office. He sat behind a plate of glass, which was floor to ceiling. At that moment, he glanced up from his report and caught her eye with a knowing look. Alexis ducked her head and lifted her hand to hide the grin that threatened to overtake her.

"See? Taken." Janelle elbowed Alexis before swinging open the door for the parking lot.

Alexis gave her an incredulous look and shook her head in denial. "You're crazy. We're old friends and nothing more."

"Uh-huh." She led her to her truck and unlocked it so they both could slide in. Janelle quickly turned the engine on to circulate the air conditioning and fanned her face.

"I never get used to this summer Texas heat."

"Fall is only a few weeks away." Alexis adjusted a vent to blow on her face and neck.

"Speaking of Texas heat." Her eyebrows moved up and down in suggestion.

Alexis laughed and waved her off. "Shut up."

"Okay, okay. All I'm saying is that you can't go anywhere without T.J.'s eyes following you around like you're his last meal."

Alexis blushed at the reference, yet said nothing. If there was one thing she knew, it was to keep her life private. There was no reason to give power to anyone else's speculation about the heat that burned through her core whenever she sensed his eyes on her.

Janelle slowly pulled through the parking lot and finally broke the silence.

"So, tell me what you're researching?" She turned onto the main strip toward a few restaurants. "It's no secret you're after a desk or field job."

"Who told you that?" Her head whipped around to face her.

Her friend shrugged. "No one. I just assumed. It's not hard to Google someone. I've seen some of your work. It's dated, but good. And, your eyes seem to teleport viewers to another place. I can't imagine you'll be behind the camera for very long."

"Thank you," she said, blushing. "I wasn't promised anything when I came here. Even if Tyler – T.J. and I are old classmates."

"I'd say you were more than that." She lifted a brow.

Alexis gave her a look. "Come on. It's not like that. That is the last assumption I need people making."

Janelle giggled. "No, I know. No one else has said a word. And you know how rampant the gossip is up there. I just know him pretty well. He took a chance on me when no one would, and I watch out for him. That's all."

Alexis hid a smile. She liked knowing Tyler had people he could count on. She knew how hard he worked and appreciated seeing how he inspired loyalty from his team.

That's because he's a good guy. She told herself as guilt penetrated her thoughts. She should have given him more of a chance.

"So why weren't you a safe bet?" Alexis' snapped back to their conversation.

Janelle cocked her head, and said, "Enough about me for now. Your research?"

"It's personal."

Her friend's eye lit up. "Oooh. The best kind."

"Well, it's mysterious that's for sure."

As Janelle parked at the local taco bar, she caught her up on everything up to date that she'd learned about Evelyn, which wasn't much. The two snagged a corner booth near the window and placed their order as Janelle stared across the table at her with wide eyes.

"You have that look you get when you have a hot lead and are about to jump on a news story." Alexis giggled at her co-worker's exuberance.

"Well, this sounds like a fantastic story!" Her voice hitched.

"Not yet. I don't know anything. Even my Uncle, who is Gram's step-son, is in the dark as to how she came to live on their ranch."

"So, do you have the letter?" She anxiously leaned over the table, ready to get her hands on it.

"Yeah," she said, digging in her purse. "I've got a copy of it. The police have the original for now." She slid it across the table.

After Janelle consumed it, line by line, her face almost burst with surprise.

"This is juicy stuff. So, there's no other info? No last name or clues?"

"Just the envelope it came in." Alexis shrugged.

"Any postmarks?"

"No, just stamped with the letter W. I assumed it stood for his first name, William." Alexis reached for her glass, her hand shaking.

Janelle took pity on her and pat her hand for reassurance. "Honey, never assume. Do you have it?"

"No, but hand me a pen, and I can sketch it."

As Alexis went to work, Janelle tore into her double macho tacos and waited until she finished the drawing. Once Alexis pushed the napkin toward her, Janelle's eyes went wide with recognition.

"Girl!" She swallowed a bite, almost choking. "Don't you recognize that?"

"No. Why would I?"

"Because anyone from around here would."

"You forget." Alexis shook her head. "I just moved back. Plus, I'm from Purity, which is outside city limits. No one in my family would recognize it."

Janelle turned in her seat toward the window and pointed toward the parking lot. "Look across the street, and tell me what you see."

Alexis blinked, turned to scan the view, and gasped at the large 'W' that sat atop the sign for a large retail chain. It was almost identical to one she'd drawn.

"Wylars? Do you think? I never come into town this way. I never imagined or thought of it," she whispered in awe. "It could be a coincidence."

"I've lived here all my life. William Wylar is the son of the founder of Wylars. He used to be the CEO. It can't be a coincidence."

Alexis' stomach dropped. "Oh, my gosh. Is he still alive?"

"As far as I know. I know there's some family drama at the moment – but he still makes it in every day to walk the store and make sure his grandson is still running it according to his wishes."

Unable to take her eyes from the W that stood tall in the sky, she stared at the store that could play an integral part of her grandmother's history.

"Girl, that's the answer to your research." Janelle reached for another bite, pleased with herself until she glanced at Alexis. Janelle narrowed her eyes. "You've got that faraway look again."

"Huh?" Alexis met her stare head-on. "Yeah, thanks."

Alexis bit into her taco without tasting a thing. All she could think about was how soon she could plan a shopping trip and what she would do if she came face to face with the old man who broke her grandmother's heart.

21

For the rest of the afternoon, Alexis fumbled almost everything she touched. Her camerawork was so sloppy that more than once, she was reprimanded by her producer through her earpiece. Her producer finally stopped cutting to her camera and gave her a stern look once the 5 p.m. newscast was over.

"Sorry." She grimaced toward Grant after they wrapped up.

He shot her a cocky grin. "I'm getting to you, huh? I have that effect on women."

"Hardly." Her deadpan look should have been enough to put him off, but she'd quickly learned not much did.

He jogged after her. "Hey, I was just joking. By the way ... Uh, we never got that drink."

"I never said we would." She stopped and placed a hand on his arm. "Look, you seem like a nice guy."

"Oh, here we go." He rolled his eyes.

She sent him a questioning look.

"You know," he continued. "The 'it's not you; it's me' excuse."

She sent him an apologetic look before giggling and saying, "Oh, no. It's you."

She wasn't trying to be rude at all, but how would he ever learn? Surprisingly, his face lit up with appreciation.

"A woman who tells it like it is. I like it." His broad smile showcased his straight teeth.

Alexis paused, thinking another woman could truly appreciate it. Still, for her, there was only one man that made her do a double-take, and Grant wasn't him.

"Do you want my advice?" She waited. When he shrugged with acceptance, she continued, "Don't try so hard. Relax and let the ladies come to you. You're cute and funny, but sometimes, well, most of the time – you're a bit too much."

"Alright." His deep voice softened. "I'll take that into consideration. You're sure I'm not the one for you?" He peered into her eyes with interest.

She put her hands up and laughed. "I'm sure. We can be friends, though."

He nodded and slung his arm around her to give her light squeeze, but quickly dropped it when he saw T.J. approaching.

"Am I about to get fired again?" he whispered into her hair.

As Alexis belly laughed at whatever Grant said, Tyler took a deep breath and counted to ten. He approached with caution and cleared his throat. Although he wanted to send Grant packing, he didn't. He promised Alexis friendship and was trying hard to stick to the rules, but friends watch out for one another.

"Am I interrupting something?" He sent Grant a look of warning.

"No, sir." Grant grinned. "Alexis was just giving me a few pointers that I plan on taking very seriously." He sent her a secret look and a two-finger salute before spinning on his heel toward the exit.

Alexis was still grinning at Grant's back when Tyler gently pulled her to the side. Before she knew it, he slipped them into a vacant room next to the studio, where the lights dimmed, and no one would be able to see them.

"Do I have anything to be worried about?" His stomach swirled with jealousy.

Her sultry laugh beckoned in the dark. "This better not be another attempt to kiss me."

"Just answer me," he said a little too quickly.

She frowned and crossed her arms, saying, "Give me some credit."

"Hey, I'm allowed to look out after you." He called after her as she opened the door for the studio.

"We've gone over this." She stopped and put a hand on his arm. "Do you mind if I cut out a little early?"

"Everything okay? I saw your work today. It wasn't your best. You were all over the place."

"Yeah, about that." She bit her lip. "I need some time off for something personal."

His eyebrows shot up as concern flushed through him. "Is Lani okay?"

"Yeah." Her heart warmed at his concern for her daughter. She was quick to reassure him. "I just need to look into this whole William thing. I may have a lead."

"Can I help?"

Although Evelyn was his business, she took a step back and lightly shook her head.

"Not yet, but I'll let you know something soon."

Tyler's gut burned. He wanted to understand, but getting shut out didn't sit well at all with him.

"Alexis, she was my family too," he urged.

"I know. Just give me a couple of days, and I promise I'll tell you everything."

He didn't like it, but he let her go. "Okay."

"Are you still bringing Lani by tomorrow? She's making great progress. I was planning on taking both of you on a picnic by the river. I thought we could ride."

She nodded. "Lani will be there."

He stepped forward and took her hand in his. "And you?"

"I'm not sure yet. If I can't make it, Anderson will take my place."

Tyler made a noise that sounded like a laugh, but she could tell it was half-hearted.

His voice was laced with disappointment. "Well, he won't be the company I'd hoped for, but at least Lani will have a good time."

"Come on, T.J." She paused. "This is sounding dangerously like a date you've planned, and we're building a friendship."

"Alexis, we're alone. You can call me Tyler."

"No, sir. Not at work." Her voice was clipped and laced with professionalism. Although she was teasing him, it backfired.

He pursed his lips and narrowed his eyes. "Take the time off you need, but send it through to your manager for approval."

"Tyler," she groaned, knowing she'd bruised his ego. When he didn't turn around, she called out after him. "Thanks for understanding."

Tyler exited the studio without an ounce of understanding. He was trying to be patient, but she was all he could think about. His one saving grace was that she spent anywhere from five to seven hours a day on his team, and most weekends during his lessons with Lani.

It may not have allowed time alone with her the way he'd prefer, but at least she was within his reach when he needed a glimpse of her. Alexis had a lot to offer, yet the fact that she continued to keep him at arm's length when he could see the heat radiating from her eyes was infuriating. She had feelings for him, and yet, she still held him in the friend's zone.

As he stood at the window and watched her slip into her truck, his assistant slowly crept to his side. "So, are you going to tell me about what's going on between you two?"

He gave her a look that was meant to intimidate her, but she'd known him when he started as a fresh-faced reporter and wasn't the least bit frightened.

"You may be able to fool everyone around here with your grouchy boss routine, but I see the way you perk up when she's around. Yet lately – you've been ..."

"Look," he said, cutting her off. He ran his hand through his thick dark hair and dropped into his chair with a sigh. "There's nothing to tell."

"Well, whatever it is or isn't, you sure have been on an emotional roller coaster these last few weeks." She glanced out the window before turning her attention back to her boss, who leaned further into his chair.

"I'm not." He sent her a look.

"Yes, you are, but I forgive you because you're like a son to me. Do I need to knock her over the head so she can see what's in front of her?"

Her motherly concern was touching. Tyler winked at her. "No. She knows. She just needs time." He looked at the papers she brought with her. "What's next on the agenda?"

She sighed wistfully, wishing she could do something to ease his mind. Her boss was a good man, who deserved a strong, yet, kind woman at his side. It's not like most available women within these walls hadn't vied for his attention. T.J. had always been all business - until now.

She slid a few papers across his desk and sat across from him.

"Jake just flagged two potential stories from the police scanners, and three calls came in that would be good human-interest pieces."

"Thanks. You can head home for the night. I'll be here for a while."

"Promise you'll get out of here soon?" When he didn't respond, she quietly excused herself.

As Tyler scanned his assistant's notes, he couldn't focus on anything other than the story that may be developing with Alexis and why she was keeping it from him.

22

Alexis' pickup flew down the dirt road as gravel rocketed in its wake. When she finally came to a stop in front of her home, she killed the engine and stared across the way to the cemetery as Evelyn's words still echoed. She squinted her eyes at the memory, wondering if she genuinely heard her grandmother or if she was going crazy.

A soft tap on her window broke her from her daze, and startled, she turned in her seat.

"Oh!" Her voice raised an octave as her hand flew to her chest. She threw her door open as Anderson jumped back.

"Geez, Sis. You about took me out with your door." Her eyes blazed, sending him in a fit of laughter. "What's got you in a huff?"

"Wouldn't you like to know?" She smirked before almost being tackled by Lani.

"Mommy's home!" Lani squealed with glee as she threw her arms around her mother's waist.

"Hey, sweet pea!" Alexis lifted her daughter for a bear hug. "I missed you so much today."

"I missed you too." Lani's solemn eyes spoke volumes.

"Did I miss dinner?"

As the two interacted, Anderson stood by with a sense of longing. Other than his immediate family, he had no one he could call his own. His job didn't really allow him the flexibility for a relationship.

"Come on," he said, leading the pair up the stairs. "Mom saved you a plate, Lex."

"What'd she make?" Her animated face shone toward her daughter.

"Steak and potatoes." Lani giggled when her mother's nose wrinkled.

"Ew." Alexis pretended to be disgusted, but with her daughter's giggles, she found it hard to keep a stern face. She soon joined in, chuckling and set her daughter down before entering the kitchen.

Amelia heard them coming before she saw them. She pushed a plate toward her daughter. "You'll eat it, and you'll like it, young lady."

Alexis' heart warmed as the words she'd heard a million times as a child came full circle.

"Yes, ma'am." She sat across from her mother and reached for a fork. "I could eat anything today. I'm famished."

"I saw the five o'clock news." Anderson leaned on the counter next to her and smirked. "Were those out of focus shots yours?"

Alexis shot him a look of disdain. "Yes."

She was about to explain when her dad limped in with his arm in a sling. She studied his bruises and laid a hand on his shoulder as he groaned in pain.

"What happened?" Her concerned eyes shot to her mother for an explanation.

"Nothing. He fell off the back of the truck." Amelia shook her head. "He was unloading some supplies and got tangled up in some rope."

Anderson bit his lips to muffle a chuckle.

Amelia sent him a glare.

"What?" He shrugged. "Dad knows I don't mean anything by it. I'm sorry he got hurt, but he made a ruckus. I saw Dad hopping on one leg, and then down he went over the side."

"All that got hurt was my pride," Hank grumbled.

"Besides, he landed in some hay." Anderson reached for a green bean from Alexis' plate, only to have her swat it away.

"Dad," Alexis moaned. "Are you in a lot of pain?"

"Nothing your mother can't help with." His eyes twinkled.

"Ewww." She rolled her eyes. "Can you two stop acting like teenagers for one minute? I've lost my appetite."

She dropped her fork to her plate in time for Anderson to claim it and inhale a few more bites.

"Seriously?" She sent him a look. "I swear! Nothing changes around here."

"Mommy." Lani crawled up into her lap.

"Yes, baby." She dropped a kiss on her forehead, thankful for the reprieve.

"Do you believe me now?" Her inquisitive eyes beckoned.

"About what?"

"Great Grams." She cocked her head to the side.

"I never said I didn't believe you," Alexis said.

"I thought that since you've heard her for yourself." Lani watched her mother's mouth drop open and patted her arm. When her mom said nothing in response, she kissed her cheek and stretched for her ear. "It's okay," Lani whispered. "You get used to it, Mommy."

As her daughter scrambled down from her arms for the front porch, Alexis felt faint. How could she have known?

"What was that about?" Anderson asked, popping some food in his mouth.

Unwilling to rehash something even she didn't understand, she shrugged her shoulders. "I have no idea. You know how she is sometimes."

The group nodded in unison and went about their tasks. Hank, who was still licking his wounds, curled up in the lounger and turned on the television. Amelia finished loading the dishwasher, while Anderson scarfed the rest of Alexis' dinner down.

Alexis stared at him. "Don't let me stop you."

"You said you were done," he mumbled, his mouth full.

She was about to pull her plate back when Lani began yelling through the screen door.

"She's here! She's here!" Lani danced on the front porch. "Come on, Mommy. Come meet Gizelle."

"Who's Gizelle," Alexis whispered to her mom. "Should I know her?"

Amelia sent Lani a wave. "We'll be right there, baby girl." She turned to Alexis. "She's the little girl who lives on Tyler's land. Her mother and grandparents run the stables."

Alexis thought she remembered Tyler mentioning something about her, but to date, they'd never bumped into them during any of her riding lessons.

"Oh, yeah." She craned her neck toward the screen door.

"I'm surprised you've not met her yet as much time as you've spent at Tyler's place." She shot her a suggestive look.

Alexis wrinkled her nose. "Only for Lani's benefit, mother."

"Mmhmm," she hummed and folded a dish towel before heading for the door. "Well, come meet Gizelle. She's a sweet girl."

As both women stepped onto the porch, Alexis noticed Gizelle's mother pulling a wheelchair from the back of her minivan. She sent her mother a look of confusion.

"She has a slight condition, and from what I understand - she doesn't have many friends. So..." She shrugged.

"You thought it would be nice for Lani to play with her? That's a great idea, Mom. She'll start school soon, and it will help to have a friend."

Alexis stepped down to join her daughter, who was already asking Gizelle a million questions. Once the two were settled under the tree with her daughter's favorite tea set, Alexis stuck her hand out to introduce herself to Gizelle's mother.

"Nice to meet you. Thanks for bringing her over."

"Hi. I'm Bonnie." She wiped her hands on her jeans before shaking with Alexis. "Thanks for having her."

"So, you live at Tyler's place?" Alexis eyed the woman, who looked to be only a few years older than her. Bonnie stood about half a head taller than Alexis and had a plain but pretty face. Her eyes were warm and inviting, putting Alexis immediately at ease.

"Yeah," she said, blushing. "Well, not at his place. We rent it from him."

Alexis laughed. "That's what I meant."

Just then, Anderson appeared next to them and waited. His eyes were glued to Bonnie's face and shone with interest.

"Hey, Anderson." Bonnie blushed.

"You two know each other?" Alexis wagged her finger between them.

"Yeah, you could say that." Anderson's voice held veiled humor.

"It's a long story," Bonnie explained before turning to Amelia. "Well, again – thanks for the invite. I have some errands to run. Can I pick her up around seven?"

Amelia waved her off. "It's no problem. See you then."

"If I can't be here by then, I'll have Tyler swing by. When he found out we were coming over, he offered."

"Of course, he did," Alexis mumbled under her breath.

Anderson chuckled at the look on his sister's face before nodding to Bonnie.

"I'll walk you to your car."

"Don't be ridiculous. It's ten feet from here." Bonnie sent him a look before crossing the yard for her daughter. "Be good for Momma. See you in a few."

"Bye, Mom." Gizelle squeezed her neck as her mother kissed her cheek.

"You girls don't have too much fun without me." She winked at Lani and turned to leave.

As Bonnie backed her car from the drive, Alexis leaned over to her brother and said, "Crashed and burned?"

Anderson winced. He looked out to the field where Evelyn's accident took place and sighed.

She followed his gaze. "Bad choice of words." "But not untrue."

"Why don't you ask her out?" Alexis thought a little fun might be good for Anderson.

"Since when do I have time for that?"

Alexis turned and peered into his eyes, which used to be filled with humor but were now hooded with something she couldn't put her finger on.

"Normally, I'd say never. But," she paused. "You seem to be sticking around instead of hightailing it back to wherever you came from. Not that I'm allowed to ask, but…"

He cut her off. "Normally, no, but I know you all have been wondering why I'm still here."

Amelia stepped in next to her son and laid a hand on his arm.

"I wasn't sure if I should ask."

"Mom, I don't know where to start." He spun to sit on the bottom step of the porch.

"Start at the beginning." Alexis shrugged. "That usually works."

"I don't know how or where to begin." He lifted his gaze just as a hawk descended toward its prey. His heart generally delighted at the sight, but today it just reminded him of how fragile life was. "And I can't tell you everything."

"Because it's classified," the women said in unison.

"Let's just say I'm looking for a new beginning, and I may not be sending any postcards from cryptic places any longer. At least, I don't think so."

"Oh, honey." Amelia settled on the step next to her son and gave him a hug. "You know you're always welcome here."

"Looks like both your kids are home for a while, Mom." Alexis grinned down at her brother. "They're stupid for letting you go."

"They didn't." His face twisted. "I'm just taking a break for a bit, and that's all I can tell you."

Neither Alexis nor Amelia pushed for anything more. As her mother stroked her brother's back, Alexis reached down to ruffle his blond curls. "So, I guess that's why you let this mop grow back out?"

He beamed up to her. "The ladies like it this way."

"I'm not so sure about that." Alexis jutted her chin toward the driveway and continued, "One lady, in particular, didn't look too impressed. In fact, you almost ran her out of here."

"Give her time." He squinted toward the bend where Bonnie's car had disappeared. "Speaking of someone's love life. I think I see someone else turning down our drive. I wonder who that could be?"

Alexis didn't even need to look over her shoulder. The familiar rumble of Tyler's engine beckoned. She swore under her breath, her stomach clenching in response.

"Lani, sweetie," Alexis called.

"Yeah, Mom?"

"Your Uncle Tyler is here to see you."

Tyler got out of his truck just in time to hear Alexis addressing her daughter.

He looked at the two girls who were having a tea party under the oak tree and waved in their direction.

"I'll be right with you, Lani." He ruffled Lani's curls in passing, before approaching the others. Tyler nodded to Amelia and Anderson in greeting before he took Alexis by the hand.

"Actually, I came to speak to you. Do you mind?" He led Alexis until the two were slightly out of earshot.

Alexis wanted to wipe the smug look on her brother's face as Tyler ushered her toward his truck, but there would be time for that later. When she dared to stare into Tyler's warm chocolate eyes, she thought she'd melt on the spot. Instead, she held her ground and shrugged as if his boyish charm had no effect.

"Sure. What do you want to talk about?"

"Care to take a drive?"

"I'm still in my work clothes. Can you wait till I change?"

He scanned her from top to bottom, leaving her as if she'd been scorched along every inch. When he finally dragged his gaze back to meet hers, he nodded and said nothing.

Alexis swallowed, trying to get rid of the lump that had grown in the center of her throat and reminded herself to breathe. Without looking at Lani, she hollered over her shoulder, "Uncle Tyler wants to join your tea party."

Tyler could tell she was affected and fought the urge to kiss her in front of all of them. The more time they spent together, the more he could sense she was losing the fight against their chemistry.

As they continued to stare at one another as if in a trance, Lani's yell broke the spell.

"Tyler! Come have some tea."

"Just what every manly dude wants to do to impress a lady. Do I have to lift my pinky up when I sip from my cup," he whispered to Alexis.

"You don't have to." She smirked.

As he started for Lani, Alexis placed a hand on Tyler's arm and said, "And by the way, you ... having tea with my daughter is exactly what would impress this lady."

Tyler's heart lurched.

"Then, I'll be here for tea every day if that's what it takes."

As Lani watched her mom go inside, she beamed in Tyler's direction as he approached. She then quietly leaned over to Gizelle and said, "He's going to be my new daddy."

23

A warm breeze flowed through the partially open windows flirting with Alexis' blonde locks. Tyler studied the look of content that crossed her face and fought the urge to take her hand in his.

"Has anyone told you how beautiful you are?" Tyler pulled his truck to the side of the road.

Alexis' heart surged, but she shoved down any emotions other than gratefulness. She didn't want to bask in his praises, but underneath her internal strife, she did. Almost bashful, she looked up at him from under her lashes and parted her mouth as if to say something yet couldn't.

Tyler tightened his grip on the steering wheel before gaining composure.

"I'm trying here, Alexis." His voice was raw. "I am playing by your rules, but it's hard."

"Tyler." She blinked. "I've got a lot of emotions here, too."

"Then share them with me. We could always talk. I'm a good listener. When you left today, it killed me that you shut me out of your life. That's not how we work."

She dropped her head back and sunk further into her seat. "I feel more for you than I should." She turned in time to see desire flash through his earnest eyes. "But, I have a lot on my plate too."

He angled in his seat to face her. When he finally took Alexis' hand in his, he said, "We all do. That's why it's important to have people you can lean on."

"That's why I came home. You don't know the half of what I've been through."

"Tell me." His voice was soft and thick with emotion.

His compassion tugged at her senses, sending peace like a river flooding through her. Although she'd not been to church for quite some time, his acceptance reminded her of a verse from Isaiah, which talked about that exact thing – peace like a river. At that moment, she knew it was safe to tell him without judgment.

"After Clay and I ran off, I thought we'd come home to Purity to live, where he grew up with his father. It's where he seemed the most at home. It's why he stayed to finish school when his mother remarried and moved away." She swallowed. "His dream was to be a police officer. Since Purity was a safe town, I had no qualms about him joining the academy and living his dream out in our lazy town. Nothing happens here."

"You got that right. Why do you think I work in Dallas?"

"Well, turns out his step-dad and mom offered him a free place to stay above their garage in Michigan, where they ran a bed and breakfast." She gulped. "But I put my foot down. I was not going to live someplace cold and riddled with crime."

"I can see why."

"Instead, he joined the military, and we got to travel. It was incredible. He was stationed on Oahu and a few other places, like Virginia, where I got my start in broadcasting. No matter where we lived, it was always near a beach." Her eyes glowed. "This farm girl was in heaven. I had no idea how good life could be, but our marriage wasn't as ideal."

Tyler noticed the shadows that crossed her face and waited.

"There was always this barrier, almost like resentment between us. Clay felt like the second choice. Then we had trouble getting pregnant. There was a miscarriage." Her voice fell.

"I'm sorry." He laid a hand on her shoulder and drew her in.

"Then Lani came along, and everything changed for the better."

"She's a great kid." His heart warmed for the little girl he was coming to love.

"She is." Alexis' smile lit up her face. "And she was everything to us. Seeing Clay, as a father, well, my love grew for him by a thousand percent. We became parents and had a whole new relationship that took us to a place we never knew existed, which was good. But part of me wondered if we loved her more than we did one another." Alexis dropped her chin and stared at her lap. "I never talked about it to Clay, but I know he sensed it too."

Tyler tightened his arm around her and kissed the top of her head. "He knew you loved him."

"I know, but-" As she tried to finish, tears streamed down her face.

"Shhh." He hugged her gently.

"No, I need to finish," she muttered through the tears and slowly pulled away to face him. Alexis wanted him to know what he was getting himself into if he were serious about pursuing her.

"Okay," he said.

"Once she was born, we were good. Then, his stepdad's health started to fail, and his mom started begging him to help her. Clay was at a point where he could put in four more years or leave the military. So, he got out without consulting me and moved us to the one place I dreaded going."

Tyler sent her a grave stare. "He didn't even talk about it with you?"

"No." She wiped her face dry. "But looking back - it's hard to place all the blame on him. I was so invested in being a mom that I hardly ever spent time with him. Why would he consult me? He was always on his own."

"Lexi, a man owes it to his wife to ..."

She quickly cut him off. "I know, and I held a grudge. Believe me, I did." She half laughed through her tears.

"So, what happened next?"

"I left my burgeoning career. We moved in with Clay's parents to help with their business. Then, Clay graduated from the police academy and started working the night shift on the streets of Detroit."

"Wow," he whispered before letting out a breath.

"I wanted to work again too, but helping his mom was a full-time job."

"So, you lost a part of your identity when he …"

"Yeah, but I thrived being with Lani all day. She was such a joy. Trust me, she was the only thing bonding my mother in law and me together."

"You two didn't see eye to eye?"

Her mouth flattened. "Hardly. Everything I did was nitpicked or questioned, but not when it came to Lani. I put my foot down there. I was Lani's mother, and no one would tell me what was best for her. When she was born, it was like a whole new part of me was too."

Tyler's face shone with joy. "You're a great mom."

He quickly pictured how she would be with a child of their own but shook the thought away. He had to win her over first. *One step at a time.*

"It was like I was in sync with her like no one else, and there was no way his mom could compete with that."

"Do you think she saw your relationship as a competition?"

"Yeah," she said. "I believe she did. And after Clay's death." Her voice dropped.

"I'm sorry, Lex. If this is too hard." He brushed another tear from her face.

She nodded with acceptance at the gesture and took his hand in hers. "No, it's a relief to finally talk about it. I've been so cut off from everyone for so long."

"What about your family?" he offered.

She made a noise. "They know a few things. I think my mom knows more than she lets on, but I've never told them how miserable I was. I ran off and got married like a brat. So, how could I admit how bad things were?"

"Even with Evelyn?"

She sent him a sad stare. "There was nothing I could hide from her. She read me like a book. It was like my heartache spoke volumes to her no matter how cheerful of a voice I put on when she called."

"So, what happened to Clay? If you don't mind me asking."

The air around them immediately stilled. Although Alexis' voice broke through the eerie silence, it sounded as if it was a thousand miles away.

"I've never told anyone this." She looked up and blinked a few times, trying to keep the moisture gathering in her eyes at bay.

Tyler squeezed her hand, saying, "It's okay if you can't."

She took a deep breath and said, "The night he died, we got into a huge fight. I blamed him for moving us to the pit of hell, where I had to worry about him on the streets each night -and into a hostile house, in which I couldn't move without scrutiny." She paused and turned to stare into Tyler's dark but compassionate eyes. "I told him I was leaving him."

Tyler held her gaze. It was steady and full of warmth, giving Alexis permission to go further.

"Before he left for his shift, he begged me to reconsider, but I was stubborn and childish. I was a stranger among his family, well, except for Lani." She took a breath. "She was my one saving grace."

Alexis turned from Tyler and stared into the night that quickly enveloped them. She bit her lip and dipped her head, shaking it with regret. What she said next almost broke Tyler's heart.

"And only two hours later, he was dead."

He reached for her hand, as she continued, "When we heard the knock on our front door..." Her voice broke, but she tried again. "When I opened the door, I saw the police lights and knew in my heart I had killed him."

"Lexi. No." Tyler placed a finger beneath her chin, forcing her to look at him. "His job put him in danger every day. That's not your fault."

Her childlike eyes loomed. Even in the dark of night, he could see they were racked with guilt.

"But it was me that had him off his game that night," she cried. "If it weren't for our fight, maybe he would have come home alive instead of getting trapped in the line of fire. If only…"

"Look at me." He gently shook her shoulders. "Lexi!"

When she was unwilling to listen, he cupped her face, found her eyes, and spoke the words she needed to hear.

"It's not your fault."

Alexis sadly shook her head. Although she appreciated the effort, deep within her heart, she still knew the truth. She wiped one last errant tear from her eye. "His mother blamed me every day afterward." She sniffled.

Tyler exhaled, saying nothing. He couldn't imagine the hell they all were living through, but for that woman to blame Alexis seemed to do nothing but heap hurt upon heartbreak. It was unfathomable.

Alexis wasn't sure how to interpret Tyler's silence. She prayed what she revealed hadn't changed his opinion of her, but she wouldn't blame him if it did.

"Apparently, she heard us fighting and knew I was the reason Clay was distracted on the job."

Tyler's soft voice interrupted. "Anyone in their right mind would know you weren't at fault."

"No." She stared outside through the windshield, unable to bear the pity in his eyes. "So afterward, instead of packing up and leaving as I so desperately wanted to do, I stayed because that's what Clay would have wanted. He wouldn't have wanted his mother to be alone, and she needed the extra help."

"Oh, Lexi," he moaned and pulled her toward him.

As she placed an ear on his chest, Alexis listened to his heart. *It beats strong and faithful, just like him.* She knew it beat wildly for her, yet he deserved better than what she could offer.

"In the end, I shut off my emotions, so I could make it through the day. Lani was my sole reason for surviving. I kept my little angel happy by putting a smile on my face and making it through each insult that woman would hurl at me. By the time she became sick, I didn't even care." She gave Tyler a look, her eyes brimming with tears. "Who does that? Who had I become that I wouldn't even care if someone lived or died?"

"You're human." Once more, he lifted her chin with his tender touch. "You were being verbally abused daily and did the best you could."

"To top it off. His mom forced us to attend church. On Sundays, all I wanted to do was crawl into a hole and sleep. It was the only day in which I wouldn't have to be around my mother-in-law, but to keep her happy, I put on a cheerful face and toted my little girl to a place where deep down I knew Lani should be."

Tyler stroked her hair, wanting to comfort her but had no words.

"I resented Clay's mom for making me out to be a bad mom, after all I'd done for her."

After a few more moments of silence, Tyler took a deep breath and finally asked, "So is that why I don't see you with your family at church? Because you're still angry with her?"

"Ugh!" She rubbed her temples. "I don't know. I guess. I've been so mad at the circumstances in my life. When I know it's not His fault? I've just been..." She paused, but before she could finish, Tyler said it for her.

"Alone."

She turned to him with a look that tore at his heart and said, "Yeah."

"You're not." His brow wrinkled. "You've got a lot of people who care about you. You've got a God who is bigger than all of it. And you have a man at your side who would do anything for you." He lifted her hand to his lips.

Tingles danced down her arms as he laid claim to each fingertip with his warm lips.

"Tyler," she groaned. "I just don't know if I'm ready for this. I've got so much to work through."

"Okay." He lowered their hands on his leg, fingers still entwined. "I've been there. I get it but know that I'm not going anywhere. And, when you're ready, I'll be right here."

"Thanks." Her mouth upturned, showcasing a small dimple on the side of her cheek. "I needed this."

"So, are you going to tell me about this clue you've uncovered with Evelyn's letter?" He started his engine up once more and looked at the clock on his dashboard.

"I think you've earned that." Alexis raised an eyebrow.

"Good, because I'm late picking up Gizelle. Fill me in on the way back." He lifted her hand once more to kiss her palm before pulling back onto the main road.

~

As Tyler's truck pulled away, Evelyn stayed behind in tears. She knew her granddaughter was torn in those last few months while in Michigan but had no idea how bad it had become. She sighed for the loss of Alexis' innocence. She knew what it was like to suffer and find yourself in troubled waters that were difficult to navigate.

Suddenly, a soft voice sounded behind her.

"Do you know yet why you're here?"

Evelyn spun around to find Clay, who had a wistful look on his face.

"Clay?" She reached out to touch him, forgetting they were both spirits without boundaries. As her hand passed through, she chuckled. "I still don't have a handle on all this yet."

"Me neither." He shrugged. "You'll get the hang of it. Focus on your touch while at the same time, sending every ounce of love you have within, and it won't pass through. Like this." He reached for her hand and squeezed it gently.

Evelyn saw the admiration that shone in his eyes as his spirit sent swells of peace to surround her. She relished every second and wished he could do the same for Alexis.

As their hands dropped, she said, "It's good to see you. I met your son. He said you were resting."

His eyes sparkled. "I get out now and then. I've found my peace with what I could and couldn't do after I passed. I rest easier now knowing you might get through to Alexis."

"With what?"

"I tried so hard to reach her after I passed – to let her know it wasn't her fault. Her heart was so torn, and her mind was so hardened that it was an impossible task." He stuck his hands in his dress blues. "Lani, on the contrary, was able to hear me while she slept. We had some great talks."

"She's a special little girl." Evelyn's spirit lit up with warmth.

"That she is, but she was so tiny. I couldn't tell her anything about her mother and me. It's a burden I refused to pass on. Instead, I utilized my time with her to tell her how much I loved her. I tried to give her some acceptance of my passing – not that it would be easy."

"When do you know your job is done?" Evelyn sighed. "How long until I can rest easy?"

Clay grinned. "You'll just know. I can't explain it. And then you'll rest and wait until He comes with a few free passes now and then, like for me, tonight." His dimples were like bookends to his broad smile.

"So, you wake up from time to time when you're needed?" She squinted, trying to take it all in.

"Something like that."

"So, I'm supposed to help her heart to find peace."

"And to fall in love." Clay sighed. "I tried most of my life to do that, and even in death, I was unsuccessful. Tyler. He's always been the one, Evelyn."

"She loved you, Clay." Evelyn stared him down with a wag of her finger.

"I know, but she deserves more. I want more for her. And you're the one to help her find her way back to the man who can give it to her."

"You're something else, Clay Mathers." Evelyn let out a ragged breath and turned toward the taillights of Tyler's truck, which were drifting from the horizon. When she turned back to Clay, all she saw was his form fading away.

"Keep her safe, Evelyn. See you soon." His smile was the last thing she saw.

24

As the golden hour settled around her, Alexis put her shovel down and wiped her brow with the back of her forearm. The soft amber rays shone from above, casting a glow across her family's property.

Her eyes drifted toward a new foal nuzzling its mother by the trough. She wished she had a camera to capture the intimate moment. Her heart lifted at how the love of a mother translates even in the animal kingdom. It was something she may not have taken note of before she was a mother. With Lani in her life, everything had a new meaning.

As she straightened her oversized work gloves, she gripped her shovel to continue her chores. Anderson stepped in next to her and looked like he'd finished a marathon. He reached for her canister of water and took a deep slug before saying, "You're out late today. Something on your mind?"

The truth was she was burning off nervous energy. She'd been thinking of ways to approach William Wylar but was unsure the direct approach was the right one. In light of how her grandmother died, she thought a little reconnaissance was in order but wasn't sure how to start.

"Just thought I'd give Mom a break. I've been at the station a lot lately."

"Finally, pulling your weight?" His lopsided grin stalled when he realized she wasn't responding in kind.

"Something like that." She sent him a sincere smile as she could muster.

Anderson narrowed his eyes. "Since when have you ever volunteered to muck the stalls? What's really going on?"

Alexis wavered. "I'm working something out for work," she added a little too quickly.

"Uh-huh." He took one more gulp, letting the cool water slide down his throat, but kept his gaze steady.

"Why are you looking at me like that? She shoveled another load into her wheelbarrow. "Keep it up, and the next pile I shovel will land on your head."

His quiet calm met her as she continued to clean the floors. She spun around to face Anderson, unable to bear the silence that hovered like a storm cloud. With a hand on her hip, she said, "Okay - look. I found out who Grandmother's mystery man is."

He expected her to break. She never could stand the quiet, but what came out of her mouth wasn't even on his radar. When he choked on the water he was swallowing, she jumped forward to pat him on the back while asking, "Are you okay?"

He coughed once more and stood to face her. He took a deep breath and attempted to speak, but his voice caught. He cleared his throat once more and took a quick sip before he slowly added, "When were you going to tell me?"

"Well, it's not like you were helping me with anything."

He sent her a look of warning.

"Okay. Okay." She muttered. "I know you left the government, but I didn't know about your job change until the other day. And besides, I just discovered his name!"

She threw her hands up.

"Who is he?"

Alexis clamped her teeth down on the inside of her lips before she wrinkled her nose and made a face Anderson knew all too well.

"You're not going to tell me, are you?" His face turned to stone. "She's my grandmother, too, you know."

"I will. I just don't know how to talk about it yet. Let's just say I'm processing it."

"Yeah, you said that already. Your idea for work?" He pursed his mouth and spun on his heel.

"Anderson," she called out to his back as he exited the barn. "Don't tell anyone yet."

"Are you kidding me, Alexis?" He turned back to her shaking his head. "The police need to know! I can't believe for one second you'd consider keeping this from Mom."

Alexis dropped back onto the hay and slipped off her work gloves, groaning in reply, "Anderson."

As he paused by the exit, a look of fatigue crossed his face.

"I didn't mean to yell." He wiped his brow. "I've been up since sun up baling hay with the guys. Since Dad got hurt, I'm trying to take on his chores too."

"I'm sorry," she murmured.

"No. I am, but that doesn't mean you're off the hook. If you don't tell the family, I will. And you have to promise me not to go off at half-cock with any of your crazy ideas."

She rolled her eyes, saying, "Like I would do something like that."

He gave her a doubtful look and said, "Uh-huh."

She leaned her shovel against the wall and dropped her gloves on the hay before slipping on a ball cap to secure a few loose strands that had fallen around her face.

"Wait up." She jogged over to catch up to her brother. "I'll walk back home with you. You look like you could use a shower."

He sniffed and said, "You smell like you do."

"Shut up!" She laughed and shoved his shoulder.

"Seriously, you do." He stared down at her boots. "And I'd take those off on the back porch, or Mom will skin your hide." The mischief in his eyes had returned before he took off running. "First one home gets the bathroom!"

Evelyn watched her grandchildren with pride. Even as adults, glimpses of the kids she helped raised appeared every now and then. She grinned, thinking that no matter what your age, you are who you are from the day you're born. Those two were living proof.

Worry wrestled from within as she knew she'd have to keep a vigilant eye on Alexis, her reckless grandchild, who fell into trouble whether she was looking for it or not.

25

Daniel Wylar answered his cell on the fourth ring to hear his cousin's scathing voice whining through the line.

"The police just left, asking about the Bozeman woman. I thought you said the accident couldn't be traced back to us."

Daniel sat down on his threadbare couch and let out an angry hiss. His cousin, younger by three years, was a brilliant man, but by no means smooth. He just hoped Henry didn't give them away.

"What did you tell them?" He narrowed his eyes at the red light that blinked at him from his answering machine. He shook his head as his voicemail, chocked full of debt collectors, mocked him from afar. The red light symbolized roadblocks he'd faced his whole life.

His existence was the polar opposite of Henry, who bore the Wylar name and had every door open to him. Daniel, however, was born on the wrong side of the family, and he paid for it at every turn. His meager existence seemed destined for the status quo until Henry's very recent visit to his job site.

As he waited for his cousin to answer, Daniel relived the defining moment when Henry stopped by the stockyards in his high dollar, designer shoes, and tailor-made suit.

He'd never forget the image of Henry ambling across the dusty road toward the surrounding fence line. Daniel had even blinked and rubbed his eyes, wondering if he was a mirage. The only time he saw his uptight cousin was at family reunions or funerals. And, those events were far and few between.

Daniel stuck another pinch of snuff in his lower lip, rested a mud-caked boot on the fence, and waited for Henry to state his business. He scrutinized his cousin's approach, thinking he looked a bit like fine china tossed in the middle of a junkyard. Why was he stopping by?

Henry cleared his throat and sent his cousin a half-smile. He lifted his hand with an awkward attempt to shake, but when Daniel didn't reach for his in return, Henry shoved his hand in his pants pocket.

Henry grimaced, asking, "How are you?"

"Since when do you care?" Daniel spat out some chewing tobacco, barely missing Henry's fancy shoes.

"Um, I guess I don't." He glanced at his shoes, mouth twisted, hoping they would withstand this unforeseen visit.

"Why are you here?" Daniel sneered.

Henry laid a manicured hand on the fence and made a face. "I have nowhere else to go."

Daniel gave him a look that said otherwise.

Henry tugged at his collar and breathed in, unsure of how to start.

"Out with it," Daniel growled. His hard eyes bore down on him like a clamp.

Henry resigned with a deep sigh. "The family business has hit a snag."

When Daniel turned his back and walked away, Henry quickly followed him, sidestepping a huge pile of manure before begging. "I need your help."

Those four words stopped Daniel in his tracks. He slowly turned with a sneer and mentally recounted the times his cousin taunted him for being less of a person because he had a smaller bank account.

Daniel closed the gap and poked him in the chest. "You. You need my help? That's rich." His throaty laugh filled the air.

With care, Daniel pulled a small grey and white-faced calf toward him by its ears and spoke to it as if it could understand.

"Did you hear that? He needs my help." He laughed and stroked the calf's nose between his eyes before turning his gaze to his cousin.

Henry, who was at the end of one of the most disparaging looks he'd experienced, shifted from one foot to the other and took a deep breath.

"Look. I apologize if I ever upset you when we were kids. You know the whole my dad is better than your dad thing."

"Upset me? No, not if you count rubbing your money in my face every time you saw me, knowing my family didn't have two cents to our name." Daniel dusted his hands off in front of Henry's face. "Now if you will excuse me. I have a real man's job."

Henry took the pot-shot in stride and bit the inside of his cheek. The last thing he wanted was to ask for help, but he couldn't go to anyone else. Daniel was the only one he could think of that could help with something this underhanded.

"What if I make it worth your while?" His voice brimmed with determination.

Daniel's steely black eyes filled with a veiled curiosity.

"Just what kind of trouble have you got yourself into, little man?" He folded his arms across his muscular chest.

"I like to bet now and then." Henry winced. "And it just so happens that I owe some intimidating people a bit of money."

Daniel's stony grin revealed a lack of dental care as it hung beneath his crooked nose. It made Henry wonder just how many altercations his cousin had been in.

"Well, you have plenty. It shouldn't be a problem to pay them back."

"Well, now see. That's where you're wrong." He ducked his head and rubbed the back of his neck. "I've uh, run through a lot."

"Why don't you just ask your grandfather for it." Daniel leered at his cousin.

Henry lowered his voice and ran his well-manicured hand along the fence. "That ship has sailed. I've asked one too many times, and last time." He paused and shook his head. "Well, last time, Grandfather said I needed to get my gambling under control or else."

"You're asking me to help you – how?" His eyes narrowed.

Henry sighed, wishing he had other options. Baring his soul to his cousin was the last thing he wanted to do, but he had no one else to turn to.

"I hired an accounting temp under the pretense of finding any loose ends in our billing. I had her work at night and pad her cash, so she wasn't on the books. You know, to stay under the radar." His brow shot up. "I thought if I could inflate a little here or," he paused and ran his hand through his fashionable cut. "I - uh- I was trying to find anything I could. You know, to siphon something from the Wylar store accounts that would look legitimate."

Daniel frowned. "Why are you telling me this?"

"Because I found something unexpected. Right after the temp discovered this account... well, it's a trust, really. Right after that, I let her go. I didn't want anyone else privy to what came next."

"I'm not good with math, Henry. I don't do finances." He waved his arms to the stockyards around him.

"Just wait. This trust. It was set up by my grandfather, and the rules were very specific."

Henry rushed to catch up with Daniel, who had left for another stall. In his haste, Henry stepped in a fresh pile of cow droppings and groaned, shaking his foot free.

"Great," he whined. Exasperated, he put his hands in the air and yelled. "Daniel! Stop."

Daniel spun on his heel and lifted his chin. "You don't get to tell me what to do. I'm on the clock here. And unless you're about to offer me the position of a lifetime, I have a job to do."

Henry raised an eyebrow and sent him a knowing look. "Would half a million dollars be enough to help?"

Daniel paused, eyes wide. He blinked, spun to close the gate behind him, and threw an arm around Henry's shoulders as if the two were best friends. "Now, you're talking. Our bad blood is water under the bridge, cuz. What do I have to do?"

Daniel's short-lived flashback faded as his churlish cousin's voice cleared the phone line. It sounded as if he was choking, which wasn't far off. The next thing he heard was Henry's inhaler when he took a puff of his medicine.

Daniel rolled his eyes. His cousin may have been book smart, but he'd never have the street sense that Daniel did.

"Answer me, Henry. What did you tell them?"

Henry stammered in return. "W-What do you think I told them? I told them I'd never heard of anyone named Evelyn Bozeman."

"Okay. Then the cops left? There's nothing to connect us, right?"

"Well." Henry's voice squeaked.

"What do you mean – well?" Daniel's blood pressure skyrocketed.

"The trust has her named as the recipient of grandfather's funds. They had a subpoena for our files."

"What?" Daniel jumped from his couch, yelling into his cell. "How could you let this happen? I thought you said there was nothing to tie us. Now they'll know you lied about her."

"Well, technically, the trust wasn't anything I ever knew of. I didn't know about Evelyn either. And it was so deeply hidden; I doubt they'll find it. Remember... I hired the accountant with cash, so no one can connect us to the money. It was run by my grandfather's lawyer, and he's been in the Cayman's all summer."

Daniel finished Henry's train of thought. "Which is how we broke into his office without his knowledge. Yeah, yeah. Okay," he breathed. "Maybe we're safe."

"We should still be okay." Although Henry was reassuring Daniel, he was speaking more to himself than his cousin.

"If all of this was for nothing. If I go back to jail ..." Daniel exhaled and reached for a pack of cigarettes.

"You're worried about you going to jail? At least you've been and know how to survive! I can't go to jail. You know what they do to men like me? I'd be someone's b–"

"You already are. You're mine." Daniel stuck a cigarette between his lips and lit up. "From now on, we do things my way. Got it?"

When there was no reply except another intake from Henry's inhaler, Daniel continued, "We lay low. Just because the police came to us, doesn't mean they or the Bozeman family know anything. Stay as ignorant as you already are, Henry. You know this means I can't do anything about your precious grandfather just yet."

Henry sighed with impatience.

"You got it?" Daniel asked.

"Yeah, but I need that money soon. I can't put these guys off much longer." Henry shuddered, trying not to focus on how many ways the loan shark's thugs could break him.

"One step at a time." Daniel needed to protect himself, but he also had to protect his investment. And Henry was his means to an end. "We have to avoid jail time first. And you need to lay low for a while. Do you have vacation time coming so you can steer clear of your loan shark?"

"Yeah, but I never take time off. There's no one else I trust to run the store. Since Grandfather left me the reins, I'm it."

"Find someone." Daniel closed his eyes and exhaled, sending smoke through his nostrils. "Then, you crash at my place."

He glanced at his meager surroundings with a laugh. While Henry would be a pain to have underfoot, the thought of his cousin slumming it in his tiny apartment was intriguing.

Henry closed his eyes and rubbed his temple. "I can't. I have inventory coming up. Besides, won't that look suspicious to the police?"

Daniel cocked his head. He had a point. "Yeah, probably. Just watch your back. Truth is - nothing may come of this."

"I hope not."

"You'll be fine, Henry. I'll be in touch."

Daniel's reassurance did nothing to ease Henry's nerves. He sincerely hoped his cousin was right. Although Henry thought himself the smarter of the two, his cousin had more experience with this sort of thing.

As he slid his cell into his shirt pocket, Henry glanced at his office. File cabinet drawers were haphazardly pulled open after the police searched the room from top to bottom. The pit in his stomach churned. Surely things couldn't get any worse.

26

"What do you mean the police are at a dead end?" Alexis flattened her palms on the table and stood, challenging her parents. "I knew I should have handled this my way."

Anderson raised his eyebrow and glanced from his parents to the wild look of rebellion that crossed his sister's face.

"Calm down." He tugged on her arm. "We did the right thing by telling them." Anderson nodded to his parents for backup.

Amelia rolled her eyes. "Don't be so dramatic, Alexis. Just because they can't find anything now, doesn't mean they won't. Sometimes things like this take weeks. Months!" She threw her hands up and stood to finish the dishes.

"Like you're the voice of authority on this sort of thing, Mom?" There was an edge to her voice that had her father immediately on his feet.

"Alexis!" he barked. "Don't you dare."

She hung her head with regret. Her dad was the strong, silent type until anyone, even one of his kids, stepped out of line. She shook her head and sat back down.

"Look. I'm sorry." She sighed and picked up her fork, pushing the last of her mashed potatoes to the edge of her plate. Her eyes flashed with fire as she connected with her brother's gaze. She mouthed, *thanks a lot.*

Anderson put his hands up and left the room. This was not his fight, and he wasn't about to get in the middle of one of his sister's battles. He did enough of that with his job. The last thing he planned on doing was mediating for his family.

Amelia watched the silent banter between her kids and sent her husband a look of gratitude. She loved that he always had her back. So many women she'd known over the years were quick to flaunt their man's money or positions in life. While she and Hank may not have a glamorous life, they always had each other, and it was still more than enough.

Hank squeezed Amelia's hand before limping back to retire into his easy chair for the evening. As he passed Alexis by, he popped her on top of her head. "Show more respect."

"Yes, sir." She bit her lip. No matter how old she got, he still was bigger than life. "Love you, Daddy." Her voice trailed as he turned the corner. Her heart lit up when she heard him reply, "Love you, darlin'."

Amelia settled into a chair next to her daughter with a chortle. "I guess all a woman has to do to clear the room is show a little emotion." Amelia's laughter magnified. "Or, in your case, a lot."

Alexis hid her laugh and said, "Shut up."

Alexis' lips twitched. She shouldn't be joking at a time like this, but her mother's mood was infectious. When her mother raised a brow at her, Alexis took in her mother's luminous eyes, thinking her to be the most beautiful woman in the world. When her mother laughed, her face lit up like a golden light after a hard rain.

She opened her mouth to pay her mother a compliment when Amelia suddenly sobered and brought the subject back full circle.

"So, what are you going to do about all this?" Her mother gazed at her lap as if she was afraid of the answer.

"What do you mean?"

Amelia's long lashes fluttered as she brought her eyes back up to meet her daughter's. The two were a mirror image, separated only by years.

"Come on. I know Anderson had to talk you into telling us. If the police aren't finding anything, I know you'll try." Amelia's soft voice quivered. "It's who you are."

"Who is that right now, Ma?" Alexis made a sound. "Because I'm not sure anymore. Other than Lani's mom, I don't really have a place or a purpose."

Amelia took her daughter's chin in her hands and stared into her eyes with tenderness.

"You're the girl, who at ten years old, who followed a stranger down that back road on your bike because you didn't think he looked like he belonged. You didn't tell a soul what you were doing. You dialed 9-1-1, told the dispatcher there was a strange man on our property and hung up to ride after him."

Alexis bit her lip to keep from laughing as she recalled the memory. "I just wanted to make sure he got to wherever he was going safely."

"Alexis Olivia! You just wanted to keep him away from all of us. You were our protector even back then. You're our champion." Amelia's soft chuckles subsided. "Your heart is full of purpose and passion. And it can be very powerful for a good cause when needed." Amelia's eyes clouded. "Or, it can be perilous when you don't heed caution."

"Mom, I've always been careful."

"Like you were with that stranger? Who turned out to be a new neighbor taking a walk, but he could have been a mass murderer for all you knew. You went off without thinking."

"Mom, I'm not ten anymore." Alexis pushed her chair back.

"Okay, how about when you ran off to marry and told no one?"

"Mom!" Alexis threw her hands up. "Why am I on trial here?"

"You're not. You've always had your reasons, and you're an adult. But you have a daughter now, so please think about your actions before you do anything."

"Who says I'm going to do anything?" Alexis raised her voice but kept her tone within reason.

Amelia sent her a look that was laced with experience.

Alexis lifted her hands with resignation. "Okay. Okay. I promise I won't do anything dangerous. I won't follow anyone around. I won't even sneak off anywhere without telling anyone."

"You promise?" Amelia's motherly tone rose an octave.

Alexis crossed her heart and stood to kiss her on the head before taking her plate to the sink.

"Need help with the dishes?"

Amelia shook her head as Alexis left the room, already knowing the answer.

"Okay, then. I'm going to pick up Lani from Gizelle's place. Her mom asked her to stay over after her riding lesson with Tyler."

"I think it's great she's got such a sweet friend."

"Me too."

"Alexis." Her mother called after her. As her daughter turned with an expectant look, she continued, "You promise?"

"I'll be good. No planned clandestine activity." Alexis sent her an angelic grin before sailing out the door with her keys in hand. "That doesn't mean I can't go shopping, though," she whispered to herself.

After Alexis slipped into the seat of her pickup, she promised herself a little retail therapy very soon.

27

A cloud of dust trailed Alexis' small pickup, as she barreled down the road to the adjacent farm. Tyler's chest constricted with anticipation, the closer she came to the stables. When she slowed to park, a grin broke across his face, and a sense of longing tugged from within.

He turned back toward Lani and Gizelle, who was riding a couple of trail horses within the training circle and nodded to Bonnie in dismissal.

As Alexis hopped out of her truck, the sun's evening rays streamed through her golden locks, making it seem as if she wore a crown.

Alexis swung her door shut and sent him a hesitant wave before closing the gap between them. "I'm here for Lani."

Tyler briefly glanced over his shoulder, where both girls rode their horses around the pen, before smirking at Alexis.

"And here I thought you were here to see me." He chuckled as her face took on a light shade of pink. "I'm just kidding. They just finished dinner and came back out for a last-minute ride."

As her face warmed, she ducked her head and tucked a few curls behind her ears in response.

Tyler dropped down on a handcrafted bench outside the fence and patted the spot next to him.

"You know you're welcome anytime."

She nodded, easing in place as he draped an arm over her shoulders. Against her better judgment, she relaxed into his muscular frame.

Emotions he couldn't identify swirled within as her hair tickled the top of his arm. Tyler laid his cheek on the top of her head and inhaled. She smelled of fresh florals and sunshine. He closed his eyes, happy to just be in the moment, and that's how they sat for a few moments, without words, content to be in each other's company.

"Mmmm," she murmured with eyes closed.

Tyler ran his fingers through her hair, sending shivers down her spine, rendering her useless. Between the stress of her grandmother's investigation, being a single parent, and the butterflies in her stomach whenever Tyler was around - Alexis was worn slick. At this moment, though, it was good to let go and just enjoy the closeness they shared.

As if he could read her mind, he whispered in her ear, "When was the last time you took care of you?"

In haste, she opened her eyes to find she was on the end of an intimate stare, which was entirely too close for her liking. As if she were poked with a hot brand, she jerked back and stood, putting a safe distance between them.

The disappointment that displayed across his face did nothing to ease her conscience. She hung her head, disappointed with herself too.

Why can't I just stay away from him? It's not fair to either one of us.

"Everything okay?" Tyler stood and squinted, searching her face.

She inhaled and sagged against the fence as her daughter emphatically waved from her horse.

"Hi, Mom!" Lani yelled.

"Hi, Mrs. Mathers!" Gizelle echoed, waving a hand in the air.

Bonnie, who was holding her daughter's reins, lifted her free hand in greeting as Alexis smiled brightly for the benefit of her daughter.

"Hi, girls." Alexis cupped her hands. "Lani, we have to go."

"Please! Five more minutes. I still have to brush Jax when I'm done."

"Don't worry about that, Lani." Bonnie grinned and patted Jax on the nose. "I've got Tyler for that."

Tyler lifted an eyebrow and chuckled. "Lani, take as long as you want. Your mother and I have to talk."

"Thanks, Tyler!" Lani pulled her reigns and dug her heels into the horse's side.

"Be careful!" Alexis hollered.

"Jax is as docile as they come. He won't do more than a canter. Don't worry so much, Alexis."

She turned to him with an evil eye. "Take as long as you want? It's a school night, Tyler."

He motioned to the horizon. "The sun is almost down. Jax won't budge when it's dark. She'll be done in ten minutes - tops."

Alexis couldn't help but laugh. No matter how infuriating the man was, he always found a way to lighten the mood. "You crack me up."

His eyes teased her from under his cowboy hat. "Anything I can do to hear more of that."

When Tyler stroked her cheek, she inhaled. "Tyler, we've talked about this."

"What?" He put his hands up. "You had something on your face. Can't a friend help you out? You had a smudge."

She rubbed her cheek as if savoring the imprint he left behind. Although his hands were now safely shoved in his pockets, her face still tingled where his fingers trailed her cheek. She narrowed her eyes and studied his dark eyes, wondering if she could ever allow anything more between them. No, at least not right now. There were too many distractions.

Tyler could tell she was considering her options. Her eyes even held a bit of hope until she analyzed herself to death. The instant she went from a place of possibility to one of doubt, he knew. His heart dropped. As patient as he had been, he was beginning to wonder if she'd ever come around. It dawned on him he may have to face a future without her. His heart burned at the thought.

Tyler was an all or nothing man. While he'd made great strides as her friend, this middle ground was about to kill him. It was like getting stuck behind a large bus in the middle lane without the ability to change lanes. While he wanted to see what their future held, if that wasn't a possibility - he might have to let off the gas and switch to a slower path or aim for the fast lane and move on. For now, though, he'd settle for being her confidante.

Tyler tossed her a curious look. Something was beneath her stormy eyes - outside her usual objections. He shifted his gaze toward the horizon, resting his forearms on the fence line and waited.

When she began to fidget, he asked, "Are you going to tell me, or do I have to drag it out of you?"

"Tell you what?" She shrugged.

"Come on. I always know when something is brewing behind those liquid pools of yours." He pointed at her eyes.

She glanced down to her boots and kicked the dirt before leaning on the fence next to him. She closed her eyes and let the setting sun adorn her with its last descent before taking a deep breath.

"The police took a copy of my letter, but so far it's a dead end." She twisted to face him. "They haven't really uncovered anything more."

"No clear ties to the Wylars?"

"You mean other than the letter which should be the glaring proof of foul play of some sort?" She paused. "No, no direct ties. And, I'm so frustrated I can't see straight. What other proof do they need? That letter is pretty incriminating."

"To some extent, it is, but use your investigative reporter skills, Lexi. It's an important clue, but not inconclusive proof."

"Whose side are you on?" She pushed off the fence.

"Yours." He spun her around. When she stopped just a few inches from him, he slid his hands to her hips. "You should know that by now. I'm always looking out for you." His voice dropped to a raw whisper.

Unable to move and afraid of what came next, she blinked and opened her mouth to speak, but nothing came out. All she could think about was how the pressure of Tyler's hands on her hips made her wish he'd explore more with them.

"I'm sorry. I've tried, but this 'friends' thing is for the birds. I've fallen too hard, Lex." He laced his fingers through her curls.

Alexis wanted to object. She knew she should, but desire kicked aside every ounce of logic that usually screamed from within. When leaned in and brushed his lips across hers, waves of euphoria flooded her senses. Instead of putting distance between them, she found herself wrapped her arms around his neck for more.

Tyler expected her to object. So, when she matched him kiss for a kiss, with a passionate response, he almost couldn't believe it.

As she ran her hands through his thick hair, he groaned in response and pulled back to search her face. As they parted, he studied her dilated eyes and wondered what ran behind them.

"Alexis?" His voice was almost inaudible.

She touched her fingers to her lips, which still hummed from the kiss they just shared.

"Lani," she said as if in a trance before wrapping her arms around her midsection and taking a small step back. It might as well have been a leap to the moon as far as Tyler was concerned because what seemed to be a few feet felt like miles.

Alexis scanned the pen to ensure her daughter didn't witness their public display of affection only to find Bonnie leading the girls and their horses into the barn.

"Did you think I'd kiss you with an audience? I wouldn't jeopardize anything with Lani. I know better." Tyler sighed and shook his head. Whatever walls he'd crashed through a few moments ago were immediately thrown back up with reinforcements. What he wouldn't give to earn her trust.

Alexis flattened her lips and cast her eyes downward in shame. "Thanks."

"Can I call you later?"

"I don't know, Tyler." She frowned and stepped backward toward the barn. "This is all happening too fast."

"Too fast?" He almost choked. "We've been dancing around this thing between us since we were in high school. If that's too fast, then I'll be in my fifties before you finally let me in."

Alexis shook her head and gave him an evil eye. So, what if he was right? It didn't give him the right to make light of the inner struggle she had when it came to him. No matter how much she wanted him, the guilt she held for Clay held her back.

"Well, a lot has changed since we were kids." She glared and put her hands up to keep him from following her.

"You're not the only one with a past, Alexis!" he hollered at her back.

As Alexis turned the corner to the barn, she snuck a glance over her shoulder in time to see him kick gravel toward the road in frustration.

"I'm sorry, Tyler," she whispered with a heavy heart.

Although she regretted sending him mixed messages, Alexis couldn't allow him to cloud her judgment any further. How could she permit herself to move forward with a relationship when she wasn't even sure how to steer her life out of reverse and into drive?

Ever since Clay's passing, she was in limbo. The minute she thought of Tyler as more than a friend, the guilt from Clay's accident saturated any hopes of moving forward. As the remorse washed over her, Lani's laughter greeted her as it traveled across the barn to the entrance where she stood. Her daughter's exuberant spirit was like a salve to her soul.

Alexis started through the double doors when the sound of Evelyn's humming stopped her in her tracks. She shook her head free from the song that echoed from Bonnie's radio and drew in a sharp breath. Was it possible that Evelyn's smooth melody was emanating from her memory?

That must be it.

However, once the chorus played from within the barn, her

grandmother's soft voice picked up where it left off. Her hum permeated Alexis' senses. Alexis spun to search over her shoulder while every nerve along her spine lit up as if someone had flipped a switch.

While Evelyn lit up the air around her with a song, she prayed it reached Alexis on some level. When her granddaughter turned back with an expectant look, she gently laid a hand on Alexis' back. The pain that tore through Alexis' heart sent shockwaves up Evelyn's arm. Evelyn shook her head at Alexis' needless struggle as she opened her hands, trying to send waves of peace over Alexis' body.

"I want you to listen," she whispered.

Alexis paused and leaned against the outside of the barn. She turned ever so slowly, afraid of what she'd find behind her. When there was nothing but the setting sun in her wake, Alexis blinked and steadied herself against the wall, thinking she was losing her mind.

Evelyn watched from a distance as Tyler crossed the yard to his truck and drove off. She then stroked Alexis' back, saying, "I know you've lost a lot." She leaned in to whisper in her ear with the hopes her message would land somewhere within her granddaughter's subconscious. "But if you're not careful - you'll lose him too."

As Alexis watched Tyler's truck disappear around the bend, her grandmother's words imprinted upon her heart. Suddenly, a chill rolled over her skin. Even though it was the middle of summer, she rubbed her arms for warmth.

Evelyn's spirit wrapped around Alexis like a bitter winter wind before soothing her with the likes of a mother's touch. Alexis' eyes widened as warmth replaced the goosebumps that barraged her skin.

"What am I supposed to do?" Alexis' heart filled with despair at the empty road that led to Tyler's home.

When she heard nothing in return, she said, "Other than go crazy, maybe?"

"Mommy, you okay?"

Much to her surprise Lani snuck up behind her and slid her small hand into her own. When Alexis looked down at her sweet, but concerned face, she had to laugh. "I think so, baby. How long have you been standing there?" She leaned down to kiss her cherub cheeks.

"Just got here. You look like you've seen a ghost." She lifted an eyebrow with a knowing look.

Alexis' eyelashes fluttered. "Nope. I didn't see anything."

"You sure? Because she's here." She looked behind her mother with an assurance that Alexis envied. Lani lifted her fingers and wiggled them.

Alexis watched her daughter's eyes dance with mischief and nodded.

"Are you waving hello or goodbye to her?" She let out a resigned sigh.

Lani giggled. "Goodbye. She said she hopes you heard her through that thick skull of yours."

Alexis didn't know whether to be offended, scared, or shocked. To be truthful, she was a little of each.

As Lani watched her mother's face ripple with emotion, she let out a snort, and said, "I bet you believe me now!"

"Would you think I was bonkers if I said yes?"

Her daughter's bubbly laughter came almost immediately.

"Of course not. You'd be normal because Great Grams hangs out with us all the time."

She squinted and squatted next to Lani. "She really does visit?"

Lani threw her arms up. "Just what do you think I've been trying to tell you all this time? I'm not some dumb kid, ya know?"

"I would never think that." A steady warmth blanketed her heart as Lani's little arms tightened around her neck. As she breathed in her daughter's scent, a combination of lilacs and leather, a sense of unity overcame her. The bond between them gave her center like nothing else could.

As Lani pulled back, she yelled over her shoulder, "Bye, Gizelle. See you later!"

"Thanks again." Alexis waved toward Bonnie, who was pushing Gizelle toward them in her chair.

"She's welcome anytime." Bonnie's bright blue eyes beckoned. "Wait up. We'll see you two out."

Both Lani and Alexis fell into a slow pace alongside Gizelle's chair, giving the young girls a chance to visit on the short walk back to the driveway. As their daughters chatted about school, Bonnie whispered over their heads and sent Alexis a look.

"So, you and Tyler?"

Alexis bit her lips, which tingled from the effects of his kiss.

"You saw that, huh?" A look of dismay splashed across her features.

Bonnie's eyes twinkled. "Not so much saw it as I saw it coming. I know when a man looks at a woman like that. Why do you think I got the girls inside when I did?"

Alexis' eyes went wide. "Was it that noticeable? And just how does he look at me?"

"Like you're his." She shrugged nonchalantly. "And I see how he affects you too, so why don't you just let it happen already?"

Alexis lifted a finger to her lips and shushed her before addressing Lani.

"Sweetheart, why don't you show Gizelle your new coloring book? It's in the back seat."

"Can I push her to our truck?" Lani's eyes lit up with hope.

"You sure can." Bonnie released the handles of Gizelle's chair and waited for a few minutes before asking, "So does he have the plague?"

"No!" Alexis laughed.

"So, what's the problem? He's free. You're free."

Although Bonnie seemed kind enough, Alexis wasn't up to a heart-to-heart.

"I could ask you the same thing." Her eyebrow shot up as she sent Bonnie a smirk.

"I'm not into Tyler!" A confused look danced across her features.

"No, that's not what I meant." Alexis tried again. "It's no secret that my brother has an interest, and he's a pretty good-looking guy, and you're single." Her voice rose.

Bonnie crossed her arms and shook her head. "It's also no secret that I have my hands full."

Alexis looked to both their girls. "There's no difference between us that I can see. We both are single moms. So, I get being cautious about who you bring around Gizelle, but you can trust Anderson."

"It's not that." She sighed, wondering why she left herself open for this conversation. "Look, why don't we both just agree that we're permanently single at this time?"

Alexis nodded in agreement and lightly touched her lips while frowning.

"Understood. And from now on, whenever my brother asks about you, I'll change the subject?"

"That would be wise."

Laughter danced in Alexis' eyes. "So, apparently, we both have issues?"

Bonnie chuckled. "It seems so."

Alexis smirked. "Someday, we can swap stories."

"I'd like that. Just not here." She nodded toward the girls, who had stopped chattering and started listening to their mothers.

"On that note." She winked and waved her daughter inside the cab of her pickup. "Let's go. You've got school tomorrow."

"Aw, Mom," Lani whined.

As the two climbed inside and waved goodbye, Lani stared at her mother's profile with a poignant expression.

As hard as she tried, Alexis could no longer ignore the little eyes that were begging her to answer an unspoken question.

"What?" She twisted toward her daughter's suspenseful face.

"What kind of issues do you have?"

Alexis made a noise as air blew from her mouth.

"Um ... Okay?" She sent her daughter a look of confusion.

"You said you and Gizelle's mom both had issues. What kind?"

"Not anything you need to know about." She turned in toward their front-drive as the memory of Tyler's kiss sent her stomach into a fit.

Lani grinned as Alexis' cheeks took on a pink tinge.

"How come adults never want to clue us in on what is right in front of your face? We may be kids, but we see things too. You know?"

"Oh yeah? Like what?" Alexis was almost afraid of what Lani would say in return.

"Like the fact that you get all fidgety when Uncle Tyler is around. And the fact that you blush when you're thinking about him."

"Lani!" Alexis batted her daughter's arm as she killed the engine.

"What?" Her voice rose an octave. "It's okay to like him, Mommy. From what I can tell, he likes you a lot, and he's nice."

Alexis sighed and chewed the inside her cheek before tapping her daughter on the nose.

"Get inside, o-wise one. Start your bathwater, and I'll be up in a few minutes to check on you."

Lani leaned over to give her mom a kiss on the cheek before sliding from her seat to run up the porch steps, almost knocking her grandmother over.

"Slow down there." Amelia scooped her into a quick embrace and kissed Lani's cheek before sending her inside.

"I swear. That kid," Alexis murmured to her mother, who stepped down to lend a helping hand.

"She's something special." Amelia reached for Lani's books as Alexis gathered the rest of their things.

"She just spent the drive over trying to convince me to go on a date with Tyler."

"She's a smart girl, too." Amelia's eyes danced.

"What? Is this a family conspiracy?"

"It's been a long time, Sis." Amelia's voice fell.

Alexis' gaze snapped up to meet her mother's hopeful eyes. "And I'm still not ready. Especially with him."

"Why is the idea of being with someone who obviously is head over heels with you and your daughter, so bad?"

"He's not head-over-heels for me!" Even as the words flew from her lips, she knew they weren't true. When her mother clamped her mouth, looking as if she were biting her tongue, Alexis conceded. "Okay, maybe he is a little bit."

"Honey, it's okay to let yourself live. Clay died. You didn't!" Amelia let out a sound. "There! I said it."

"Wow, Mom. Don't hold anything back." Her eyes watered.

"You've thrown yourself into making sure her life is everything it should be." Amelia's arm flung toward the house. "Just like any good mother would, but it's okay to want something for yourself too."

"I have everything I want, Mom. I have you guys. I have my daughter. And I had a man who loved me very much."

"What about experiencing that kind of love too? I know you loved Clay. He was a great guy, but ..." Amelia stopped short of saying it.

"What, Mom? Are you saying I didn't love him as much as I should? Don't you think I've tortured myself every night thinking if I'd only been a better wife?"

"Honey! That's just it!" Amelia cried. "You were an excellent wife. It's not your fault about what happened. You shared your heart with Clay the best way you knew how to. Was he your soulmate? No! You loved him by choosing to love every day despite your differences."

Alexis wiped away her tears and twisted toward her mom with an armload of Lani's dolls.

"I appreciate what you're trying to do, but it doesn't help when I know the last thing I did for him was get him killed."

"Alexis," she moaned from behind.

As she watched her daughter carry Lani's belongings inside, Amelia wished she could lighten the burden Alexis carried within. She raised her eyes toward heaven for silent prayer, knowing it was all she could do to help.

28

Early the next morning, Alexis arrived at work with a renewed vigor to uncover what happened to Evelyn. She was determined and unyielding to anything except an outcome that would be a personal and family victory.

As someone entered the bathroom behind her. The door screeched, echoing through the aging bathroom, which was layered from floor to ceiling in tile. Although musty and filled with mold, the space was big enough that she usually found herself alone with her thoughts.

"Talking to yourself?" Sharena sashayed next to her and pulled out a lipstick. She generously applied it to her full collagen-filled lips.

"Yeah." Alexis barely lifted the corners of her mouth and sent her a disingenuous smile. "That makes one of us who is nice to me around here."

Sharena grunted, rolling her eyes.

Alexis spun for the exit, but before she left, she turned on her heel to face her once more. "I just have to ask."

Sharena pursed her lips and glanced in the mirror at Alexis' reflection, eyebrows raised.

"What did I ever do to you? That you go out of your way to be rude to me?" Alexis asked.

"Well, I don't know what you're talking about." She blinked her innocent eyes and made a face. "I don't know why anyone would expect me to be nice when she has the boss twisted around her finger. We all know you're sleeping with him to get a promotion."

"What?!" She inhaled as her blood curdled, sending enough adrenaline through her veins, she thought she could rip the door from the hinges. She balled her fists, trying as hard as she could to keep her hands at her sides. "That's not true!"

"Well, Lord knows we've all tried. And he hasn't given us a second glance. A man who looks that good, should be enjoyed, but he's such a goody-goody, going to church and all. Yet, when it comes to you, he is obviously flustered."

Sharena's throaty laugh stopped short as the pieces fell into place. She spun around with a knowing look and said, "Now I get it. He wants you but can't have you. Why didn't I see it before? Honey, why wouldn't you go for a man like him? I had more respect for you when I thought you were sleeping with him."

Every emotion Alexis had been clamping down on over the last few months - no years - of her life came flooding to the surface in an instant. Instead of taking the high road, which the logical side of her told her to do, she sunk lower than she ever thought she could. Without much thought, she reared back and punched Sharena square in the face.

Shareena's curdling scream, coupled with the blood that was spurting from her nose, had Alexis wincing, immediately regretting her actions.

"Sharena, you're on in ten minutes." Janelle's jaw dropped as she stuck her head through the doorway. "What the–" Her eyes rounded as she glanced between the two of them.

Sharena, who was wailing and crying, grabbed a few paper towels to stop the bleeding while Alexis, who looked mortified, hightailed it from the bathroom.

"You! You broke my nose!" Shareena yelled as Alexis flung the door open.

Sharena's screams could be heard down the hall, but Alexis didn't stay to see the outcome. She scanned the newsroom as curious bystanders made their way toward the bathroom and suddenly had the urge to flee. She turned the corner for the back door, knowing that leaving the scene of the crime meant she had probably lost her job and her chance at being a full-time journalist, but so be it.

As she leaped into her pickup, a text came in from Janelle.

Where are you?

When she didn't reply, Janelle sent another.

Look, we all would have jumped at the chance to be the one who got that punch in, but you need to come back. Sharena is talking about filing a complaint, and Tyler's looking for you. He looks like... well, I won't tell you what he looks like. You just need to come back.

Before she could respond, the surround sound system in her truck blasted with what sounded like an alarm. The ring tone she'd assigned to her mother was blaring through the speakers, making it seem like an incoming missile was tracking her. It was loud enough that she almost ran her truck off the road and into the front lawn of the news station.

"Ugh." She hit ignore before shoving her phone in the cupholder when Tyler's ringtone, which sounded like a spring, started popping around her, resounding like a continuous pogo-stick.

"Everybody. Just stop!" Alexis yelled. "Especially you, T.J." She let out a huff and powered down her phone before driving from the property with only one thing in mind.

∼

AFTER AN HOUR of observing the comings and goings of the many shoppers, who walked in empty-handed yet left with multiple packages in tow, Alexis finally shut off her engine and laid a hand on her door handle. Her bladder had been screaming at her for over twenty-five minutes, so her only option was to go in. Besides, she'd come too far to turn back now.

You can do this. Alexis exhaled, unaware of how the next few minutes of her life would play out, but it didn't matter. She needed closure for her family, but mostly for her grandmother, whom she now swore was surrounding her every move.

Ever since her encounter at the barn with what she thought was her grandmother's spirit, Alexis kept looking over her shoulder, expecting to see Evelyn's bright, shiny eyes smiling at her.

Alexis stood outside the entrance as if in a trance, staring through the beveled front doors, wondering what she would find inside. Would William still be at work? Or, would one of his family members be on staff? Would they be open to talking to her? Or, would they admit to knowing her family?

Just as she was about to pull the oversized door open, a large Cadillac pulled to the curb and parked. She squinted through the tinted windows, wondering who was inside as the driver exited to usher someone from the backseat. When the rear car door opened, a smartly dressed man, about her age, stepped to the curb and almost knocked her over. He was on his cell phone, unaware of anything or anyone around him.

"Excuse you," he growled. As his laser-sharp gaze pinned Alexis down, the color drained from his face.

"Excuse me? You almost knocked me over." She recovered after stumbling against the marble column behind her.

The man's driver quickly came to her aid with an apologetic look.

"Pardon us, ma'am." He took her by the elbow, stabilizing her. "Mr. Wylar is on a tight schedule today."

"Mr. Wylar?" Alexis shot him a look.

When Henry noticed her, he did a double-take, thinking he'd recognize her anywhere. Although Evelyn was dead, his cousin had seen to that, the young woman standing before him was the spitting image of the photos he'd found among his grandfather's belongings.

Henry ducked his chin and whispered into his phone, "I'll have to call you right back." He slipped his phone into his jacket pocket and slid his hand toward hers for an introduction. "Henry Wylar, at your service. I'm truly sorry for almost taking you out." The corners of his lips lifted at the irony of his words.

"Alexis Mathers." She lightly grasped his for a shake and nodded politely.

His gut tensed. Although her last name wasn't Bozeman, she had to be related. Henry made a mental note to have his cousin find out more about Miss Mathers. It couldn't be a coincidence that she was standing at the front of his store. Henry casually tossed a smirk to let her know they were done.

"Well, have a good day." He waited for his driver to open the front door and turned his back to enter the store.

"Actually." Alexis lifted a hand and waited.

Henry's face fell, but he put on a smile before spinning to face her. He knew what was coming next, which meant he and his cousin could no longer wait until this went away. They could no longer sweep this under the rug.

29

"Why didn't you tell her to wait here, so that I could have taken care of her right away?" Daniel stormed forward with hands clenched.

"Keep your voice down." Henry looked at the smattering of workers, who were loading the last shipment on his docks. He tugged his cousin to the edge of the building. "Have a little finesse, would you?"

When Daniel closed the gap between them to tower over Henry, he swallowed. When his cousin pushed his sleeves up his massive ink-covered arms, Henry could only imagine the measures he'd take to keep their secret.

"When you called me in a panic and asked to meet, I thought the loan sharks caught up with you. Why didn't you tell me someone from their family came by?" He tapped his jacket, where his handgun was snuggly tucked in his holster. "It's a good thing I came with this on me. So, they know?"

Henry shook his head. "I can't know for sure. And who knows to what extent?"

"Well, what *do* you know?" He snarled between his teeth.

"I recognized her. She looks just like the old photos. Genes run strong in that family."

When Henry started to babble on with unnecessary details, Daniel rolled his eyes and pushed Henry's shoulder, hoping he'd stop.

"What did *she* know?" Daniel stared him down.

Henry winced under his cousin's hand and glanced behind him to sit on an empty crate.

"She asked me if I was related to William. I admitted he was my grandfather."

Daniel gave him a look, pushing him for more.

"She seemed excited and asked if she could talk with him. I told her he didn't come in much anymore, due to his age."

"And?"

"She asked how she could get in touch with him. I asked her what it was about, of course." Henry swallowed. "She just shook her head and said it was personal business to which I replied that my grandfather couldn't be reached at the moment."

"You left it at that?" Daniel's brows arched.

When Henry nodded, Daniel reached inside his jacket to stroke his gun and paced the dock like a man on a mission. After what seemed to be an eternity, he murmured a few things to himself and spun around to face Henry. "Here's what you're going to do."

~

ALEXIS WAS ALMOST HALFWAY home when she remembered her phone. Without taking her eyes off the road, she powered it back on. The second she slipped it into her cup holder, it started vibrating like Morse code against the hard surface. She winced, hoping the number of missed calls or texts was minimal.

Alexis exited the highway into a vacant parking lot at the edge of Purity. She glanced outside her window to an old sign that read, 'The Dixie Cup.'

Her eyes shone as memories of working her first job as a carhop came flooding back. This place was also where she received her first kiss from Clay. Now she would remember it as being the first place where she hid out from her family after her erratic behavior.

What was wrong with her? She made a disgusted sound as she scrolled through multiple texts she'd received from not only Tyler but also her mom and Anderson.

"Fine mess you've gotten yourself into," she muttered before hitting the home button on her smartphone. Her guilty conscience kicked in knowing she'd be frantic if her own child went off the radar and didn't return her messages.

She lifted the phone to her mouth and spoke into the mouthpiece with a resigned sigh. She held down the home button. "Call my mother."

It only took one ring before her mother's concerned voice filled the truck's sound system.

"Alexis, where are you? Are you okay? We've all been worried sick. I knew something like this would happen."

"Like what, Mom?" Her stiff voice almost broke.

"That you'd go postal at work! No," Amelia paused. "No one could predict that. What were you thinking?"

"I wasn't – obviously. Besides, that girl had it coming. She's been pushing my buttons for weeks, and her holier than thou attitude was on my last nerve."

"You're an adult, Alexis. This isn't the schoolyard. I would expect something like this from Anderson, but you?"

"Because he's a man? Aren't women supposed to defend themselves too?"

"Was that what you were doing? Because according to your boss," Amelia refrained from saying Tyler's name. "She's pressing charges, saying you attacked her!"

"Ugh." Alexis pressed the bridge of her nose with her thumb and pointer finger, warding off a migraine. "Just back me on this, Mom."

"Of course, I will, honey." Amelia's concerned tone softened. "We're just worried about you. You've not been the same since you've been back."

Alexis had recently revealed the mental trauma she'd endured at the hands of her former mother-in-law. Amelia knew how that could change someone, along with the guilt that ate away at Alexis' soul over Clay's death, but until now, didn't know how far it had pushed her.

"I know." Alexis teared up. "I'm fine, Mom. I promise. I just lost it back there." The memory of Sharena's bloody nose had her wishing she'd shut off her anger sooner. "I shouldn't have lost my temper. She just..." Her voice fell.

Amelia listened, hoping for more. When nothing came, she asked, "Are you coming home? Tyler's been here looking for you. He looked like he would move heaven and earth to find you."

Alexis closed her eyes, knowing that look full well. It was the same look he got when he got the lead on something newsworthy. He was driven to be the best with everything he did, including finding her apparently.

As if his ears were burning, his name popped up on her caller ID to which she promptly hit ignore.

"Was he mad?" Alexis' heart dropped. She knew how much she'd screwed up and understood she jeopardized her job but couldn't stand the thought of losing his friendship too.

"No." Amelia blew into the phone as a sigh escaped her lips. "He was worried about you, honey. You can tell that - he cares about you very much." The last part of her sentence came with caution.

"I know," she groaned. "I can't think about that, Mom. How's Lani?"

"She's fine. And as for Tyler, I disagree. That's a talk for another time, though. We must get you out of this mess right now. Come home."

Unable to think about Tyler at the moment, she ignored her mother's sentiment.

"Thanks for taking care of her, Ma."

"Lani's none the wiser. As far as she's concerned, you're at work like any other day. She won't have reason to worry until after dinner. I won't turn the TV on to keep her from thinking about you." Amelia cleared her throat. "Alexis, please make your way back home."

Alexis' face twisted. She hated that her family had to lie to her kid because of her bad behavior. Her mother was right. She needed to head back to the ranch to sort things out. As she was about to pull into town, a number, which looked like the one from Henry's business card, displayed on her caller ID.

"Hey, Mom. I'm going to have to call you back. That's a call I've been expecting."

"When will you be home?"

"Later."

Amelia knew a brush-off when she heard one. "Make sure you call Tyler. He's been worried sick."

"Yeah, sure." Alexis' finger hovered over the answer button on her steering wheel. She ended the conversation with, "Talk to you later."

When she switched over to the next call, she said a silent prayer.

"Mrs. Mathers?" Henry's voice boomed through her vehicle.

"Yes. Is this Henry?" She'd remember his distinctively snappy voice anywhere.

As if he was offended, she had to ask, he forged forth.

"Grandfather says he'd like to meet you. Can you be here at five? We've got inventory this afternoon and have closed early. Since he's coming in to supervise, it'll be the perfect time for you to visit."

"Sure. I'm only forty minutes away, so I'll be there a few minutes before."

"Great. He'll see you then."

Alexis dropped the call and pumped her fist, which was still a bit bruised from her right hook. She grabbed a towelette from her bag and cleaned it before sending Tyler a quick text.

I know I'm in trouble. I am sorry I hit Sharena even if she had it coming. I will turn in my employee badge tomorrow. Please just give me the day come to terms with it all.

Tyler's response came immediately.

. . .

As your boss, I should demand you return immediately to face the music. As your friend, I'm going to let you have the day. I'm swinging by your place tonight after the six o'clock news, and I'm not taking no for an answer. We need to talk.

Alexis ignored the text, threw the towelette into the seat next to her, and turned left for the highway. *Okay, Grams. Here we go. Wish me luck.*

Evelyn, who appeared in the passenger seat, dropped her head into her hands for silent prayer. If she were here to help navigate her granddaughter on a better path, she was doing a horrible job of it. Not only was she running from Tyler, possibly getting into legal trouble with an assault charge, but now she was heading into dangerous waters with the Wylar family.

If she didn't know any better, she'd say that her first husband, who thankfully passed before his time, was playing havoc from beyond. His horribly deceptive genes could have been rearing their ugly head, inspiring Alexis' fiery side. Still, Evelyn was confident his final punishment kept him bound in chains, somewhere no one could escape.

Her first husband was her biggest regret, however, if it weren't for his passing, she would have never met William. And if it weren't for the heartbreak William caused, she never would have ended up on the Bozeman ranch, where she belonged all along.

Reminiscing and revelations aside, her priority was to keep Alexis from danger. If she didn't stop her – she sensed something horribly wrong was about to happen.

"Alexis." Evelyn narrowed her eyes, willing her granddaughter to listen. "Turn around. You don't know what's waiting for you."

When Alexis seemed unaffected, Evelyn sent all the emotions she possessed through her hand and laid it on the radio to work a bit of her newfound magic. As the frequency erratically skipped to another station, Alexis frowned when it came to rest, and Frankie Goes to Hollywood's tell-tale voice belted out, *Relax. Don't do it.*

As the one-hit-wonder engulfed the small space around her, Alexis abruptly shook off a chill that traveled across her skin like ants and pushed the power button. She stared at the now silent radio in awe, unable to put in words what she'd just experienced.

"Grams, if that's you, knock it off!"

Even if Evelyn were trying to communicate, it wouldn't do any good. The urge to move forward for the sake of her family was stronger than any warning from beyond. She owed it to herself to uncover what happened in Evelyn's life that lead up to that letter. It may not help her solve her grandmother's death, but it would at least give her and her family closure about Evelyn's life and how William played a part.

"To infinity and beyond," Alexis quoted a line from one of her daughter's favorite movies, as she depressed the blinker and turned left toward the highway.

30

Tyler pushed through the papers on his desk and turned to read his cell, scanning Alexis' last line of communication, which wasn't much. He ran both of his hands through his hair in frustration, praying God would clue him in as to where she was. It was a long shot, but he was a praying man. He prayed that when he found her, he'd have patience and wisdom to know when to kiss her - before or after he wrung her neck.

After two hours of searching, Tyler was at his wit's end while still putting on a polished smile for his staff. Even though his gut wrenched at the thought of Alexis walking out of his life, he couldn't lose face with his team.

When Alexis left, it proved two things. That he still wasn't the person she turned to when everything came undone and that he was lost without her. Even with the current nefarious circumstances, Tyler never wanted to be in these shoes again. Next time, if there was a next time, she had to know he was where she could run.

Tyler frowned. Alexis needed to stop acting outlandish and return to the secure girl he once knew instead of the woman who was ready to react without thinking of everything around her. It was one thing to pop Sharena in the nose and walk out, but it was another to run off to heaven knows where and avoid her family. Even though most of his staff would have given her a high-five if she'd stuck around, Alexis couldn't give in to this type of behavior. Especially when he was the one who had to deal with the fallout.

"Where are you, Alexis?" he whispered as he studied the monitors in his office.

If it were up to him, he'd send Chopper Charlie in the air and cruise the main streets, looking for her little red pickup. Except, he would get in serious trouble for wasting company resources. Besides that, their helicopter pilot was already filming a house fire slated for the lead story on the five o'clock news.

Just then, Fran popped her head into Tyler's office.

"Tyler, we just got a lead from the police scanner." Her sober face gave him pause, but what she said next had him reeling. "There were shots fired at Wylars department store, and it may be a potential hostage situation."

Tyler swallowed, hoping for a random coincidence. Still, in the last two hours of his search for Alexis, he'd had plenty of communication with her family. He knew enough to know this couldn't be good.

"Did you say, Wylars?" He blinked.

When he asked God to clue him in on where Alexis was, he never imagined this would be the answer. In his gut, he knew she was there. He just hoped the shots weren't meant for her.

"Yes." Fran spun toward the newsroom, ushering the anchors toward the desk with some copy.

Tyler grabbed his phone to text Alexis once more while praying for her safety. He yelled toward the newsroom, saying, "Fran, tell Janelle to pull Chopper Charlie from the fire and send him to Wylars. Call me when you know more. Who's heading to the scene?"

"Steven!" Fran hollered over her shoulder.

"Call him and tell him I'm riding along."

"Why?" Fran approached with a look of confusion.

"I have a feeling about this one." No need to tell her what his suspicions were now. He prayed he was wrong, but his intuition told him he wasn't.

"You're the boss." She cocked an eyebrow and reached for her cell to call Steven while Tyler ran for the back door.

~

I<small>F</small> A<small>LEXIS HADN'T EXPERIENCED</small> it, she wouldn't have believed it. After jabbing her elbow into would-be captor's ribs, she slammed into his jaw, snapping his head back. The second he was the most vulnerable, she kicked him where it counted, barely buying enough time to run for the back door of the department store.

Daniel never imagined someone with her willowy frame could put up such a struggle. Once he took a blow to his jaw, his head jerked back, and he landed on the bumper of his van. After the crushing blow to his groin, he bent forward, seeing stars.

A string of curse words sounded from behind her, sending Alexis scrambling, taking the dock stairs two at a time before Daniel pulled at her from behind. As she stumbled back, she swung her bag in his direction. When the corner of it made contact with his temple, Daniel lost his hold on Alexis and fell against the pavement.

This was becoming more trouble than it was worth. As Daniel squinted through the pain, she scurried up the steps and shoved her way through the back door to the store.

You've come too far to turn back now. Daniel pushed off the pavement to stand.

What was supposed to be a simple grab-and-go just spun out of control. Daniel charged forward grumbling accusations at his cousin under his breath, but when it came down to it - he couldn't blame his cousin. Henry had done his part by inviting her back to the store with the promise of meeting William. It was up to Daniel to finish the task of getting Alexis out of the way.

No, Daniel was the one who had failed. All he needed to do was to shove her in the van, which he parked near her vehicle. However, he never imagined her to be such a fighter.

He took the steps as fast as his throbbing head would allow. What did she carry in that thing? Bricks?

As he yelled more obscenities at her back, Alexis scurried through the dock entrance and fortunately found an open door that led to the storage room of Wylars. As she flew inside, looking for a place to hide, a stunned young man working the stock stood frozen in place, unsure of what to do. All he knew was that a hurried and disheveled woman had run in gasping for air.

"How do you lock this thing?" she yelled. "Hurry!"

Not sure if she was getting ready to attack him or if she was in trouble, he stammered, "Who are you?"

"Hurry! He's after me." Alexis pulled the heavy door closed just as Daniel reached the other side and pounded on the heavy metal.

"You bitch!" He yelled through the weighted door and lifted his gun to shoot the handle from the outside.

The stockroom employee clambered into action and slid the lock into place and then pushed a large shelving unit in front as a barrier.

At the distinct scraping sound echoed through the door, Daniel hung his head. It was clear they had barricaded the entrance from the inside. He pounded on the exterior yelling obscenities when he heard her on the other side.

"We're calling the cops!" Alexis frantically searched for her phone but slowed when the stock boy dialed 9-1-1 on his cell.

"I have them on the line now," he whispered, taking her by the hand. "This way. Let's go up front."

Daniel scanned the docks looking for another entrance with the understanding that he was all in. The fact that he was probably going back to jail was glaringly obvious, but at this point, his pride had taken over. His motivation was to finish the job, no matter the outcome. For a minute, he considered texting Henry to give him a heads up but knew there wasn't time for that.

The sound of gunfire behind the store had everyone on edge. Henry jumped, praying their plan wasn't unraveling but had a suspicion it was. A handful of employees huddled together and stared at the back wall in shock.

"What was that?" a few murmured.

Henry didn't question it. His half-cocked cousin had just put the last nail in both their coffins. He looked for the nearest exit, wondering if he had time to pull whatever funds he had left to skip town. It was now or never. He darted for his office to grab his belongings. While there, his first instinct was to call for his driver, but before he could dial, Daniel stormed in with a gun in hand. Henry was trapped.

Henry studied him from head to toe, noting the absence of blood and let out a sigh of relief. Whatever shot he'd taken either missed or wasn't close enough to stain him with any evidence.

"What's the rush? Going somewhere?" Daniel waved the gun at him, his eyes voice of emotion.

"You were supposed to take her somewhere else and take care of it," he said between his teeth.

Daniel jaw clenched. "She's a lot tougher than she looks."

"Apparently." Henry raised a brow and motioned toward the gun. "Will you stop pointing that thing at me?"

"We're going down, Henry. No one saw me sneak in, but they'll know soon enough if you don't listen to me. Go lock the doors." He motioned for Henry to take the lead, his gun still trained on him. "Come on. Hurry before the cops arrive."

"If you shot her, then all you need to do is get out of here. You're in the clear. Go!" He waved his arms toward the door.

"Don't you think I'd do that if I could?" He grabbed Henry by the arm and pushed him out. "She escaped and is somewhere in the store. Lock her in so we can find her."

"She's in here?!" Henry's voice climbed an octave. "She can't be here. This is going to ruin us!"

"If we can find her. We can use her as leverage."

"I can't go to jail!" Henry cried in a panic.

"Hey, stupid. We'll take the girl hostage and get out of here if you listen to me!"

"No, no, no. N-n-no." Henry stammered and began to pace until Daniel smacked the back of Henry's head.

"Look. I'll make you a deal. If it looks like we're going down, I'll kill the girl and make it look like I was working alone. You'll be free to access the money we need."

Henry rubbed his jaw and stared Daniel down. "There's still the matter of my grandfather. He must be taken care of first for us to get that money. And you can't do that from jail!"

Daniel thought about it for a second. "That can be part of my demands. I can ask that he be brought in and take care of Uncle Willie inside." Daniel's eyes lit up. "Yeah, this will work. Trust me, Henry."

"You're crazy. You promised this wouldn't get dirty. You promised to handle it."

"Well, I am handling it. Not everything goes according to plan. Sometimes you have to improvise, like MacGyver."

Henry's eyebrow shot up. "He's usually working against the bad guys, not with them."

"Shut up. If you do anything other than what I ask and we get caught, you're going down. You understand?"

Daniel thought Henry's head looked like a bobble caught in the tides when he nodded it up and down in agreement.

"Good," he said. "As far as anyone knows, I've asked you to lock up, and you're my prisoner, just like the skeleton staff you have here."

Henry rocked forward, reached for the key from his bag, and allowed Daniel to follow him, gun pointed. As they stepped inside the main floor, he held his hands up and looked at the five employees that turned to him with eyes wide.

"Everyone - keep calm. It's going to be okay if you just stay calm."

One of his assistant-managers leaned toward a female sales associate and said, "I knew we should have left when we heard the shot outside."

"Are you kidding?" She shrieked in horror. "For all we knew, the gunman was outside the front door. We were supposedly staying safe by staying indoors."

"Oh, crap," another associate murmured as they passed by them.

Daniel waved his gun toward the group and yelled, "Everybody in the office." He pointed them forward. Once inside, he yelled, "On the ground!"

Once they gathered together in the corner, he studied each face with a nagging sense that something was amiss. *Weren't there six of them?*

Daniel was about to ask but paused and glanced at the clock. He had to stay on task. Finding a missing employee wasn't his concern. Alexis Mathers was.

"You." Daniel waved the gun at Henry. "Go lock the doors and hurry back. The rest of you. Scoot your phones in my direction."

The five of them immediately responded, sliding their phones across the floor. Daniel stashed them in a small bag with a mix of excitement and trepidation, shivers trailing down his spine. A sense of nostalgia overcame him when he realized this was like his bank heist in Austin. He clenched his fists. That job was what put him in the pen the first time.

This probably wouldn't end well, but if he could get Henry out clean, then he still had a shot at the money. One more time in jail would be worth it if he came out a rich man.

31

The second Stephen pulled on the premises and parked next to the curb, Tyler jumped from the SUV and approached the nearest officer.

"Sir, you need to get back." The officer held up a hand, preventing him from moving past the barricade.

"I think my girl, one of my employees, is in there. My name is TJ, and I'm with the KTXT news." The words fell from his mouth like they were rapid-fire.

Although the officer could see the anxiety written across his face, rules were rules.

"For your safety, you need to stay back with your news crew. We're allowing all the networks to set up over there." He pointed across the street, which seemed miles away as far as Tyler was concerned.

Stephen jogged over with his photographer in tow to set up next to Tyler when Tyler shook his head and pointed across the street.

"Not here," he said with regret. "We're restricted to the lot over there." Tyler back to the officer and asked, "Okay, before we go, what do you know so far?"

"We're waiting for our hostage negotiator. We've not made contact yet, but the doors are locked, so there's no way in or out. There's been only one shot reported by the 9-1-1 caller."

"Was it a woman?" he asked in haste.

"No, it was a young kid, a male. He apparently works there and is still inside, for all we know."

Tyler scanned the street and the lot across from them and said a silent prayer of thanks. The fact that she wasn't the caller, and there was no sign of her truck from what he could see settled his swift pulse.

"What about the dock entrance?" Stephen asked. When Tyler frowned in response, he added, "My wife used to work here. There's a large lot behind the store for loading and unloading and employee parking."

Tyler nodded at his photographer, Grant. "While Stephen and I interview a few people here, will you set up and let me know if you have a clear view of the lot?"

"Yes, sir." Grant packed his camera and tripod and ran for the section where another network was about to set up. "B-roll footage coming up."

"And let me know if you see a red pickup!" Tyler yelled to his back.

After Grant set up his camera, he began filming the area for supplemental footage. When he panned the lot by the dock, one vehicle, in particular, caught his attention. He zoomed in, instantly recognizing Alexis' Ford truck. It sat next to an unmarked van. When Grant noticed the van's side door was wide open, his heart sunk.

"What in the world?" he murmured to himself.

He waved Stephen over, who was attaching a small microphone to the inside of his shirt.

"I didn't think much of it at the time when Tyler asked me to look for a red truck."

Stephen sent him a frown. "And?"

Grant nodded. "That's not just any red truck. That's Alexis'."

"Did you tell Tyler?" Stephen reached for his phone.

"I just saw it."

"I'll text him really quick. We're live in two minutes." He tapped his earpiece. "Janelle's already giving me the heads up."

"I'm ready when you are."

Stephen slipped his phone in his pocket. "Sent. I hope she's okay. Let's roll."

As his guys started their live shot, Tyler's phone buzzed. He reached for it, hoping it was Alexis, but when he saw Stephen's text, his heart dropped.

"God, please let her be okay," he whispered. "Please."

"You know someone in there?" a bystander asked.

"I'm afraid so."

"I was supposed to be at work tonight." She nodded to the storefront. "Hi. I'm Casey." She crossed her arms and sent him a weak smile.

Tyler nodded in greeting, unable to focus on much other than Alexis. He sent Casey a half-hearted smile and said, "Nice to meet you. If you'll excuse me?"

"Sure. Not much to do but wait and pray."

We'll see about that. The prayer he agreed with, but Tyler couldn't just sit and wait.

Tyler stepped up to the same officer he'd visited with before hoping for more assistance. He looked at the name badge and asked, "Officer Kerry?"

"You again." He frowned. "We can't do our job if you keep interrupting."

"Any luck with the hostage negotiator?"

"He's stuck in traffic."

"I know someone who used to be in this line of work with the CIA. if you'd like me to call him." Tyler reminded himself to text Anderson either way because Alexis' family would need to know.

"No, thank you. We stick with our own guys."

"The girl I mentioned? Who I think is inside? It's his sister."

"Even more reason to keep him off my back. I don't need some stuffed suit with a personal agenda breathing down my necks. If you'll excuse me." He turned his back on Tyler to place a call. "How far out are you?"

At a loss, Tyler picked up his phone and texted Alexis, praying she'd answer, but before he could send it – her face popped up on his caller ID.

∽

AFTER SEARCHING through a few departments and a couple of dressing rooms, Daniel was getting desperate. He locked Henry up in the manager's office with the rest of the employees to make it appear that Henry was one of them, but at this rate, it made more sense to use him to search the store. Especially since he was familiar with every nook and cranny.

As he dug in his pocket for the key Henry gave him, he heard the hushed whispers on the other side of the door.

"We can take him!" one of them said. "There's more of us than him."

"No!" Henry, the voice of reason, chimed in. "No, don't do anything that could get any of you hurt."

Daniel finally unlocked the door and flung it open while pointing his gun in the air. "If any of you try to take me, this is what they have in store for them."

He aimed toward an overhead light and pulled the trigger. As they screamed and hunkered down for safety, he asked, "Who is brave enough to mess with a bullet?"

When no one made a sound, he chuckled at the startled looks on their faces. "I didn't think so."

Next, Daniel waved the gun at Henry. "You. Get up and come with me. I need help. The rest of you - stay quiet, if you know what's good for you."

∽

FROM THEIR HIDING SPOT, Alexis and the stock boy listened to the commotion inside the store. Alexis studied the dark closet when she noticed the kid next to her. His brow furrowed as if he were either praying or freaking out. Either way, she needed to reassure him.

"Hey. We're going to be okay." She reached for his hand. "What's your name?"

"Francis." He opened his eyes and pulled his knees into his chest. "But everyone calls me Frankie."

"I'm Alexis."

"What's going on? After the shot, I thought whoever it was would stay outside. When we saw him enter the store with a gun..." His jaw dropped.

"Well, it's lucky you pulled us in here." She sent him a weak smile. "What is this place?"

"It's where we keep the displays for the window. It's not somewhere an outsider would think to look." He shrugged. "At least I don't think so. The door is flush with the back wall of the window display, and you have to enter the front staging area to get inside. The only other entrance is from a back hall that's kind of out of the way."

"Good. Now, we just need to stay hidden until the cops find us."

"How will we know?"

"We've already heard the sirens. It's just a matter of time."

"But what if they don't make it inside? What if we don't make it out? I'm only eighteen! I've never asked Casey out. I never got to skydive!"

Instantly, Alexis thought of Tyler. "I work at the news station. I can text my boss to give us updates."

As she was about to pull out her phone, another shot rang throughout the store. Alexis threw a hand over Frankie's mouth to silence the scream she knew would be coming.

"Shh. Stay quiet," Alexis warned. When he nodded his head, she slowly took her hand from her face and dug through her purse for her phone.

ARE YOU OUTSIDE? She texted.

Yes! Are you safe? Where are you? Was that a gun?!

Yes, but I'm okay. I'm hiding in some sort of closet. Someone tried to kidnap me, and I got away. Then, whoever it was followed me in the store.

TYLER TAPPED the police officer on the shoulder and lifted his smartphone for Officer Kerry to read.

"Just thought you'd want an update."

Once he finished reading their texts, Officer Kerry signaled for one of his men to come over. "Stay with–"

"T.J.," he reminded him.

Officer Kerry nodded toward Tyler. "He works at the news station and has news from the inside. He may be our way in. Find out everything he knows. I've got to check in with our negotiator. He just pulled up. Come find me and tell me everything he knows as he gets it."

"Yes, sir. Officer Cho at your service." The younger officer took Tyler's phone to read what had transpired so far. When he handed it back, he asked, "What else can we find out?"

Tyler's fingers started once more.

Can you call me? Or is it too dangerous?

Alexis read his last text and wondered if any conversation would give them away. She put her ear to the closet door and listened. When silence answered her in return, she took the risk.

As soon as her face popped up on his screen, he answered. "Tell me you're okay."

"I am for now," she whispered.

"Alexis." He paused and turned from the officer. "If anything happens to you..."

The desperation in his voice made her heart skip a beat. If she were honest, it clarified how scared she really was. Although her motherly instinct kicked in, giving her the wisdom to keep Francis calm, she was shaking. The sound of Tyler's voice had her wishing she could run to him for safety.

It was then that she decided. To make it through this, she had to distance herself from emotion. To do that, she had to put on her reporter persona. Alexis inhaled and nodded.

"Patch me through. Let's go live," she said.

Tyler blinked. "Are you sure?"

"Remember my interview when you said you wanted to be number one?"

"Yeah."

"How many other stations are set up outside?"

Tyler glanced over his shoulder. "Two more, so three including us."

"Do any of them have a reporter on the inside?"

Tyler grinned. Her fiery spirit was about to win them some ratings.

"As long as you're careful. Promise? If you hear anything, stop reporting, and we can cut to Stephen outside. Got it?"

Alexis looked to Francis, who stared as if she'd gone mad. She patted his arm for reassurance before addressing Tyler.

"Got it."

"Okay, here goes. Stay on the line. Once Janelle picks up, she'll give you the go-ahead."

She waved Francis to the door. "Let me know if you hear anything, okay? Even if it's just a whisper of a sound, signal for me to stop. Understand?"

As Francis gave her the thumbs up, she waited for what seemed like an eternity for Janelle to pick up.

∽

Tyler watched the monitor from his news van as Stephen wrapped up his update and introduced Alexis. When her sultry voice sounded, his gut wrenched.

"Please keep her safe," he prayed.

"This is Alexis Mathers, reporting from inside Wylar's department store, where a lone gunman is terrorizing a handful of employees. Before the hostage situation, the gunman approached me as I was exiting my car for the store and tried to force me into his van."

Tyler signaled for Grant to cut to the van in the parking lot. When he noticed the open side door, Tyler drew in a sharp breath - thankful she got away.

"Once I escaped his capture, I ran into Wylars for safety, where I locked the back door. It is unclear at this time what his motivation is other than ..." When Alexis went silent, Tyler signaled for Stephen to pick up the broadcast and began to pray.

When Francis sent her the signal, Alexis held her breath.

Please don't let it be him. Please don't let him find us, she prayed.

When the door flew open, much to her surprise, a young woman flung herself inside and lightly closed the door.

"Bella." Francis gasped with awe. "How did you get away?"

Out of breath, she panted, "He never saw me. I've been moving to different hiding places to keep from being discovered. They're looking for someone." Her eyes panned the small dark room and landed on Alexis. "I assume it's you they're looking for?"

"They?" Alexis' skin crawled. "I only saw one man."

"Yeah, but he has Henry looking with him. At first, I thought Henry was being forced to, but he looks just as upset as that other guy, whoever he is. And they seem to know one another."

Suddenly, the pieces fell into place. Through the dark silence that surrounded them, a sense of déjà vu overcame Alexis. This had to be about the letter. Why didn't she listen to her grandmother's warning?

Alexis punched the screen of her iPhone once more to text Tyler.

Another employee is hiding with us now. She says the owner's grand-

son, Henry, might be in on it, but not sure. Don't release that until I'm sure.

TYLER SIGHED with relief and searched the sky before closing his eyes. *She's okay.*

It was then that another officer, someone Tyler assumed was the hostage negotiator, stepped from behind a police van and pointed the megaphone toward the front of the building.

"We've got you surrounded!" The negotiator started. "We know you have some people inside who are very scared and would like to go home to their families. Let's do everything we can to make that happen. We're going to phone in. Pick up."

Tyler, who stood next to his team, said, "Dear Lord in heaven, help us."

Grant, who was filming the negotiator and his team from afar, said, "Amen. I'd give anything to know what was going on inside right now. Can't they send in one of those robotic things like in the movies?"

"If the feds were involved, maybe," Stephen chimed in.

Casey, the young girl who had spoken with Tyler earlier, wandered over and said, "I gave them Henry's cell phone number so they could call in."

They all three looked at her with questioning eyes.

"You know," she paused, shrugging. "In case you need more information for the news. They were having a hard time calling into the store just now because Wylars has an automated phone message. You know – press one for home goods, two for women ..."

She paused when she realized she was babbling and asked, "You know someone inside?"

It wouldn't do any good to remind her that he'd already answered that question earlier when they met. Instead, Tyler lowered his eyes and nodded.

"I know them all." Casey's eyes watered. "I'm sure the police will get them out alive, right?"

Tyler stared at the young woman, who couldn't have been more than nineteen or twenty and pat her on the back.

"They're the best at what they do." He prayed his words were on target. He turned his back on Casey and stared at his phone before sending one more text.

Are you okay?

Yes, came the reply.

They're starting to negotiate now.

Yeah, I heard the announcement from here. You think the gunman did too?

Tyler looked to the negotiator, who was speaking to someone on the phone.

I believe he's talking to whoever is inside now. I'm praying for you, Lexi.

Tyler took a deep breath and texted one last line.

I love you. Get out of there please so I can tell you in person.

When three dots popped up on his screen, his heart lifted. He'd not planned on declaring himself this way, but if he didn't say it now and something happened, he'd never forgive himself.

Alexis started to text but paused, unsure what to say in return. Finally, she let go of all the reasons that held her back this far and told him what was on her heart.

I know. I am struggling with it all. I want there to be an us, but I'm not sure how to make that happen.

Tyler knew it was as close as he was going to get to her telling him she loved him. And he was okay with that, for now. It was a start.

We'll take this one day at a time. Just get out of there in one piece, okay?

I promise. Keep praying. We all need it. I want to feel your arms around me as soon as I'm out.

Alexis couldn't believe she said as much as she had, but these were dire circumstances, and she loved Tyler. Although she couldn't bring herself to tell him, she was lightheaded at the prospect of what could be. Guilt or no guilt over Clay's death, she didn't want to die without at least giving Tyler that much.

32

Daniel tossed Henry's cell back to him with a frustrated grunt. "I just asked the cops to bring your precious grandfather to me as part of my demands." He slid the gun in his holster and placed his hands on the counter with a glazed look. "This isn't the way this was supposed to happen, but we can still make it work."

Henry looked over Daniel's shoulder to the door, where his employees were locked up.

"You won't hurt any of them, will you?"

"I don't plan on it." Daniel's lip lifted into a snarl. "Unless they cause problems. What's it to you?"

"They're innocent bystanders in all this. They have families to go home to."

"Like the girl doesn't?" He snorted. "You started this, and I'll finish it. Just play along and get our money."

It was then that they heard a knock from inside the office door and a yell from one of his sales associates.

"Can we get some water in here?"

"No!" Daniel's loud voice boomed across the room.

"Come on," Henry urged. "They won't cause problems if you keep them comfortable."

"Fine." Daniel tossed the key across the counter. "Grab a few bottles of water from wherever you keep them, throw them inside, and lock it back up. And hurry! Your grandfather should arrive any minute, and we still have to find the girl."

Once Henry scurried to the break room, Daniel turned on the small TV on the counter and froze. He expected there to be live news feed with the cops outside, but he would have never expected to a still photo of his intended target on-screen.

What is she doing on television?

The second he heard the female reporter voicing over the live broadcast, he knew it was her. Alexis was reporting from wherever she was inside the building. Daniel scanned the sales department, wondering where on earth she could be hiding. Wherever it was, she apparently wasn't running scared. And, she was a reporter?! From what it sounded like, she was rubbing it in his face, daring him to find her.

"Is that her?" Henry slid up next to his cousin and stared at the television.

"Apparently, she thinks she is safe to broadcast to the whole world." Anger coursed through Daniel's veins. He hated being made a fool. He turned to Henry and asked, "We've searched everywhere you can think of, right?"

Henry's brow scrunched as he mentally searched the layout of his building. Finally, his eyes lit up with recognition.

"There's one more place, but only employees would know about it."

Daniel slammed a hand on the counter. "Take me!"

∾

ALEXIS SIGNED off from what she thought was one of her most brilliant pieces of work.

If that doesn't secure me a spot on-air, I don't know what will. She hit the end button on her screen with a nervous smile.

Even with the incident involving Sharena, this might be enough to sway the powers that be to let her stay and move into a prime spot. If she got out alive, that was.

Just as she was about to text Tyler, Francis waved her back in the corner, whispering, "I hear someone."

Bella's soft whimper echoed through the dark. The young girl reached for Alexis' hand as Alexis slipped her phone into a hidden pocket in her jacket.

Suddenly, the door creaked open, reminding Alexis of every stereotypical horror movie she'd ever seen. The group shielded their eyes from the bright light in the hallway when Daniel and Henry filled the doorway with a look of surprise. When Alexis saw the gleam in Daniel's eyes, her breath hitched.

"So, I see you've had some help." All three cringed at the sound of his voice.

Daniel waved the gun in their direction. "Get out here!"

Alexis squeezed Bella's hand before moving in front to shield the pair.

"You think you're some kind of hero?" Daniel snarled, taking a step closer.

At the sound of his voice, Alexis, swallowed, pushing the panic down that clawed at her throat. If she let fear win, she wouldn't be able to breathe. To get out of this alive, meant she had to keep her head.

When Daniel reached for Bella's arm, a look transpired between both girls. They were both scared, but Alexis had a calming presence that Bella clung to.

"You're next. Go!" He pushed Francis toward Henry, who gave him an apologetic look.

Henry ducked his head and whispered, "He's making me, but I'll make sure you're safe."

"Now, you." Daniel slowly twisted toward Alexis. "You. I have plans for you."

His beastly stare sent shivers down her spine.

God help me get out of this. Please. She inhaled through her nose, almost shivering.

Daniel snarled, thinking her fear was more tempting than the curves that gave her figure her allure. Just before he laid a hand on her, he called over his shoulder, "Henry!"

"Yeah?" Henry looked from Alexis' tight face to the desire that crossed Daniel's.

"Go lock them up with the others. Take your time coming back."

Alexis found it hard to breathe. When she swallowed, it was as if she were forcing a rock down her throat. Backed into a corner, she had nowhere to run.

As if he could read her thoughts, Daniel said, "You can't escape this one." His eyes lit up. "You're a feisty little thing."

He closed the gap between them and stroked the side of her face with the barrel of his gun.

Alexis winced as he dragged the cold steel from her cheek to rest at the top of her cleavage. His stale breath rolled down the side of her neck as he brushed his lips along her jawline. Alexis shivered and turned from his touch.

"I like my women running hot," he whispered in her ear. "I can only imagine what you would be like."

No, she had to get back to Lani and the rest of her family. She made a promise to Tyler. It was then that her fear morphed into something more. Everything inside her told her to fight.

"Keep dreaming," she grunted between her teeth right before she brought up her knee.

When Daniel doubled over gasping for air, she tried to pry herself loose from his grasp, but his brute strength was no match for her petite frame. No matter how much pain he was in, his muscular arms didn't waver as he pressed her against the wall.

"That's twice," he choked. "There won't be a third." When his dark eyes bore into her soul, what she saw was pure evil.

Just then, Henry cleared his throat and hit the mute button on his cell.

"Sorry to interrupt." He stepped inside. "The cops are asking for you. My grandfather is outside waiting."

Daniel glared at Alexis with a look that said it was only a matter of time. The second he let go of her, it took everything she had not to slide into a pile onto the floor.

"We're not done yet." He pushed her toward Henry as he lifted the phone to his ear.

∽

Tyler tried to text Alexis twice with no response. He paced the lot next to the police camp dampening the worst-case scenarios that were running rampant in his mind.

"What's going on, boss?" Stephen stepped in next to him.

"She's not answering."

"Maybe she can't, but is still safe?"

"No, something's wrong." A sickening twist pulled at Tyler from within. Alexis was in trouble.

Grant whistled across to both men to get their attention and waved them over.

"Someone just arrived in a limo and is being ushered to the van. It looks like they're putting something on him."

"Film it, but tell Janelle we're saving it for later. Who is that?" Tyler strained to see.

Stephen stepped up on the running board of their van to get a peek. "That's the old man. Mr. Wylar."

"William?" Shock rang through Tyler's entire being. This wasn't good if the negotiator was using him as a bargaining chip. It meant only one thing. Alexis was dead center in the middle of the family drama that led to Evelyn's death, and now, she could be next.

"Yeah." Stephen stepped down. "What do you think they want with him?"

"I know, but I wish I didn't."

Both men looked to him for answers he wasn't sure he could give at the moment. He just shook his head and walked off.

Endless Possibilities

~

WILLIAM WYLAR WAS NEVER MORE concerned in his life than he was right now. In all his years of living and all he'd survived, he never imagined he'd be walking into a lion's den with a button cam on his jacket. If it were discovered, it could be the end of his life and possibly everyone else still inside.

After the police ended their conversation with whoever was on the inside, they ushered him to the front door, where Henry unlocked it and slid up the metal cage door to allow him entry inside.

"Henry?" William's shaky voice beckoned. "Are you alright?"

His sentiment should have been touching, but Henry was left unaffected. His grandfather was solely about his business, and never once did he share a piece of himself that left Henry any room for emotion.

"I'm just great." He sent him a nasty smirk and then paused, thinking his grandfather genuinely looked concerned. "He wants us in here."

"What is going on? Who is it?" William took Henry's arm, allowing himself to be pulled inside.

"Stop talking, old man," Daniel said from behind a corner. He knew enough to stay out of sight, knowing a S.W.A.T. team would be prepared to shoot on command if he came into view.

"That sounds like-" William stopped short as he rounded the corner. "Daniel?"

"In person."

The gleam in his eyes sent shivers down William's spine. He never did like that boy. Even if Daniel was his nephew, he didn't claim him. Anyone could see that Daniel was malevolent to the core.

~

EVELYN WATCHED from the other side in shock. What little control she had was almost deadlocked as her emotions overrode her abilities to meddle. It was as if she were frozen in place.

"William?" Evelyn whispered as he passed.

William stilled, wondering why all of a sudden it seemed as if Evelyn was nearby. He glanced over his shoulder, expecting her to appear then shook his head free from such thoughts. As Evelyn's spirit shadowed him down the hall, chills permeated his skin.

Henry nudged him forward. "Keep moving."

A young woman, who could have been Evelyn's twin sat on a couch next to the elevator. Her wrists were bound, and she was clearly shaken. He blinked in awe.

"It's you." He sat next to her and studied her face.

Alexis took in his warm eyes with wonder. Did he know who she was, or was he reliving something different altogether?

"My name is Alexis. I'd shake your hand, but..." She shrugged and showed him her wrists, which were bound by women's hosiery.

"Alexis?" His voice faltered.

"Evelyn is – was my grandmother." Her eyes filled with a mixture of sadness and something else that he couldn't quite put his finger on. Sympathy? Or was it just stress?

"Oh. I see." William studied her face one last time before casting his eyes down.

For a split second, as he approached, he saw Evelyn's compelling eyes unaware that this young lady was someone twice removed. He blinked. He was getting old, and his mind often played tricks on him. After all, it wasn't far from this very spot where he first met the love of his life.

"How did you know I knew your grandmother?" William sat in thought. Her eyes had more of an almond shape than Evelyn's, but the rest of her was the spitting image.

"I found the letter you wrote in her desk after she passed."

"Enough!" Daniel waved an arm. "Both of you. Shut up!"

"So, you know our story?" William ignored him. He'd always wondered if Evelyn ever thought of him after he pushed her away, and this was his chance to find out.

"No. I know nothing except what was in your letter." Her eyes glanced at Daniel as she spoke out of the side of her mouth. "How did the two of you meet?"

"I said, 'shut up!'" Daniel cocked his gun. "Speak one more word, old man."

Henry paced the floor behind Daniel, getting more nervous with each step. This wasn't how everything was supposed to go down. Henry could stomach Daniel taking care of the loose ends alone, but here in front of him was just too much.

"Do you have to do this now?" he yelled at his cousin.

"What do you mean? Is there a better time to finish this? Everything has led up to this moment, and if we miss our window-" Daniel's warning stare pinned him to the spot.

As the two argued over what would come next, Henry's phone rang. He sent his cousin an evil eye and answered. "Keep them in line."

Daniel left for the women's department, where he could hide behind a few mannequins and peer unseen through the front windows. Now, all he needed to do was buy more time with the police until he could think of what to do next.

Alexis nervously eyed Henry as he sat on the counter a few yards away. When it appeared that he was more preoccupied with his thoughts than he was with the two of them, she saw her window of opportunity and scooted closer to William.

"Hurry," she said. "How did you two meet?"

William lifted the corners of his mouth and took in a short breath.

"Your grandmother was a vision, much like you. She used to work for me right here at Wylars."

Alexis' eyes went wide. "She worked for you?"

"I'll never forget the first time I saw her in her oversized overalls." His eyes took on a faraway look. "She worked here on the cleaning crew. As soon as I saw her, I knew I had to get to know her. She was sassy and classy and," William sighed, "...well, anyone could see she didn't belong in work coveralls. With one look, I knew we were meant to be."

"Then what happened?" she whispered.

"I arranged for her to work on the floor in sales so that I could see more of her. As the store manager, I had more contact with her during the day than at night, when I was at home with my parents. To keep them from suspecting anything, I got her a day job, so I could run into her whenever I could."

"Why would they care?" She frowned.

"Because I was engaged to someone else, someone my parents would approve. Patricia, my fiancé at that time, came from money and had a name." William clasped his hands. "After I broke it off with Patricia to be with your grandmother, I discovered Evelyn was pregnant. I asked if it was mine. I wanted it to be mine so badly." His eyes watered.

Alexis sat in awe, unable to speak.

"I already knew she was a widow before she met me. Out of curiosity, I had done a little digging before I got involved with her."

"She was married? To whom?"

"A two-bit con man who drank himself to death. No one would hire a single pregnant woman from the wrong side of the tracks, which is how she ended up cleaning toilets and watering plants. But anyone could take one look at her and see she was better than that."

"Oh, my gosh," she exclaimed before covering her mouth in shock. "So, this con man was my...?"

"Grandfather."

"What was his name?" She had to know.

"Jack Skinner. There was no love lost when he passed. From what I understand, he raised his hand to Evelyn a time or two."

"He hit Grams? How do you know?"

"Because she confided in me after we started seeing one another. When I found out what she'd come from, I wanted to do anything and everything I could to give Evelyn a better life. I even moved her into an upscale apartment near the store."

"Before deserting her when she needed you most?" Alexis' accusing eyes did nothing to punish him. He'd done enough of that to last a lifetime.

"I did it to save her." He shook his head. "Once my father found out, he blackmailed me. He said he'd strip me of every cent I had and blackball my name from here to California. If I stayed with Evelyn, I would be unable to find work to support my wife and child."

"Who does that?"

"The Wylars. Why do you think these boys think so little of me that they'd plan my demise?"

Alexis shot a glance at Daniel's tattoo-laced arms and piercings and asked, "So, he's a Wylar, too? He looks a little far from the family tree."

William chuckled. "You remind me so much of your grandmother. She never minced words either."

"I get that a lot." She rolled her eyes.

"He's my nephew on my wife's side." William touched his forehead and chest before tapping each shoulder, to complete a cross-motion. "God rest her soul."

He then narrowed his eyes in Daniel's direction and said, "He doesn't have the Wylar name, but he's Henry's family. We don't really have many family members left on either side, which is why I left my grandson in charge of my business. From the looks of things…" William eyed Daniel with a shake of his head.

"I should have hired anyone other than Henry. And, as far as the few family members I have left, the whole lot of them only care about what happens to my money when I pass. Now that Evelyn is gone, the account I set up for her goes to your family. That is… until I die. Then, that account goes back to my grandson, Henry."

Alexis' eyes widened. "Is that what this is all about?"

William nodded. His eyes filled with regret. "Since you're here, it looks like you're in their crosshairs too."

"Oh, no. I was just trying to find out more about you. I don't care about the money." She violently shook her head. For a minute, as she listened to her grandmother's story, she had almost forgotten her circumstances. But the cold reality was that she had to find a way out of this predicament. "I have a child to go home to. A life to live. We can't let that happen, Mr. Wylar."

"Call me, William." He began tugging on the stockings that bound her hands together.

When Daniel ended the call with the police, he turned in time to see the old man untie Alexis' wrists. He leaped forward. "Uh-uh. No way. Henry, I told you to keep an eye on them!"

"I w-was," Henry stammered as if in a daze.

William ignored and continued to untie Alexis. "What is she going to do to you, Daniel? She's a helpless girl."

"I've seen what she can do." He pointed to the lump on his temple. "Henry, tie her up again."

Although hesitant, Henry stood in place, wondering how much longer he needed to be a part of Daniel's plan. He'd much rather be inside the office with his employees, unaware of what happened next.

"Henry!" Daniel yelled. "Now."

It was then that her cell vibrated in her pocket. To cover the sound, as minimal as it was, she started a coughing fit and bent over.

"I need some water," she gasped.

"Henry, get the lady some water, please." William glared at Daniel before turning his attention back to his grandson. "Prove to me you're better than this."

"Enough!" Daniel backhanded William across the jaw, sending him toppling sideways into Alexis' lap.

"William!" Alexis screamed.

When there was no response, she cradled William's head in her lap, protecting it as if he were her own flesh and blood. No matter how badly this man broke her grandmother's heart, he didn't deserve to be beaten. Alexis lifted her gaze to the ceiling and prayed for a miracle.

"Get her some water, Henry." Daniel's monotone voice dropped half an octave.

Alexis cocked her head. A shift took place in Daniel's demeanor. Not only did her captor seem to be on autopilot, but he seemed to be boring a hole in the wall behind them as if in a trance.

Alexis narrowed her eyes, wondering what Daniel saw. She glanced over her shoulder, but the only thing behind her was a blank wall. He'd become so detached it was as if he were on a different planet.

Before too long, Daniel spun and pointed at Henry. "On your way back with water, head to the front door. The cops are sending us some pizza. After that, we'll wrap everything up here."

Daniel hadn't fully checked out but needed some distance between him and what came next. When he took out Evelyn, it was from a distance. He'd never murdered someone in cold blood.

This time, he'd take two lives - up close and personal. It wasn't that he was unwilling, but he certainly hadn't mentally prepared for it. Daniel nodded, hatching a new plan. After Henry returned with the pizza, he'd eat a few slices before pulling the trigger. Murder wasn't something he would do on an empty stomach.

When it was clear that Daniel was alone with his thoughts, Alexis leaned forward to whisper in William's ear.

"Are you okay?" She stroked back his silver hair as he moaned in her lap. "William?"

"I believe so," he whispered. "Just let me lay low here while I work out our options. Let them think I'm out cold."

Alexis exhaled, nodded, and prayed he'd come up with something to hold them off. From what it sounded like - they didn't have much time.

33

"He looks stressed." Officer Kerry observed Henry's movements on the surveillance screen.

"I can flip him." Officer Cho pulled a bulletproof vest over his pizza delivery uniform and looked at his boss with excitement.

"Maybe." Kerry rubbed his temples. "Do we even know if this guy is involved?"

"It sure looks that way." He pointed to the screen as Daniel pulled Henry aside as if the two were conspiring.

"Do we have an ID on this guy yet?" Kerry turned to his team, who were scurrying to get him the information he needed. "You heard the audio. The old man said the gunman was related to the Wylars. From the looks of his tattoos, I'd bet he's served a stint or two. If not nearby, then somewhere."

"I have what you need right here." A detective came from nowhere and offered a tablet to the team. "Our Sergeant sent a photo from your live feed to my partner and me." He pointed to the screen that still displayed the pair in a heated conversation before nodding to the woman, who stood next to him.

Officer Kerry nodded in acknowledgment to the woman before

eyeing the tablet's screen. "Looks like he's done time in Austin for armed robbery, among other things."

"Henry Wylar seems to be involved. I'm telling you; I can flip him. He's showing classic signs of anxiety. He's in way over his head." Officer Cho tapped the monitor where Henry's face tightened with distress.

"He's part of it." Tyler's deep voice came from behind.

"You're making a bad habit of this." The lead investigator smirked in Tyler's direction.

"You said to keep you updated." He shrugged and handed his phone to him. "She asked me not to reveal this to the public just yet, but you all should know."

"Is Officer Cho suited up yet?" Another officer approached with a few pizza boxes.

"What's going on?" Tyler's eyes darted between the two men.

When Kerry sent Tyler a dismissive smirk, Officer Cho pulled Tyler aside and said, "They've asked for food, so I'm going in as a pizza delivery guy. Maybe we can get the upper hand."

Tyler grasped Cho's arm. "She's not responding to my texts. Can you tell me anything?"

Cho shook his head and looked at Kerry, who glared at him in return. He turned from his superior's gaze and said, "Sorry, man. I know you're worried, but we've got it under control."

Cho pitied him. If it were his girl, he'd do anything to get her out of this mess. Once his supervisor was safely out of earshot, he nodded for Tyler to follow him to the other side of the compound.

"You didn't hear this from me. So far, Alexis is safe. We sent Mr. Wylar in with a button-cam, so we've been able to see everything since then."

"Is she hurt?" His pupils seemed to dilate to the size of quarters.

"Not that we can tell. That's all I can say."

"Cho! You're up!" Kerry yelled from across the group and waved him over for the pizzas.

∼

Henry wiped the sweat from his brow and reached for the lock on the heavy front doors. As he pushed a door slightly ajar, he peered through the space that led to the sidewalk. The commotion that had accumulated across from his property had his stomach in knots.

Seven police vehicles surrounded the front. One was an oversized, dark tactical van. As he scanned the rooftops across from him, Henry saw a few strategically placed snipers. He tried to swallow, but his mouth was too dry. His throat narrowed as if his airflow was about to be cut off.

"Hey there." Cho motioned to the pizza box.

Henry eyed him, wondering who he was. Surely, they wouldn't let someone from the restaurant mosey up to a hostage situation. He looked too calm.

"You're a cop," Henry whispered.

Officer Cho saw no use in lying. He shrugged his shoulders, saying nothing to the contrary.

"You'll need to lift this gate from outside the doors if you want me to hand over the pizza." Cho eyed him cautiously, before asking, "How are you doing?" He thought Henry looked about ready to pop. "You don't look so good."

"How do you think I am?" He seethed in response. "We've got a madman in there with a gun."

"Seems like he trusts you enough that you can come and go as you please. Any reasonable person with that amount of liberty would run for the hills if they valued their life. How come you're not running?"

Officer Cho watched his eyes skirt back and forth as Henry tried to cover his tracks. When a bead of sweat trickled down Henry's temple, he knew he had him.

Henry's stomach swirled with uncertainty. Although frightened, he wasn't about to admit to anything. "I'm in charge of my employees. If I leave, he'll kill them."

He inhaled, hoping the lie was believable.

"Okay." Cho rocked back on his boots and gripped the pizza boxes with a knowing look. "I'll tell you what. I'll let you in on a little secret. We have had eyes on you guys this whole time. We know more than you think we do."

Cho waited patiently. The next words Henry spoke would tell him everything he needed to know on whether he would cooperate or not.

"You have a camera in here? With sound?" Sweat perspired on his upper lip. "You're lying."

"How else would we know that your cousin is holding something over you? Someone of your stature would never be involved in something like this."

Henry's breath hitched. "He's forcing me." Henry's mind spun faster than a pinwheel in a hurricane. His options were limited. "What do I need to do? I'll do it – as long as you can cut me a deal."

Although Cho was tempted to let out a celebratory yell, he stayed calm.

"Your cooperation will speak volumes. I'm sure the district attorney will take that into account when she files charges."

"I can't turn on him. He'll kill me. I know it." He looked over his shoulder, hoping Daniel didn't suspect anything.

"No one is saying you have to be a hero." Cho nodded toward the metal gate that still separated them and pushed the pizzas forward. "All you need to do is lift this gate, take these pizzas, and forget to pull it back down or lock yourself in."

"He'll know." His hands shook as he lifted the gate.

"No, he won't." Cho held his grasp on the boxes before giving them fully over. "Will this gate slide down halfway without crashing down?"

"Yes." He glanced over his shoulder, taught with distress.

Cho finally released the pizza. "Pull it halfway down. From inside, it'll appear that it's to the ground. Your cousin?"

"Daniel."

Cho nodded. "Daniel will think it's down if he happens to look. We'll be able to sneak in, stay quiet, and get you all out alive."

"You're sure?"

"Could I trust you to ring me up when I shop here next? Yeah, I could – because you have done it probably your whole life, right?"

Henry nodded.

Cho grinned. "Trust me. We do this sort of thing every day. I've been doing this for a long time. Let us help you, Henry."

He hesitated before slowly nodding and pulling the gate down halfway.

"That's it," Cho encouraged. "Now just act as normal as you can and get those pizzas inside."

Cho watched him disappear through the menagerie of mannequins and said a silent prayer.

∽

For Henry, the rest happened fairly quickly. In a matter of minutes, soft shuffles surrounded him. When Cho and the other officers snuck inside, Henry went into survival mode and ducked behind a rounder of clothing before the pandemonium broke loose. What he saw next was the sting of betrayal in Daniel's eyes as a string of obscenities flew from his cousin's mouth.

"You couldn't just play it cool?" Daniel glared and pointed the gun toward Mr. Wylar, who had now regained consciousness and sitting upright.

Daniel thought about his options as a harsh voice from somewhere within the store ordered him to freeze. Instead, he pulled the trigger and aimed at his uncle. Before he could get off his second shot, bullets barraged him through and through until he lay on the ground in a pool of his own blood.

Alexis' painful gasps were the only thing that could be heard when the shooting came to an end. Everyone in the room stood motionless as they glanced at Daniel's lifeless body next to Alexis, who had slumped to the ground and was struggling to stay conscious.

William gingerly pushed Alexis' blood-matted hair back from her temples and cried in a soft voice that she alone could hear.

"Please hang on. Please." The pain in Alexis' eyes tore at his heart.

He knew she might not have much time left and selfishly added, "Tell Evelyn she was the only woman I ever wanted."

"Please," Alexis puffed. "My daughter…" Her voice fell as she fought the pain.

∼

When Daniel pointed the gun toward William, all Alexis could think was to get them both safely home. She lunged to protect William just as Daniel pulled the trigger. When a bullet tore through her chest, it was as if she'd been struck by lightning.

Immediately, images of her loved ones flashed before her eyes. Everyone she wished she could say goodbye to slipped from her like sands in an hourglass. As her eyes narrowed and her breath shifted, all she remembered were the yells of the officers, who had finally come to their rescue. She only hoped it wasn't too late for her.

"Get the EMT's in here! Now!" Officer Cho hollered over his shoulders.

As the medics rushed inside, Tyler dropped to the curb and groaned in prayer.

"Please don't let it be her," he pleaded. "Please, God."

He lifted his head when the sounds of raised voices and the clatter of the stretcher came toward him. As the medical team clamored to get their patient to the ambulance, he strained to see who it was, but there were too many people surrounding the body.

Once they turned to lift the stretcher into the back of the ambulance, Tyler got a clear look. Alexis' pale skin was now gray. Her blonde hair was now red from the blood that sprayed across her chest and face. When they secured her inside, her eyes fluttered, and she fell limp.

Tyler ran toward the back of the ambulance just in time to slam his palms on the back windows as the vehicle drove off with sirens blaring.

34

Evelyn may have been stunned into inaction for most of the standoff, but when Alexis was in immediate danger, instinct took over. When her granddaughter pushed William to safety, Evelyn dove forward and cradled her heart, preventing the bullet from hitting any vital organs.

"I got you, baby," she whispered into her ear as Alexis' groaned in pain.

As the medical team hooked Alexis to an IV and gave her oxygen, Evelyn had a sense Alexis was going to make it. She wasn't sure how, but as Clay had told her earlier, she just knew.

When the ambulance, carrying her granddaughter, drove away with sirens blaring, she noticed Tyler struggling to find his phone. She appeared next to him, wishing she could offer comfort, but he wasn't in a place to receive it. Instead, she focused on where she was needed most.

∽

TYLER'S NEWS team ran to get closer to the scene. Grant zoomed in with his camera to film the departing ambulance and made sure to keep Tyler from the frame.

As the ambulance sped off, TJ dropped to his knees as if he were the one who was shot. As much as that imagery would make for a stellar broadcast, Grant respected TJ's privacy too much to include him in the footage.

"What do we do?" Grant turned to Grant in shock.

"We take care of our own. Keep shooting B-roll and upload it to Janelle. I'll get TJ to the truck."

Stephen took off his mic and ran to help his boss and friend from the ground.

"I'm here," he murmured as he placed a hand on TJ's back. "What can we do?"

"I've got to call her family." Tyler shook his head. "They're going to kill me for not calling sooner."

"It's not like you've haven't had your hands full." Stephen's eyes shone with compassion.

"No, I should have called." Tyler's face filled with grief.

Tyler dialed Anderson as Stephen ushered him to the station van.

"Let's get you back." Stephen nodded to Grant, who was packing up his camera.

"Take me to the hospital," Tyler ordered. He pinched the bridge of his nose and exhaled as the phone rang in his ear. It didn't take long for Anderson to answer.

"Anderson?" Tyler paused. "You might want to sit down."

∽

AMELIA WAS in the kitchen with Lani, when Anderson walked in with a grave face. After today's events, she knew it had to be about Alexis. Instinctively, she patted Lani on the head and almost sang, "Lani, sweetheart. Why don't you go to your room and bring me some of those books we were talking about?"

Lani watched the looks between her family and could sense the tension that rippled through the room.

"I want to stay with you guys." She frowned.

Anderson dropped to a knee with a reassuring grin and pulled her close.

"I need to speak to my mom privately. It's grown-up stuff. Can you please give me a few minutes?" Her bottom lip protruded, and he added, "For me?" He raised his eyebrows as he put on a silly face.

She stifled a giggle and nodded. "But only for a few minutes."

When he was sure Lani was safely out of earshot, he ushered his mom into a chair.

"You're scaring me." Amelia's voice shook. "Your dad should be here for this."

As Anderson gravely nodded, Lani listened on from around the back entrance to the kitchen. Though the adults thought she'd gone upstairs, she'd snuck out the front door and rounded to the back of the house. She quietly crouched on the top step of the stoop, where she could hear everything that was said.

"Big ears can get you in trouble." Evelyn appeared to sit next to her.

Her eyes watered. "I think something's really wrong. They have that look."

"What look?"

"The one that everyone had when my dad died, but no one wanted to tell me. Is my mommy okay?" Her voice quivered.

"Sweetheart, she's going to be fine." Evelyn wrapped her arms around her great-granddaughter's hunched shoulders.

"But something has happened. Right?"

Evelyn nodded.

"And she could die," she whispered, straining to overhear what her family discussed inside.

As Evelyn comforted her, Lani closed her eyes and willed herself to be strong. She leaned into Evelyn's embrace, thankful for her presence.

"That feels nice." Lani's thoughtful eyes searched hers.

"Your mom is not going to die, but she did get hurt. So, I need you to put on a brave face for your family because they don't have that sort of assurance. If I were you, I would say some prayers for her that she recovers one hundred percent. Okay?"

"You said she was going to be okay."

"She's going to live."

"How do you know?"

"Call it my guardian angel antennae. I just know."

Lani bit on the inside her lips and sat up straight, putting on a brave face.

"I believe you. Will you watch over my mom through this?"

Evelyn nodded and disappeared.

Lani stood with a strengthened resolve. Her mother would come back to her, but she needed to do her part to help her family.

Lani slipped into the kitchen just as Amelia wiped her face free from tears, forced a smile, and opened her arms. When Lani climbed into her lap, Amelia stroked her arms, unsure where to start.

"Sweetheart." Amelia paused, searching the faces of her family. "We've got some bad news."

Lani lifted her hand to cover Amelia's lips and gave her a reassuring look that was wise beyond her years. It was as if Lani could see deep within Amelia's heart when she said, "Great Grams already told me, but she said Mom's going to make it. She said we all should pray."

"W-What?" Amelia was at a loss for words.

Hank stepped forward and took his granddaughter's hand as she slipped from his wife's lap.

"How about you and me go pray while the rest of the family visit your mom?" he asked.

"I want to see her." Her little eyes filled with anxiety.

"And you can," Anderson murmured as he leaned down to get nose to nose, "but she's in surgery right now, and unfortunately, they don't allow children."

"Uncle Marshall, are you going?" She looked to the man, who was always stoic and seemed to skirt the edges of their family while seemingly holding them together. Even at her young age, she understood his temperament and respected his place.

Unless it had to do with farming, he never involved himself much in family matters, yet at that moment stepped forward and offered his hand.

"I think your grandpa should go with the rest of them." He sent a look to Hank over her head with a nod. "You and I can take up praying in the yard."

Lani made eye contact with each of the others, unsure, yet followed Marshall's lead. She slipped her hand from her grandfather's and took Marshall's instead.

"Come on," Marshall reassured her. "You can help me. I'm not very good at this sort of thing, so you lead the way."

Lani's smile broke the somber mood. "Okay, this way."

"We'll let you know something as soon as we can." Amelia gave Lani a kiss when the two passed by and squeezed her step-brother's arm in thanks.

"I'll keep my phone on me." Marshall nodded to Amelia before guiding Lani out to the porch.

35

Alexis hovered for what seemed like hours over her body as a surgical team worked on repairing the damage to her chest.

"Clamp. Nurse, get me some suction." A hurried surgeon worked furiously to get the bleeding under control.

"And there's the bullet," she sighed. The surgeon inhaled as another nurse wiped sweat from her brow.

"You're a lucky girl, Ms. Mathers." The nurse looked at Alexis. Even though she was under sedation, she chose to believe her patient could hear her. "The bullet missed your heart by a fraction of an inch."

Evelyn materialized next to her granddaughter, whose spirit hovered above the operating table. She laid a hand on her arm just as Alexis turned toward her with a look of despair.

"Am I dead?" She eyed a wave of color swirling around her as worry poured from her spirit. She reached out to touch it, unsure what to expect only to find it evaporate like smoke.

"What is that?" Alexis blinked.

Evelyn's calm stare was full of peace as she shook her head.

"Come with me." She reached for Alexis' hand.

"But – but, what about?" She pointed toward her body in horror. If she left it behind, what did that mean for her or her family? She shook her head, unwilling to move.

"It'll be okay. You're going to pull through, but there's something you need to see first."

The ceiling faded as if it was never there. As they lifted through the air toward the billowy clouds, Alexis gaped in awe. Existence outside her body seemed so surreal. When her Grams led her toward the sky, floating high above the hospital, it was as if she were dreaming. With the last glance below, she noticed her family frantically running toward the entrance of the emergency room.

"I'm here," she whispered as they hurried inside without a glance in her direction. She looked at Evelyn and frowned. "What is happening? Why can't they hear me?"

"Welcome to my world." Evelyn shook her head. "You get used to it."

"Will I?"

"No." Evelyn squeezed her hand. "I promise you won't have to worry about that right now. Think of this as a reprieve from what's going on down there so that you can understand where the big and little pictures come together."

"So, you've been with us all this time?" She reached to touch Evelyn's face, but her hand flew through as if she were reaching for air.

Evelyn chuckled. It seemed as if she'd somewhat graduated. It wasn't long ago that she was in Alexis' shoes, but now she would be the one to send her granddaughter back to the land of the living, but not just yet.

"I have a gift for you."

As Evelyn took both of Alexis' hands in hers, Alexis asked, "How do you do that?"

"Lots of practice." She ushered her granddaughter toward an open space that looked to be a vast spot surrounded by clouds. "Look."

Alexis watched as loved ones, who had already passed, filed in side-by-side. And as each face gleamed at her with loving eyes, she was filled with amazement and recognition. Family, friends, teachers, and many others she'd known in years past, were there to welcome her. The warmth in their hearts filled her from within and poured over her.

As every fiber of her being tingled with awareness, she acknowledged each new spirit with a smile or a nod reveling in the mix of emotions that had her spellbound until one name whispered across her heart.

Frantically, Alexis searched the group for the one face she had yet to see. As if they could read her mind, the others parted, allowing her access to see the one soul she ached to connect with once again.

When she saw him, she was overcome with a mixture of grief and gratitude.

"I thought there was no sadness in heaven," she whispered to herself.

"There isn't." Evelyn blinked. "If there's time, I'll explain that later. Right now..." She paused, urging Alexis forward.

Trepidation circled her spirit. It was as if butterflies swarmed her. Just when she was about to step forward - swirls of color surrounded her, covering her spirit with what she could only describe as love. She eyed the ribbons that wrapped around her to their source. They led to Clay. His love for her was more than she'd ever experienced on earth, and she wondered what the difference was.

She stared at her grandmother with a look of confusion.

"We're not bound by earthly problems here. Everything is elevated yet more simple. Clay has always loved you that much. He just couldn't express it while bound by his body."

Alexis covered her mouth, letting a small cry escape.

"Go." Evelyn nudged her from behind once more.

Alexis outstretched her hand to Clay, unsure she could move on her own when she noticed a young child who could have been his carbon copy.

"I've got you." Hearing his voice for the first time in three years, Alexis turned her attention back to her husband.

She stood in awe and searched his eyes. They glowed with certainty and peace.

"Is it really you?" She tried to touch his face, but her hands fell through as if she were grasping at air. Her heart ached for the loss of their marriage and his life.

When Clay sensed her regret, he cupped her face. "It wasn't your fault, Alexis."

"But, if we hadn't fought. If I hadn't pushed you away."

"We could do everything over again and change it -and I'd still be standing here with you now." He smiled down at the child who now stood next to him before turning back to Alexis. "This was our destiny."

Alexis' heart warmed at the young child who had yet to speak. She noticed his eyes looked a lot like Lani's. When she dropped to her knees, her heart flickered with recognition.

"You're mine?" she asked, already knowing the answer.

Once she held in her child, something clicked. Her soul fell into tune with his leaving her without a doubt. He circled his arms around her neck, fulfilling her in such a way that she had only experienced with Lani's affectionate embraces.

"Don't cry, Mom." His eyes almost glowed as the love he possessed for her outpoured. He wiped her tears, emitting a wave of love that shook her to her core. Then he whispered, "I'm okay, and I'm with Dad."

Alexis took his chin in her hands with awe. The brightness her son held within his soul made her dizzy with affection. His spirit washed over hers, pulled her under much like an ocean's undertow.

Clay reached for his son's hand and lifted Alexis from her knees with the other saying, "Alexis, our time is short. I need to let you know something before you go."

She looked at her son and said, "I don't want to leave you."

His adoring face gleamed up at her, and when he spoke, the truth resounded through her. "I'm always with you. It's not your time. Listen to Dad. I'm going to go play with Grams."

As her child skipped off to sit in Evelyn's lap, Alexis asked, "What's his name?"

"We never gave him one."

Alexis brought her hands to her chest. Now that she knew his face, she could imagine him growing up with Lani. The thought tore at her heart, knowing that couldn't be a reality.

Clay turned her toward him and cupped her face. He only had limited time to reach her and needed Alexis to focus on what came next.

Alexis shook her head from the cobwebs that seemed to cling to the corners of her mind. Part of her still thought this was a dream.

"What is this all about? Why am I here?"

"This is a gift from a Father who loves you very much. None of us want to see you waste your life down there when you have so much available to you... and so much to give. You and Lani deserve to have love in your life."

"We had you." Her heart broke. "I had you and let you die."

Clay shook his head. He had to make her see the truth and understand.

"There is nothing you could have done. I was very good at separating my personal life from my job. It was the only thing that kept me focused. And trust me, with my beat, I had to be focused."

"But when you left - you were so distraught," she argued.

"I was," he nodded, "but once I stepped through the doors of my precinct, only the job was on my mind. It's what every cop does if they want to make it home each night. It's what I did every time to get home to you. Our fight was just bad timing. That's all."

"But-" she whispered.

Clay placed a finger on her lips to still them and finished. "That night, I was in a situation that was unavoidable." He sighed. "And fight or not with my wife, I wasn't getting out of that one alive."

When he said the word wife, she came undone.

"Shhh." He lifted her chin to dry her tears. "We were ambushed, and I risked my life to save my partner's. Nothing you did or said was part of that."

"Clay." She closed her eyes.

"Believe it and let go of the guilt."

"I should have loved you better."

"You did everything you knew how. You were the best wife a man could ask for. Alexis, you were my everything, and I want to give that back to you. Now it's time for you to experience that kind of love. You need someone who is your everything." His voice broke.

"No, that's not fair to you."

He chuckled. "I have news for you. Life isn't fair, but love is what makes it worth the risk. And I know of a man who would do anything to be your everything in life."

He looked at her red-rimmed eyes, half laughed, and finished by saying, "I release you. You deserve to live."

"Clay."

"Shhh. Hear that?"

Clay cocked his head and listened as a gentle breeze wove around them. With it brought Tyler's weary voice, which filtered in allowing them to hear his words.

Alexis drew back, confused. She frowned at Tyler's voice that whispered around them.

"How is that possible?" she asked eyes wide.

"My sweet Alexis, there are endless possibilities when it comes to this place."

As he put a finger to his lips, the sound of Tyler's voice came through louder - as if he were standing there with them. If she didn't know better, she'd say it was a prayer.

"He's..." Her jaw dropped.

"Yes, he is." Clay sent her a peaceful stare. "And he's the one for you. Let him in, Alexis. It won't take anything away from what we had. If anything, it will teach Lani how much love we can have in our lives if we let it happen."

"Are you sure?" She turned back to face him only to find he was gone.

The next thing she experienced was a tug on her hand as the little boy, whom she'd yet to name, reached for her waist to hug her goodbye.

"I don't want to say it." She shook her head.

"Then, just say I'll see you later." His wise eyes filled with mischief.

As she kneeled for one more embrace, the name, *Milo,* softly whispered within her heart. Her spirit reverberated from top to bottom as the familiarity of their bond overtook her. She kissed both of his soft cheeks and quietly said, "I know your name. I know you're mine."

Milo, the child who claimed her heart immediately, took her face into his hands and stared deep into her eyes and said, "I'll always be with you."

"I can't leave you." Alexis' heart tore in two.

"Lani is waiting." Milo released her and took a step back.

Alexis shook her head and sent him a bittersweet smile.

"You and she would get along famously." Her heart lifted at the prospect.

"We already do." His eyes twinkled.

As she was about to ask him what he meant, Evelyn spun her around. "It's time."

36

Once Alexis successfully made it through surgery, the family rejoiced by hugging and crying all at once. When the doctor updated them, they listened as she explained that Alexis was to spend the night in ICU, where only her family was permitted to visit.

Amelia saw the disappointment in Tyler's eyes and interrupted.

"Excuse me, Dr. Shay. Can he come with us?" She laid a hand on Tyler's arm.

"Is he family?" The doctor looked her gravely in the eyes.

Tyler cut them off by saying, "It's okay. I'll wait."

Dr. Shay's lips thinned as she addressed Amelia.

"Look. It was touch and go for a while. Even your time is limited. It's my job to protect my patient."

"Thanks, doc." Tyler nodded with full understanding. He wanted what was best for Alexis.

Once Anderson and Alexis' parents disappeared behind the swinging doors, Tyler thought he'd go mad with distress while he paced the visitor's room. All he could think was how unfair it was that he couldn't be inside with the woman he loved, but he wasn't family. If he had the chance, he'd rectify that immediately.

In less than an hour, the three of them filed back into the waiting room, looking worse than when they left.

"She looks so," Amelia paused, unable to finish.

"You heard the doctor." Anderson pulled his mom into a hug. "She said Alexis' vitals are getting stronger by the hour."

"Let's get you home." Hank rubbed his wife's back and sent his son a knowing stare.

"I can't leave her!" Tears ran down Amelia's face. "What if she wakes up?"

"Come on, Mom. Lani needs you." Anderson nodded above his mom's head to his dad.

"I'll stay here. You should go home." Tyler joined the effort.

Amelia sunk into the chair next to Tyler. "I can't leave her."

"I promise to call you first thing."

A nurse, who happened to overhear, approached and sat in the chair next to Amelia. "Listen to your family, hon'. You need to get your rest to stay strong for your daughter."

"Do you know anything about her surgery?" Amelia asked, hoping this woman had more insight than the surgeon, who'd only given them the data, not the details.

"I was in the surgery with Dr. Shay. She's a tough but dedicated lady. Her patients benefit from it." The nurse laughed. "But her bedside manner..."

"Leaves a lot to be desired," Amelia finished for her.

The nurse's eyes twinkled. "Let this young man take the watch. From what I saw of your daughter, she's a fighter. We'll keep him informed. Go get some rest."

Once the family successfully led Amelia out, Tyler nodded to the nurse with thanks and asked, "Is she really going to be okay?"

"She seems to be getting stronger by the minute. Are you family? Visiting hours are almost over."

Tyler dropped his gaze to the floor, conflicted. As his face twisted with emotions, the nurse took pity. She recognized a man in love when she saw one. In the name of love, she decided to push the envelope.

"There is a rule about family, but I might be able to help you out."

"You'd do that?" He sat up in his chair with a look of hope.

"She's someone special in your life?"

"She's my heart."

"Then consider it my wedding gift to you in advance, because I expect a proposal out of this."

As Tyler's brow furrowed, she saw the look of confusion and laughed, knowing he misunderstood.

"Not a proposal for me. One for Ms. Mathers." She stood and wagged her finger. "Follow me," she whispered.

As they pushed through the double doors and approached the nurse's station, she nodded to the supervisor saying, "This is the fiancé for room 333. He's staying the night."

The supervisor didn't even glance up. She was too busy with the chart in front of her to notice. She waved them by with a grunt.

Once the nurse approached the glass door, she paused before opening it and said over her shoulder, "Be prepared. She just came through major surgery. She's going to look a lot worse than you could imagine."

Tyler tried to get a look through the glass door to prepare himself, but a curtain was drawn and was blocking his view.

"Thank you, Miss?"

"Hallie. You can call me Hallie."

Thank you, Nurse Hallie."

When she opened the door, the first thing he noticed was the sounds of monitors beeping. Hallie lifted an arm to pull back the curtain to reveal a very sedated Alexis. The tube that extended from her mouth took him by surprise.

"Is she not breathing on her own?" His heart skipped a beat.

"She is, but since she's not waking up yet. It's just a precaution."

"Shouldn't she be awake by now?"

"It's early yet." Hallie grinned and pulled a chair up to Alexis' bedside. "Sorry about this." She motioned for him to sit. "This is about as much comfort as we can offer. Can I get you a blanket?"

He shook his head and stared at Alexis, willing her to open her eyes.

"When will you know if she's turned a corner?" He held his breath.

"By morning." She checked her watch. "Which is only about five hours from now."

Tyler sat down and stroked Alexis' face. The love he held in his eyes was nothing short of inspirational.

"I'm off now," Hallie whispered. "I'm not due back for a couple of days, but keep me posted on any upcoming nuptials." Her eyes crinkled at the edges as she sent him a hopeful smile.

"Hallie?" She turned when he called her name. "Thanks. I – we – owe you one."

"It's the least I could do. Get some rest." Hallie left as Tyler bent his head in prayer.

∼

TYLER'S VOICE was raw from the hours he'd spent throughout night and morning praying over her body - hoping for a miracle. He looked to the ceiling and thanked God for how far Alexis had come but prayed she'd wake up. As he squeezed her hand out of desperation, her fingers contracted in response.

"Alexis?" He sat up, fully awake. When her fingers shifted once more, he leaped from her bedside and ran for help.

"Nurse!" His yell could be heard from across the entire wing. As everyone turned in his direction, he said with excitement, "She's moving her fingers when I say her name. She's coming around. Come quick!"

He flew back inside and took his chair as a couple of nurses trailed him. The biggest of the two, who reminded him of Attila the Hun, pushed him aside and barked at him. "You need to move out of the way. Please wait outside."

He drew back with surprise and blinked. "You'll have to drag me out of here." He sent her a steely stare.

"I can call security." She looked at him from under her eyebrows while she checked Alexis' vitals.

"If you don't mind stepping outside, sir." The nicer of the two nurses pulled him aside with a gentle touch.

"But it's my voice she's responding to," he said with desperation.

"Not necessarily," Attila the Hun grumbled. "It could be nothing more than her nerves - an involuntary response."

At that moment, Alexis lifted her arm and groaned. She reached for her mouth and fumbled for the tube that was keeping her from saying anything.

"Oh, my goodness." The second nurse pointed at Alexis. "He's right. She is responding to him." She then turned back to Tyler. "But, you still need to wait outside for – just a few minutes." She gave him a sweet smile before pushing him out the door and drawing the curtain shut.

∽

When the nurse slid the tube from Alexis' throat, she groaned in agony. The pain was motivation enough to open her eyes and get her bearings. She blinked a few times and quickly came to the realization that she was in a hospital, but Tyler wasn't anywhere to be seen.

"Tyler," she hoarsely whispered.

That one word was all he needed to rush back in and push Attila from her position of authority.

"Try it." He sent her a warning glare.

As Attila stood back, apparently offended, the other nurse covered her mouth to keep her grin from showing and nudged the larger nurse. "It's true love."

Even Attila couldn't blame the man for his behavior when she saw her patient's face light up.

"If my husband had half the heart this guy did." Attila frowned and left the room muttering under her breath. "She's a lucky girl."

Tyler stroked the hair back from Alexis' face and eagerly kissed her forehead.

"You're here." Alexis struggled to get the words out.

"It's okay. You don't have to say anything. Just rest." Tyler sighed. "You gave us all quite a scare."

"My mom? Lani?" She glanced behind him toward the door.

Tyler shook his head. "Anderson and your dad made Amelia leave late last night. She didn't want to. She wanted to be here when you woke up."

Alexis shook her head and swallowed. "I'm glad it was you."

"You thirsty?" He asked and reached for a pitcher of water to pour a glass. "Here," he said, lifting her head so she could take a sip.

She swallowed with a wince before sending him a grateful smile.

Dr. Shay pushed the curtain back and reached for her chart before grinning at Alexis. "I see someone woke up." She touched Alexis' leg. "How do you feel?"

"Like someone ran over me." She tried to laugh but coughed instead. "Ow." She frowned.

"That's to be expected. You were shot. We had to open you up to stop the bleeding and find the bullet. You're bound to be sore for a while and will need to be very careful."

Alexis replayed the image in her mind and shivered.

"Can you give her a minute?" Tyler's protective nature kicked in. "She's been through a lot."

"Indeed, she has, but it's you that needs to give us a minute. She's my patient."

"She's my–"

"It's okay." Alexis touched his arm. "Give us a few minutes." She motioned toward the door.

When he searched her face, she sent him a look. She was going to be okay.

"I need to call your family anyway. I promised your mom," he whispered.

He gave the doctor a weary look before leaning over to kiss Alexis once more on the forehead.

"I'll be right back." He stared down into her hopeful eyes and paused. Something in them had changed. He wasn't sure if it was because that she had survived such an ordeal or if she was still under the influence of pain meds, but her walls were no longer screaming for him to stay away.

"I'm counting on it." She sent him a shy smile, resembling the girl he once knew. His heart surged with the possibilities.

As he left, Dr. Shay chuckled. "Your husband protective much?"

"Oh, no. He's not-" Alexis started, but stopped short of explaining. Between her voice and her condition, she didn't have the strength. Besides, she kind of liked the sound of it. "Yeah. A bit much."

"We all should be so lucky." She took the pen from the tight bun on her head and started making notes on the chart. "Now, let's talk about you."

As the doctor droned on, Alexis zoned out, unable to recall anything she said. The only thing she could focus on was how Tyler's face was the first she wanted to see when she woke. And she couldn't shake the feeling that Clay would be okay with it.

∼

EVELYN AND CLAY hovered in the corner, celebrating Alexis' return.

"Do you think she'll remember?" Clay asked.

"Probably not. If Alexis has any recall at all, she'll most likely think it was a dream."

Clay nodded. "You did a good job, Evelyn."

"I think so too. Now," she said, stretching. "How about that rest you've promised me?"

Clay chuckled and nodded upward. "I'll lead the way."

"I'll still be able to check-in from time to time?" she asked.

"Yes, ma'am." He sent her a wink before they retreated to the only home they knew.

37

One week to the day, Alexis curled her arms around Tyler's neck as he lifted her from the hospital wheelchair into his truck.

As he slid her in, he bumped his head on the door frame and grunted, "Ouch."

Alexis laughed. "I told you I could get in by myself."

"Not a chance." He rubbed his temple. "You're not going to lift a finger unless I say so."

"Mommy!" Lani's sweet voice sang from outside the truck. She grinned as her daughter flew from Amelia's grasp and ran toward Tyler. "I want to ride with Mom!"

Amelia jogged to catch up. "Honey," she said, smiling at Lani. "I need your help with all the flowers. Remember?"

"But Mom." Her sad face pulled at Alexis' heart.

"Come here, sweetheart. Give me a hug."

"Be careful of her chest." Tyler gave her a soft warning and helped lift her into Alexis' lap.

"Grama and Papa need your help. People paid a lot of money for these gifts, and we need to make sure we get them home. It means a lot to me." Alexis pushed a strand of hair behind her daughter's ear and lifted her chin so that they were eye to eye. "I have the rest of my life to spend with my family. I'm not going anywhere."

Lani's lips quivered. She nodded. "Great Grams came to see me the day you got shot. She told me you'd make it, but I was still pretty scared. And then when I couldn't see you afterward..." A tear escaped.

"I know." She wiped the tear away with her thumb and kissed her face on both cheeks. "I'm okay."

Amelia stretched out her hand and helped Lani climb down.

"Come on, sweetheart."

As Tyler and Alexis watched her family carry the gifts to their car, Alexis groaned.

"I can't believe all this happened. I messed up royally, huh?"

Tyler shrugged. "Water under the bridge. As long as you're okay, that's all that matters."

"What about my job? Sharena? I assume I still have to answer for that."

Tyler's infectious grin shone from across the truck.

"What aren't you telling me?" She squinted her eyes in his direction.

"Once the network saw our broadcast, your work, they convinced Sharena that she should drop any complaint. And, they sweetened the deal by offering her a move to a bigger market."

"You're kidding me?!" She almost coughed and then groaned with pain, lifting a hand to her chest.

"Easy there." He sent her a look before continuing, "Yup. They kicked her upstairs. Every single one of our staff came forward in your defense. Corporate decided they'd rather move Sharena than find an entirely new team for the station."

Alexis covered her mouth. "I don't know what to say." Her wide eyes filled with appreciation. "I don't know how to thank you."

"I know of a few ways." He leaned forward to claim her lips for a brief kiss. "But it's not me you should thank. Janelle had heard the whole conversation between you and Sharena before she stepped into the bathroom. She pushed for this and got everyone on board. She claimed it was self-defense, and everyone else backed her whether they believed her or not. Sharena didn't have a chance."

"Oh, my gosh!" She laughed. "So, I still have a job?"

"Honey. You have a career, and they have a contract waiting for you that offers you a pretty sweet deal."

"I'd reach over and hug your neck right now, but-" she paused and winced, "it hurts too much."

Tyler took her hand in his. "There's plenty of time for that."

As he was about to start the engine, a long black limousine pulled up next to them. Tyler raised his eyebrow and sent Alexis a questioning look.

"Don't look at me." She shrugged and winced once more. "I have no idea."

William Wylar eased his way from his limo with his can in hand, waving off his driver. His lips clamped to form a thin line as he approached the truck and waved for Tyler to roll down his window.

"I hope it's okay that I came to see you home." He placed both his hands on the door frame.

Alexis nodded. "Considering all we've been through, I believe it is. How are you?"

"Thanks to you, I'm alive. I'm so grateful you made it."

"Me too." Tyler frowned. He didn't hold anything against the old man, but if it weren't for him and his family, Alexis wouldn't have been in the middle of their drama to begin with.

William nodded, acknowledging Tyler's protective nature, noted the short leash he was given, and said, "I'll make this quick." He swallowed. "My grandson has been arrested. My no-good nephew didn't make it. And, I just signed paperwork to sell Wylars. I've had offers for years, but I thought I'd try to keep it in the family. There's no one left that's qualified to run it. Not that Henry ever was."

William's eyes dropped to the pavement.

Tyler frowned. He didn't see how this applied to Alexis and was about to say so when Alexis laid her hand on his arm.

"Good for you," Alexis reassured William through the open window.

"The reason I'm here." He let out a deep breath. "I owe you my life. I owe Evelyn my life. Once the sale is final, I'm setting aside enough money for myself and my family. The rest will go to you to your family."

Alexis' jaw dropped. After a few seconds, she said, "You don't have to do that."

William sadly shook his head. "My children have died. Henry was the last of my direct line, and he hasn't proven himself worthy. I have a few distant family members, and they'll still get an inheritance, but the bulk of it goes to you. You were the one willing to take a bullet for a man you hardly knew. If I had stayed with Evelyn, you would have been part of my family. I know Amelia wasn't my child, but I would have loved her as mine. And that would have made you my granddaughter even without the blood ties."

Alexis' heart broke for William. "Still, I can't."

"You can. And you will." He nodded firmly. "You have a ranch and a family to care for. It's what Evelyn would have wanted."

Alexis, still in shock, sat shaking her head. "I don't know what to say."

"Say, 'thank you.'" His warm eyes took her in.

Tyler started the engine. "I need to get her home. She's going to need rest."

"Of course." William backed away from the truck.

"Wait!" Alexis called out the window as Tyler slammed on his brakes and waited for William to catch up.

"Yes?" William's curious face peered through Tyler's open window.

"I still don't know how my grandmother ended up at the ranch. Do you know what happened after she left you?"

William's sad eyes spoke volumes. "I kept tabs on her even after she thought I deserted her. From what I can tell, she took my check to the nearest bank outside town. I suppose she started heading west to go home but stopped in Purity to figure out her next move."

Knowing this might be a lengthy conversation, Tyler cut off his engine, opened his door, and offered his seat to William. "I'll give you guys some privacy. I need to make some calls to the station anyway."

William waited for Alexis, who motioned for him to sit inside. Tyler was quick to extend a hand to help William into the driver's seat.

Wincing, Alexis turned in her seat to reach for William's hand.

"You need to take it easy." William scolded and waved her back to her position. "I'm all right."

Alexis blinked, thinking that for a moment, William could be as warm as they come ... until the next, when he was as intolerant as could be.

"Okay." She laughed it off. "So, she stopped in Purity?"

"My man followed her to Purity. She sat in her car at the main intersection next to the bank on the corner, where she saw a toddler playing by himself on the stoop. From all reports, she approached the child to make sure he was alright. My man stayed close enough to hear without being noticed. Apparently, she was upset that the child was alone and stormed inside to find the parents."

Alexis laughed. "Sounds like her. Always taking up for someone and taking a child under her wing."

"She was a force; that's for sure." He wrung his hands and shook his head in remembrance. "Anyway, from what I could tell, she found the child's father, who was in a heated discussion with one of the bankers. He was pleading with the mortgage lender not to take his land.

"Apparently, he was a widower and didn't have the resources or means to simultaneously take care of a child and run his ranch. He was desperate." William sighed. "I guess Evelyn's anger for the child turned to empathy for their situation. She, with her generous heart, couldn't let that happen."

"What did she do?" Alexis asked in awe.

"She handed the check I had given her to the mortgage lender and asked if it would be enough to keep the loan in good standing, which it was. She told them there would be more checks from where that one came."

"So, let me get this straight. She signed her future income over to a stranger and his child?"

"Yes, the Bozeman's. That child is your Uncle Marshall. His dad allowed Evelyn to stay at the ranch to give birth to your mother. She agreed to watch over Marshall like he was her own, raise him, and help keep up the house. She basically owned that ranch – not by deed, but by all other standards. She was paying the bills."

"So that's how she ended up with the Bozeman's? And then she ended up marrying him, Tennessee Bozeman? I guess that would make him my step-grandfather?"

"Yes." William's voice caught. "She finally found her happily ever after... until my money caused her death."

Alexis saw the pain that ran deep and squeezed his hand. "It wasn't your fault."

"Then why does it feel like it is?" His voice faltered.

"Mr. Wylar."

"William," he insisted.

"You didn't rig that tractor to explode."

"But I might as well have." He shook his head. "The guilt I carry..." He tapped his heart. "has lived here for many years in regard to what I did to Evelyn all those years ago. The guilt over her death, though, hurts the worst. At least now, I can make amends by taking care of her family."

"It's too much."

"Do with the money what you want. Give it away. It doesn't matter. But do something with it that Evelyn would approve of. That's all I care about."

Alexis liked that thought. "Okay. For her, I will."

"Take care, Alexis." William's hand shook as he reached for the door. Tyler, who was waiting patiently outside, beat him to it and opened the door offering a hand to William once more.

"Thank you, young man." He paused. "Don't take her for granted. Fight for love. It's all we have."

"Oh, believe me. I know." He slid back into position and started the engine. "Bye, now."

William nodded in return and watched them ride off into the distance hoping to God they made better choices than he did at that age.

"That was for you, Evie," he whispered to the clouds and got back in his limo.

38

One month later

A CELEBRATION WAS IN ORDER. Amelia sighed as she looked through the crowded field toward the barn that was lit up with twinkle lights. Her chest filled with awe as she watched her community pull together after another successful harvest. This year's festival was much more than that, though.

Hank slipped in behind his wife, thinking she was the most beautiful woman in the world. His followed her gaze was trained where Lani ran toward Tyler to jump into his arms, Tyler swaying them to the music that filled the starry night.

"Are you thinking what I'm thinking?" Hank's heart filled with hope for the young man that had always been a part of his family.

"Mm-hmm." Amelia looked on as her daughter's face lit up with happiness at the sight of Tyler and Lani. "Alexis deserves to be happy. I'm glad she finally is."

"Me too," Hank grunted. "Not to say she's not had a rough time of it, but I'm glad our girl finally got out of her own way."

Alexis glanced at her parents, who smiled in her direction. She waved and diverted her attention back to the man, who had become a staple in hers and Lani's lives. As he swung her daughter around on the makeshift dance floor, in the middle of the field, twinkle lights adorned them with a soft glow.

Now, this is a picture I could get used to.

As Bruno Mars' latest hit wound down and the softer crooning of Passenger started, Lani wrapped her arms around Tyler's neck and whispered something in his ear. They turned to Alexis with a wide grin. Lani hopped down from Tyler's arms, grabbed his hand, and wiggled a finger toward her mother.

Tyler's eyes glowed with warmth. Alexis approached, sending them both a look that left her emotionally stripped – totally exposed. Her love for them was so different, yet still so fierce in its own way.

"Mom." Lani giggled. "You're blushing again." She grabbed her mom's hand and put it into the one of Tyler's she'd been holding.

"You going to dance with us?" She looked down at her daughter's mischievous eyes as Lani answered with a giggle and a shake of her head.

"No, this one is yours." She tilted her ear to the music. "Hear that? It's a love song."

"I got it from here." He grinned at Lani, who promptly darted through the crowd.

"You've been hiding from me?" When leaned down to brush lips across hers, part of him was still amazed she finally chose him.

"No, not hiding." She lazily wound her arms around his neck. Alexis was amazed at how freeing it was just to be in the moment. "I've just been mingling."

"Everyone wants to wish the bride well before she goes off on her honeymoon?" He took her left hand in his while appreciating the wedding band that accompanied the diamond she'd said yes to a few weeks ago. "Talk about a whirlwind wedding."

"I'd say the harvest festival was a perfect place to hold the reception. This way, the whole town can join us on our special day."

Tyler glanced over his shoulder at the barn where they'd shared their vows only a few hours ago.

"I still can't believe you said yes." He shook his head with wonder.

"Come here." Alexis chuckled and led him toward the side of the barn, where they find a bit more privacy.

Once they were somewhat hidden in the shadows, Alexis pushed him against a wall and lifted to her toes. The expectant gleam in Tyler's eyes had her stomach flipping with anticipation. She looked at him with the promise of more and sank into his body for a kiss.

"When can we get out of here?" he murmured through their kiss.

Alexis pulled back with a laugh. "This is not why I pulled you over here, I swear."

"Such a tease." He flicked her on her nose and circled her waist, resting his hands on the small of her back. He could tell by the look on her face that she had something on her mind. He waited, giving her the space she needed.

"After I woke up, I had glimpses of these images that kept invading my dreams. And that's what I thought they were – dreams." She shook her head, trying to piece it all together. "But they were in-depth conversations with Clay and Grams. And, there was another little face that keeps flashing before me that I swear could be Lani's twin."

When a far-off look crossed her face, Tyler dropped his arms and took his hands in hers.

"When Lani said Clay came to her in her dreams," she paused. "That hurt me for a while, knowing he chose her instead of me."

"Okay." Tyler had no idea where this was going.

"Last night, I had another of what I thought were dreams. Clay... he released me. He told me that you were the one to give me the life I needed."

"That's awfully nice of the guy." His gut still clenched at the sound of her dead husband's name. He shouldn't be jealous, but he was.

"Stay with me. I have a point. I'm not trying to ruin our day."

"No, that's not it. Clay is and was a part of your life, and he's Lani's dad. I know he's going to be carried into this with us. I am not mad."

"I know." She laid a hand on his chest. "My point is that I, we have his blessing. And after I woke up in the hospital, I had that same remnant of emotion, but I couldn't tell you why. It was like deep down I knew he'd be okay with us but couldn't put my finger on why. Then last night, the very last part of my dream was my grandmother telling me that it was time to go back to you."

Tyler shook his head.

Alexis leaned up to kiss his cheek, cupping his face. "Deep down in my core, I don't think these are dreams, but memories."

"Memories?" He frowned, his pulse racing. "But your heart never stopped beating. You never died. Did you?"

"I know it's confusing. I didn't die." Her eyes went wide with awe. "But somehow I was there. I know it. And, it means the world to me that Clay chose you. I just wanted you to know."

Tyler clamped his lips together and tilted his head to the side, unsure of what to say.

"Tyler, you were always the one for me, but my guilt about it caused many issues in my marriage. Then, my guilt over Clay's death kept me from letting anything progress with you. I think this last dream or memory was a gift. It can't be a coincidence that I had it on the night before our wedding."

The knot in Tyler's chest dissipated as relief replaced the dread that had been coiling at the pit of his stomach. He covered her hands with his and brought them to cover his heart.

"God works in mysterious ways," he said.

"He does." She tilted her head back to stare up to the night sky. There she saw two stars twinkling, shining brighter than the rest and smiled.

Since her awakening, Alexis had gone back of her own volition to church. She realized what she was tired of running. God had been chasing her in every way possible to give her the life she needed, and she discovered she was shutting Him and Tyler out at every turn.

Once she finally let God back into her life, she also started seeing the light when it came to Tyler. Not that Tyler would have given her a choice. Two weeks after she was released from the hospital, he picked her up for her a routine checkup, stopping at his house on the way.

When he drove Alexis onto his property, she was surprised to see construction trucks and a crew working on the back on Tyler's home.

"What's going on?" She sat in a hazed stupor, still groggy from the pain medication.

"I'm building a master suite on the back and a playroom upstairs." He turned off the engine and slowly turned toward her with the look of a man on a mission.

"Good for you." She nodded with appreciation.

"No, good for us." Tyler put a ring in the palm of her hand. "When you were shot, my whole life flashed before my eyes. I saw the golden years we'd never share, the kids we'd never have, and I was devastated at the thought. You are my soulmate, Alexis." His eyes temporarily misted. "I know this is sudden in some ways, while in others, we've been leading up to this our whole lives. You've been a part of me for as long as I can remember, and I just don't want a life without you or Lani in it."

Alexis had felt the warm tears before she knew they'd escaped. Her heart beat wildly for Tyler, and she what he said rang true.

"I understand if you want to wait." He curled her fingers around the ring while holding her fist in his palm. "I'm here for as long as you'll have me. You don't have to say anything. Just know that these guys are building on to my bachelor pad and converting it into a family home, where Lani can play with her future brothers and sisters."

A flash of the little boy who had been haunting her dreams came and went, which made Alexis shake with a soft sob.

"Alexis." Tyler slid toward her. "I'm so sorry. I didn't mean to put too much pressure on you. If it's too soon…"

"No," she said through her tears. "There's nothing I'd like better. I want to start a family with you. I want you to be in our lives. Lani adores you, and I've," she paused, "I've always loved you."

Tyler dropped his forehead to hers and joined her with a few tears of his own.

"You just made me the happiest man on earth." He breathed in her scent.

As Alexis shook free from the memory of their engagement, she pulled her husband toward her by the lapels of his jacket.

"Come here," she whispered. Their kiss was slow and steady yet filled with the promise of a future.

"Can we get out of here now?" He slid his arms down the back of her dress and pressed her toward him.

"Yes." She laughed through more happy tears and reached for his hand to drag him toward the party.

As the two ran from their hiding place to say their goodbyes, Evelyn swung her feet happily from the tree above.

"Finally," she breathed in with a sigh of relief. "Have a beautiful life, my child."

Evelyn experienced a twinge of regret that she couldn't stay longer, but her time with Alexis had come full circle. Her granddaughter had a life ahead filled with love and laughter. There would be challenges, but she had a good man to support her.

Her eyes darted around the property as she mentally said goodbye to the rest of her clan when she noticed Lani chatting Anderson's head off in the corner of the barn. Anderson looked to be somewhere else entirely.

"Unc?" Lani pulled his face toward hers with intent in her eyes. "Have you heard a word I've said?"

Anderson snapped out of his funk and blinked at his bubbly niece. "Sorry. I've got a lot on my mind, kiddo."

"You okay?" Her wise eyes filled with concern.

"Yeah, I will be. Listen, tell your mom and grandma that I love them, okay?"

Lani narrowed her eyes and pursed her little lips. "You're going somewhere?"

"They'll understand. It's time, and I need a little space to clear my head."

Evelyn frowned as her grandson stood to kiss Lani on the head. Just when she thought she was finished watching over this family – she had an overwhelming urge to follow Anderson.

"I guess I'm off too," she whispered into great granddaughter's ear. Anderson's words prompted her to stay close to him wherever he was running to.

Lani turned to face Evelyn with a pout. "You'll watch over him?"

"Yes." Evelyn stroked the child's dark curls. "He can't sense me like your mother could, but I can still help. Make sure to tell Tyler thank you for me."

At the mention of her new stepdad, Lani's face lit up.

Evelyn blew her a kiss and trailed Anderson as he grabbed his bag from behind a bale of hay.

"Apparently, you've been planning your exit," she whispered in Anderson's ear as he turned to glance at the party over his shoulder. "Where are you off to now?"

Anderson watched their faces as his gut burned with envy. How he wished he could cut loose and enjoy life, but it seemed it wasn't in the cards for him. Now that Alexis and Tyler had started their life, he needed to find his.

As Amelia watched her son slip into the darkness, her heart whispered goodbye like it had a thousand times before. This was what Anderson did. His job kept them constantly guessing about where and when he'd show up next. Now that he was on a hiatus from the agency, she worried that his exit had him running to something even more dangerous.

The sound of his motorcycle revving to life could barely be heard through the music that filtered around them. As his taillight disappeared around the bend, her heart was torn in two.

She'd just sent her daughter off on her honeymoon, knowing she was in a good place with an exceptional man who loved her more than life itself.

There's nothing better for a mother's heart than that.

Knowing her other child wasn't in the same place had her praying that Anderson would find his way.

. . .

LOOK to the next page for a glimpse of Anderson and Savannah's story, from the second book in Kimberly's 'Spiritual Gifts' series.

39

SNEAK PEEK AT DANGEROUS VISIONS

It was hard to believe in less than twelve hours Savannah Miles' somewhat quiet life had been turned on its ear, from running a successful business to becoming a woman with a price on her head.

She peered over her shoulder for the umpteenth time, pulling her hoodie closer to her face and settling at the back of the bus. She smiled at a young mom, who settled in next to her with a newborn wrapped in a blanket.

Savannah's heart warmed at the sight of mother and child until she remembered why she was on the run. She didn't have time for idle thoughts. She needed to come up with a plan. Absentmindedly, she ran a finger along her bus ticket and blinked, unsure if any of this was real.

Savannah drew her lips in and bit them from inside, wondering when or if she'd make it back home. The urge to cry was more than she could bear, but she pushed the tears back, unwilling to draw more attention to herself.

If only she could call her friends or co-workers to let them know what happened, but a conversation could put them in danger. At the very least, she would have liked to send a quick text making them aware that she was leaving town before smashing her cell and tossing it in the nearest public trash can.

With a heavy heart, she slipped the receipt into her backpack and leaned her head against the window, staring into the dark abyss that threatened to swallow her whole.

At least I'm not totally alone. Relief flooded her heart at the thought of her cousin, Danny, who advised her to leave her phone behind and only take the necessities. As a government agent and one of her favorite and only family members, she trusted him implicitly.

As soon as Danny found out she was in trouble, he booked her on the first bus out of town and arranged for her to stay at his family's home in Nebraska away from the spotlight and the danger that darkened her doorstep.

Savannah's mind jumped to the man who'd put a price on her head. Suddenly, it was as if her stomach was tormented by fire. Benny, whom she had discovered was nicknamed 'Benny the Bone Breaker,' wasn't merely a local bookie, but had ties to a dangerous crime organization.

If only I hadn't overheard anything.

No matter how many alternative solutions she thought of, the truth of the matter was that she had. Her impeccable timing had placed her at the wrong place at the wrong time.

"Breathe," she whispered.

Savannah turned to the mom, who sent her a look of question. She gave her a bland smile before staring out toward the night once more. She could do this. She would survive.

Thank God for Danny.

Although her cousin couldn't drop everything to meet her, he promised to have someone waiting at the bus terminal in Nebraska to help her until she could return home. She just prayed the promise of home would still be a reality when it was all said and done.

As she traveled further from her life and the city lights of Nashville, Savannah hoped the tension between her shoulder blades would dissipate. If anything, the pit at the bottom of her stomach became increasingly more bothersome, especially when she noticed a heavy-set man, who seemed to be watching her more closely than he should.

Savannah shifted in her seat, putting another passenger's head in between them, much like she used to do in school when she'd left another paper at home.

Please be looking somewhere else.

She squeezed her eyes shut only to open them and peer around the passenger's head in front of her. Surely the man, who she had nicknamed 'The Beast,' would have lost interest. She was wrong. When their eyes connected, hers widened while his gleamed with intensity. Savannah gulped, but it was as if she'd swallowed a handful of gravel.

At that moment, years of instructions flooded back to her as her mind raced with scenarios of how to escape. Her father, God rest his soul, had taught her a few fundamentals in life.

'Sit with your back to the wall, so you can survey your surroundings. Look for an exit strategy if needed and be aware of things like someone who is watching you more than they should.'

Savannah sunk into her seat a bit more, thankful to at least be on the last row of the bus. Without the threat of passengers behind her, she could be sure there wasn't anyone in cahoots with the stranger a few rows up.

Next to her, the young woman nodded off with her baby securely cradled in her arms. The hum of the motor had lulled them into an instant sleep giving Savannah a short window of opportunity to search the woman's purse.

She rifled through as expertly as she could as to not wake her seatmate until she found what she was looking for. Once she secured the woman's cell phone in her jeans pocket, she zipped the purse and exhaled.

Again, her father's teachings flooded her memory. As a military brat, she'd been trained to blend in and disappear into a crowd. The key to staying under the radar was not to draw attention to yourself.

It's a little too late for that. She grimaced.

But when in need, use what you can to defend yourself.

She slid her eyes up once more, noticing the heavyset man's eyes narrowed in her direction. She could almost read the Beast's thoughts, and his eyes told her a story with an ending that didn't look pretty.

As the bus slowed to exit, she had only one option, which was to put as much distance between them as possible. She may not have known who he was, but it was clear that he was aware of who she was and had plans to finish what Benny's men had started the night before.

The Beast readied himself, looking as if he was going to pounce once the bus came to a stop. Her one saving grace was the elderly man, who sat in the aisle seat, blocking her would-be captor from stepping out to do her harm.

If she could grab her backpack and stretch around the woman and her child – she could bolt down the aisle and get to the nearest bus exit without incident.

"Please let this work," she whispered as she scanned the bus for anything she could use to defend herself. The only thing that came to mind was the elderly man's cane, which would be the last resort.

How do you even know he's after you? The analytical side of her brain antagonized her. She shook her head. She might have been paranoid, but she'd rather be paranoid than dead.

The bus stopped outside a well-lit diner just as Savannah jumped from her seat and eased by the mother and child. She held her breath, with a prayer of thanks, as she watched the elderly gentlemen swiftly rise from his seat and fumbled for his bag – cane in one hand and a duffle bag in the other. It was just enough to keep a safe distance between her and a dangerous demise.

As she fled down the stairs of the bus, she stole a glance over her shoulder. What she saw in the man's eyes sent her fleeing for the diner. She had a matter of seconds before her assailant would catch up. She tore inside and scanned the diner in haste, hoping for options to escape.

She scanned the dingy diner. The bathroom was out. Unless it had a window that she could squeeze through, it was basically a trap.

Heck, there was no guarantee there was a window at all. A second exit to her left was an option, but a dangerous one as the Beast could easily see her if he timed it just right when he entered the diner.

Savannah made a split decision and rushed through the swinging door to the kitchen and into the arms of a line cook.

"Hey, watch out! You can't come back here."

"Someone's after me." Out of breath, she could hardly get in another word. She pulled herself away from his reach and asked, "Is there a back way out of here?" She turned her warm brown eyes on him, and the rough edges around his face softened.

"Hold on. Shouldn't you call the police?" He searched her panicked face and finally nodded down a hall. "That way. It leads to two doors. Take the one on the left."

"Thank you!" She started for the hall.

"Wait!" he called after her on a whim. "There's an alley that leads to the main street. Head toward the fields and keep running. You'll find a farmhouse. It's a safe place."

"How do I know I can trust you?"

At that moment, a bell sounded alerting them to more traffic entering the diner. Her eyes went wide with terror.

The line cook quickly yanked off the chain from around his neck. "Take this. The barn is safe. It's my family's property."

Savannah nodded in haste and took the cross from his hands without much thought, shoving it into her pocket before starting for the doors and disappearing into the night.

40
BETA READER

If you'd like to be a beta reader, feel free to email me. From time to time, I look for someone new. Feel free to email me! My email is kimberlymckayauthor@gmail.com.

ABOUT THE AUTHOR

As a military brat, she's traveled the world, which has given her lots of experiences to pull from. For the last twenty-nine years, she's made Oklahoma City her home. Married with one child and a rescue pup, Kimberly works full-time in sales, has a consulting business on the side, is a writing instructor at OU, and still finds the time to write.

Her love of people and culture is what drives her to tell her stories. Please help readers find her books by leaving a positive review.

You can find out more about Kimberly at her official author website at **www.kimberlymckayauthor.com**. If you're on social media – follow her at the icons below.

ACKNOWLEDGMENTS

A big thanks to my former college professor, mentor and friend, Marcia Feisal. Your editing skills helped polish what was already underneath, ready to shine.

Another heartfelt thank you to my former co-worker and creative friend, Dana Jordan. Your ability to take direction and create beautiful things is what made this cover so special.

Thank you to Robert Trawick at Trawick Images for my new headshot. I appreciate your amazing talent!

And without these people, this book wouldn't have had come together quite as well. To all my family, friends, and beta-readers who spent time delving through this book to give your unbiased and sometimes critical feedback. Thank you to every single one of you. Get ready for the next book!

To my readers – I love your heart and enthusiasm for my books. Thank you for your emails, tweets, and Facebook posts at my page. And, a huge thank you for your positive reviews. Your wonderful words help others find my books, which is truly humbling to think about.

Made in the USA
Middletown, DE
29 April 2020